WIZARD EYES

BY Sylvie Evdoxiadis

Good or bad, all must suffer the consequences of their actions.

History Part 2 - Dragons

Wizard Eyes

This book contains legends minus one: the Bible is real!

Merci à Mélissa et à Jean-Marc.
Ευχαριστώ Ξανθούλα.

Prologue

It was a rainy night. In fact, it was exactly what one would expect of any story that begins with a rainy night. The rain poured so hard a man could stand with his face toward the sky, his mouth open, drinking it in. Like I said, it was one of those typical, miserable nights one often reads about in stories. It was a rainy night. No one in their right mind would venture outside.

Safe in a simple farm house, near the outskirts of Valley City, where one should be on a night like this, a woman warmed herself by the fire, pretending to stir the beef stew that obviously did not need stirring. Not too far away, his feet propped up on the wooden table, her husband thought of the ravages the rain would cause to the crops. They did not talk. After fourteen years of marriage, nothing new happened; there was not anything to talk about. He worked in the fields every day, trudging home at sunset, while she spent the whole day scrubbing, washing, cleaning, and taking care of the house. Yep. It was boring and they did not need to talk to remind themselves of that.

As he sat brewing about the rain, and she tasted the meager stew by the warm fire, a knock disturbed them, causing both of them to jump.

"Who in Atlantis could be out on such a wet night!" exclaimed the woman.

"Well, it must be important," deduced the man, looking at his wife expectantly.

She sighed and peeked through the window; then, her frown deepened, her eyes hardened, and her nose crinkled.

"It's one of them." she hissed.

At that, the man abruptly sat up, almost falling off his chair. Quickly, he grabbed the chair on his way to the door and shoved it under the doorknob.

Silence. Then, another triple knock. "I know you're in there. Open the door!"

"There is no way I am letting one of their kind into our house!" the wife squeaked.

"Back up." The husband reached for her and guided her to the opposite end of the room. "Maybe he'll go away."

But on a rainy night like this, those traveling outside certainly must have a good reason to be there, and in no way could anyone deter them from doing what they set out to do. A closed door cannot stop them. Simple farm folk do not stand a chance.

With a hiss and a whoosh, both the chair and the thick wooden door burst into bright blue flames. As the woman screeched pitifully and the man held her protectively, the wood fell apart, leaving their house wide open to the elements and to the unwanted guest. The fire, instead of lingering and eating the rest of the house, ceased to exist, the only trace a wisp of green smoke.

Not one, but two figures entered, both covered in thick, hooded robes. One would think it was for the rain, but the wife and husband knew that was not the case. Their kind always hid their bodies and faces, too ashamed of the changes caused by the magic. A wizard, like everyone else, starts his life as a normal child, laughing and playing; but when their power takes hold, it all changes.

"What do you want with us!?" cried the woman. "We have nothing you want!"

"And what would you know of our business, simpleton?" The taller wizard crossed his arms and shook his head slowly.

The second wizard, obviously a woman, chuckled with contempt. "Absolutely nothing."

The two hooded figures walked confidently toward the couple who blocked the entryway to a corridor. In fear, the wife stepped aside, clutching her chest for protection, but the husband stood his ground.

"If I let you pass," he said, "will you leave us alone?"

"If!?" the fiery lady spat at him.

Holding his hand up to her brusquely, the first wizard shook his head and replied, "Of course."

At that, the farmer stepped aside and the wizards strode through the entryway. Without hesitation, the first wizard opened the door on the right and entered the small bedroom. The wife gasped at the sight behind the door and began trembling.

"This can't be..." she sobbed, and fell to her knees. Quickly, she closed her eyes and covered her ears with her hands, all the while humming to herself.

In the corner of the room, Miriam, their thirteen year old daughter, lay in her straw bed, reciting four rhyming lines over and over again. Where her skin peeked out from under the covers, its appearance had become like a ghost's. Her eyes were closed as in sleep, but her mother knew that they would no longer be green. That is, they would still be green but not in the normal sense. Now, when she would open her eyes, all anyone would see is green: no white, no veins, no black irises, just green.

Under his hood, the first wizard had at first seemed confident and pleased with himself, but after paying attention to Miriam's words, his shoulders slumped slightly. His smile vanished instantly.

Over and over again, Miriam recited,

> *"Hear Atlantis, and learn:*
> *By fire you will burn.*
> *Flee, flee! For naught you hold*
> *Can stop this tale foretold!"*

Note 1

What can I say about wizards? I only knew them for a short period before they became extinct, but I must say I disliked them much at the time. Not only could you partially see through their skin, but their eyes seemed opaque, with just that one color. It was creepy. No hint of emotion ever showed through them and you always felt like they were constantly watching you, no matter where you stood. And let's not mention how superior they thought they were. What know-it-alls!

They had it coming.

Chapter 1 – Creation

Many years later, the wizards still argued about the meaning of Miriam's prophecy, but Thangard, the high wizard, had made a decision. On that sunny day, seven of them talked in hushed tones in their dark underground cave, surrounded by shelves and shelves of dusty spell books and a fireplace crackling in the corner.

"After all of our talks," Thangard finally declared, "I have made a decision."

"Miriam!" Gala, another wizard, whispered in the prophetess' ear, "Have you had another prophecy? Otherwise, I can't see how he could know what to do or act without any more information, I mean, after..."

Thangard's black eyes did not seem to move but he signaled the wizard to his right with his right index finger. With that signal, the second wizard, whose name was Kib, moved his head down slightly and Gala's rant choked off.

"As I was saying," continued Thangard, "I have made a decision. The reason I have called the six of you here is not to debate the issue any further but to help me put my plan into action."

In turn, he looked at the six other wizards until they acknowledged him with a nod. When it was Gala's turn, the talkative wizard raised his left hand up a bit and made to talk, but no sound came from his mouth. With a sigh, Thangard signaled Kib again and the second wizard moved his head up slightly.

"Hum," started Gala, "so what would you like for us to do, then?"

Thangard smiled. "The prophecy says that nothing we have can defend us from the fire that is coming to destroy us, so we must create something that will guarantee our salvation and continued existence. They will attack us with fire? We shall strike first with the same and prevent our doom!"

"But I already have fire," Ember, the wizard to Kib's right, quietly spat.

"Patience, sister," smiled Soffia, standing on Gala's left, "I am certain our leader here will divulge his plan to our satisfaction."

"Everyone outside!" commanded Thangard.

One by one, the wizards exited, Gala tailing them and talking to himself. "All cryptic as usual but at least we're leaving these damp caves. I like the outside: it's free, it's fun, even unpredictable."

Once all had reached the outside, the high wizard addressed Pita, a short quiet man who tended to walk around with his nose up in the air, seeming to think that made him taller than everyone else.

"Pita, I need crocodiles and snakes, lots of them, and the biggest ones you can find!"

The short sorcerer raised his eyebrows in a bored manner and his brown opaque eyes clouded for a second.

"I have twenty of each on their way as we speak."

After a long wait accompanied by scattered flighty comments from Gala, the horde of reptiles started arriving, crawling their way to an unspecified spot in front of Pita. The snakes, ranging from green to blue, red to yellow, plain to spotted and striped, once having reached the wizards, lay frozen, as if in hibernation. In the same way, the bulky crocodiles ceased their movement, their eyes staring into empty space.

"Now," Thangard broke the silence that had accumulated from the appearance of the creeping animals, "combine the snakes with the crocodiles to make a new kind of creature, but enlarge them, make them monstrous! After all, we want to strike fear into our enemies' hearts."

It all happened eerily fast and one would not know how to describe the process, but the end result spoke for itself. There, towering over the seven magic wielders, stood twenty frozen monsters that could strike fear into any man—or woman, for that matter. Their faces greatly resembled the crocodile's, but their elongated necks, though thicker than a normal snake's body, were long and slithery like the latter creatures. The bodies were much thicker, like the bigger reptile, and the four legs were positioned in a way that allowed the creatures to walk on all fours or sit up on the two hind legs. From the head, spikes worked their way down to the tip of the tail where two bigger sharp spikes waited, ready to skewer any passerby. Like the snakes, the new creations varied in color.

"Ember," Thangard continued, "give them the power of fire and you, Soffia, make them resistant to the fire of others."

"I can do both, Master," Ember boasted impatiently. "We don't need *her* help."

With that remark, the redhead raised her arms and a great gust of wind engulfed the area. Though frozen by

Pita's power, the monsters, one by one, began shrieking. Their scales, though of different hues, slowly burned a glowing red as their cries intensified. As one, they stretched their necks and warm steam escaped their opened mouths.

Gala, covering his ears in pain yelled as loudly as he could, "I think something's wrong. I mean, don't you think they look kind of pitiful and like they're going to blow up? Ember's good with fire, of course, but, no offense, sometimes she's a bit crazy and out of control. If they don't die, it just might drive them mad!"

No one heard him.

Soffia sighed and closed her eyes. Now, a cool breeze replaced the arid wind around them and the burning scales of the reptiles cooled back to their natural color. Immediately, their roars quieted, their mouths shut, and their eyes closed in relief.

"Soffia!" yelled Ember, "I can do this alone!"

"Enough," Thangard ordered the fire mage. As instructed, the small wizard ceased her ranting but she looked as if smoke was going to come out of her ears and nostrils; her face was so red.

"Gala, I want you to give them the ability to fly."

Raising his eyebrows and puckering his lips, Gala deliberated, "Well, I mean, I can make them light enough to fly but that would be permanent and you would find them floating around forever, going with the wind. They'd have no direction, you know. It just wouldn't work. They need some wings."

Without being asked, Pita motioned in the air, making like he was stretching strings out. From their backs, scaly wings sprouted on the monsters, large enough to cover their whole bodies.

"Well okay," continued Gala, "I guess that would work."

Though long winded when he spoke, Gala simply puffed his cheeks and blew the air out in a split second. The spell was done.

"Pita, I would suggest you release one and let it fly around for a test run. I might need to make some adjustments. You never know about these things until you try, you see," Gala said.

Closest to them, a huge green beast animated and started looking around. When it saw the others of its kind, it hissed and bared its teeth, slashing its tail back and forth.

"Fly," whispered Pita.

Looking surprised with its head lifting backwards, the creature jumped high, stretched its wings and languidly flapped them, sucking all the air under them. With little effort, it took to the air and flew in a circle around the field to finally land on its original spot. Right before returning to its frozen state, it let out a proud roar of fire, singeing Thangard's robes. Automatically, Soffia threw water from her fingers and stopped any further burning.

"I suppose we shall call this one *Singe*," smiled the high wizard.

"Pff," puffed Ember, "what's the point of giving them names? They're so dumb they wouldn't even recognize we were talking to them."

"This is where I come in, I suppose," acknowledged Kib, nodding to himself.

Thangard nodded his head once and Kib faced the creatures.

"I name you *Dragons*," he said, looking at each of their faces. "From now on, you will speak as we do, you will have intelligence as we do, and you will do as we say. We are your masters."

"It is complete," Thangard smiled. Then, he glanced at Miriam, waiting for her to speak but the prophetic woman remained silent. His frown returned in disappointment.

"Dragons?" Gala raised an eyebrow. "What kind of a word is that? If I was going to name them I would ha..."

His voice cut short and no sound dared escape the talkative wizard's mouth. Smugly, Kib smiled.

"It's a fitting name," he declared and walked away.

Gala rushed after the speech wizard with one finger raised, looking like a child does when he has a question. But when he reached him, he forgot all about not being able to talk because that was the exact moment when

Pita decided to free the dragons from his control. This caused an unexpected racket of questions, statements and declarations in roars and hisses. Singe, the big green dragon, bared his teeth and was the first to strike at a neighboring yellow dragon. Just like in a brawl, when a man throws the first punch, all the other punches seem simultaneous and uncountable; there is no separating the fighters and there is no knowing who starts what.

At first, baffled by the violence before them, the wizards stood frozen; but finally, Pita woke from his reverie and halted the scene with a wave of his hand.

"What is *wrong* with them!?" asked Ember, almost amused.

"I can change their shapes and I can control them," replied Pita, rolling his eyes at Ember, "but I cannot change who they are. Ingrained in their being are territorial creatures who refuse to share their space. We will never be able to keep them all together in one place."

Gala made to speak but had to frown when only silence came out. With a shake of the head, he punched Kib on the shoulder in a very non-wizardly fashion.

"Hum," he cleared his throat once Kib had done his magic, "they're supposedly intelligent by your own saying, Pita. Can't we just reason with them?"

"Can you reason with a hungry baby to stop crying because food is on the way? Can you reason with a farmer to stop working on his crop because a drought is coming? Can you reason with a pregnant woman to not eat so much because she is going to gain more weight than she needs to? Gala, it is in their nature."

"I suppose they are but full grown babies now," replied Gala, "but adults can be reasoned with, if they are reasonable that is, of course. Anyone can change, no matter the situation, we all have our choices. So do they, since they are smart. They can fight against their very nature, just like we can!"

"I can help things along the way with a threat and a spell," cut in Thangard.

All six sorcerers bowed their heads in respect and backed away. There was a good reason that Thangard was the high wizard. Although he did not have a strong power over any particular element of life the way other wizards did, he could detect abilities in others, help them grow and understand what possibilities these powers offered them. Moreover, with all this understanding, he could create spells about anything and once he made and wrote them down, these spells could work for anyone in turn who uttered them. Their sacred library cave, the one from which they had exited thirty minutes earlier, was filled wall to wall with his spells. He was legendary and the only one of his kind.

Bowing to one knee, the high mage drew a parchment and a quill from the pockets of his robe and deposited them on the ground. After a minute or so, he scribbled a few lines, read them over in his head and nodded. Back on his two feet, he cleared his throat and addressed the dragons,

"Dragons, hear me! I will put a curse on you. It will not stop you from killing each other but know that if you do such a thing, there will be dire consequences that will haunt you till the day you yourselves die."

Looking down at the parchment, Thangard chanted the spell,

"When your kin you kill,
On earth his blood spill,
A curse on your head:
Return will the dead!
With worms to follow,
His path he will show.
To break this here spell,
You must die as well."

Thangard nodded toward Pita who again released the Dragons from their paralysis. Instead of fighting as before, they wearily glanced at each other sideways and finally ignored each other's presence.

"Now, that's more like it," acquiesced Gala, pleased.

"Indeed," agreed Thangard, "indeed."

Note 2

Sometimes, being young can be the worst thing ever! No one lets you do the things you want to do; instead, they put ideas in your head and have great expectations concerning what you need to do, when, where, and how. Then, when you finally reach that fateful day, it just doesn't seem good enough for them.

It was definitely tough and I'll never forget.

Chapter 2 – Warthang

Sixteen years had passed. In the beginning, the wizards trained the dragons carefully, riding on their backs and explaining battle strategies. After having assured themselves that their beasts understood, they would watch from afar different combats and assaults on dummy cities and fortresses. At first, they seemed pleased and acknowledged the cunning of the reptiles, especially when they reacted wisely in unpredictable situations. But over time, and this took a few years, of course, the sorcerers separated out the creatures and began using them for more menial work, like leveling fields, building great stone defenses and patrolling areas to protect against thieves. This was not the problem, exactly. The problem was the way they treated the dragons. At first, they had almost revered them and even respected them for their strength, intelligence and power. Later, however, they treated them contemptuously and like slaves. Being intelligent, the colossal beasts did not appreciate the magic users' demeanor and resented them greatly for it.

Four years earlier, Singe had mated in secret with the yellow dragoness Ferel. Finally, at that time, one of their eggs had hatched a yellow-eyed, red-scaled baby dragon that they had named *Warthang*, since they were declaring war on Thangard and all the wizards.

Now four years old, Warthang waited impatiently for the hour when his parents would let him accomplish his purpose in life. On that particular day, a chill coursed through the baby's cave, announcing a cool winter. As usual, the small creature—that is, small for a dragon, he was about the size of a human adult—lay between the rocks and crags of the cave, in the dark places where passersby would never know that a little monster longed for one of his parents to return for some company. Once a day, one of them would visit, usually his father, but only for a short period of time. They did not want to alert the wizards of their treason.

Warthang heard a crackle at the mouth of his lair and his ears perked up. When he saw the huge figure of his father, he slithered out of his hiding place and jumped

24

up with glee.

Without a word, Singe deposited a small parchment he had clutched between two of his claws and pointed to it.

"On this next full moon," read Warthang confidently, "our ten year meeting is due. Hall Forest is the place."

"Well done, my son," said Singe. "It seems your reading is good enough for the task."

"Oh, I am ready, father! Ask me anything and I know all the answers!" perked the slim red baby.

"Who is the enemy and why?" began Singe.

"The wizards are the enemy, they are evil and despicable! They have oppressed our kind in doing things that are beneath us. They give us no freedom, no choice, they will never let us rule ourselves the way we should."

"What does the enemy look like?"

"They usually wear long robes, their skin is see-through and their eyes are all one color."

"What do you do if you see a wizard?"

"I hide, they cannot see me."

"What is your mission?"

"To crawl into their cave and find a spell that can help us defeat them."

"Where is the cave found?"

"Directly south of this cove, I go across the mountains, continue south through farmlands then grass fields until I find a river. Once I cross the river, there is a big rock that marks the entrance to the cave."

"Why is your mission crucial?"

"Hum..." stammered Warthang, "you never told me the answer to that one. I don't know, Father."

"With everything that I've told you about the wizards, I was hoping you were clever enough to figure it out on your own," glared Singe, disappointed.

"Ok, well," thought Warthang out loud, quickly, not wanting his father to think him dull, "the only weapons we have are fire, our teeth, our strength, our flight and our tails..."

"Go on," pushed the green dragon.

"The wizards can do all sorts of things, like teleport, explode objects, throw fire and water, make plants grow and...oh!"

"Yes?" Singe squeezed his eyes, looking at his son from above.

"They can control our bodies! With that power, we can't do anything! We can't defeat them!"

"Correct. So when you look for a spell in that cave, and I don't know what kind of spells they have down there, keep those things in mind to help us defeat those dictators. Without you, we cannot accomplish anything."

"Yes, Father!" said Warthang, flapping his little wings excitedly, "I will destroy them!"

Singe looked at his small charge and sighed, muttering something about not waiting another ten years. Finally, he looked down at Warthang and pointed a large claw at the small parchment left on the ground.

"Every ten years," he began, "the wizards have a meeting where they all gather. Other than that meeting, you can never find them all in one place. This is the ideal time for us to strike and get rid of all of them once and for all. Where they are meeting this time, in Hall Forest, is ideal for us to hide. The trees there are enormous and strong enough to bear our bulk. We will send one of our kind to attack and be frozen so that when your spell comes through, we will be able to see the change. That will be our signal to annihilate the wizards."

"Father," trembled Warthang, in both anticipation and fear, "The note says their meeting is at the next full moon. That only gives me a week to find the cave."

"Do not whine, Warthang!" growled the adult dragon, "I came as soon as I found out and that is the time allotted to us. You will travel with all speed and you will not fail your mission."

"Could you not just carry me to the cave and drop me there?"

Suddenly, a sharp screech undertoned by a deep growl protruded from Singe's opened mouth. With his spiked tail, he whacked Warthang across the side, sending him flying and crashing to the end of the tiny lair with a whimper.

"The wizards have a sight to help them watch the land, you fool!" With the speed of a slithering snake, Singe crawled to where Warthang lay sprawled on the dirt, yelling directly in his face. "They will watch me but they will not watch you. They do not know of you!"

With his snout, the green dragon pushed the red baby back to his feet and flung him toward the mouth of the cave.

"Now go and find a way to defeat the wizards, you idiot!"

*　　*　　*

It had taken Warthang about a day to cross the mountains and reach the farmlands. That part of the journey really came out to be the easiest since there was a myriad of hiding places for him, and really no humans of which to speak. Finally, after that first trek of slithering behind boulders and between cracks, the young dragon found himself in a new environment, wounded and hungry. His left side throbbed where he had landed in his little cave after being flung by his father, and every ache reminded him of how he had shamed Singe. He could not wait to accomplish his mission, so that he could make all dragons respect him and possibly attain even more renown than his father.

Forgetting his pain, Warthang looked out across the farmlands to see a mysterious landscape, mysterious to him, that is. In the distance, rows of funny plants stretched out for miles, encumbered only by a shack here and there. Close to these homes, small packs of animals cropped the short grasses. The four-year-old did not know what they were for he had never seen the likes of them before, but they looked appetizing. Some had curled horns and all were covered in some kind of fluffy substance that did not resemble the fur he was used to seeing on wolves and rodents. Not knowing if their horns would prove dangerous, the red reptile slid his body between the rows of tall plants to reach the closest herd, all the while remaining concealed. Among his prey, a few small babies rested, oblivious to the danger he posed.

Before he could attack, a biped creature, one he could only assume was a human, exited the cabin. When this happened, all the fluffy animals raised their heads and headed toward him with a trot, bleating incessantly, like they wanted something. The man smiled.

"Come and get it!" he yelled and threw some kind of grain from a sack he carried by his side.

The scene filled Warthang with a pang in his breast and a longing he did not understand. With downcast eyes, he slithered deeper into the plant maze and continued south on his journey. That night, however, curiosity and hunger got the better of him and he sneaked up to a window of a home ten miles away and peeked into the light. In the room sat two adults and four children, eating supper. On a taller stool, a little girl giggled, flinging small peas at an older boy.

"Mom! Tell her to stop!" whined the little boy.

"Juniper," said the mother sternly, "I know you think that being four gives you the right to do anything, but that is enough!"

Little Juniper whimpered and Warthang expected the father to slap her, but instead the mother patted the girl on the hand and both parents smiled.

The red dragon frowned in confusion and disgust. She was four just like him and deserved to be beaten for her despicable manners.

Later on that night, little Juniper wobbled outside to fetch some water. In the darkness, a small voice called out her name.

"Yes?" she asked in her little child voice.

"I am hungry," whispered Warthang, loud enough for her to hear.

"Come in and eat. We have lots of yummy food!" piped Juniper.

"No. I can't be seen. Bring me some. But don't say anything!"

"Okay!" At that, she ran back into the house.

The whole minute that Juniper spent collecting food, Warthang thought hard in his young head. Humans seemed mild and kind, nothing like what he knew of the

29

wizards. From what he had seen that day, they took care of animals that were not their own kind and treated their young with love and affection. The dragons could definitely keep humans around and use them! What he could not understand, however, was why his father had never told him anything about them. With a sigh, the baby dragon figured it was because he had to focus on his mission and not worry about anything else.

Arms filled with different victuals, Juniper returned to the dark outside and deposited the lot around where she thought the voice would be.

"You eat now!" she ordered, resting her small hands on her hips.

"Turn around," Warthang whispered back.

Without questioning him, the little girl turned around and waited while he snatched the food and brought it to his hiding place. None of the things she had brought him were familiar to him, but his stomach growled enough that he did not complain and just gobbled everything down. Once he had eaten it all, which took a whole of two minutes, his yellow eyes gazed at her frail figure in the dark.

"Mister?" she asked, "Can I see you now?"

"No!" Warthang burst, knowing that in his mission, no one could see him.

Turning back around towards the sound of his voice, Juniper folded her arms and puckered her lips.

"Mommy says that people who hide do bad things. Do you do bad things?"

"No," the man-sized dragon responded, thinking about the evil sorcerers. "I'm good. In fact, I'm a hero."

"Oh!" exclaimed Juniper, clapping her fragile hands. "A story! What did you do?"

Warthang smiled and flicked his thin tongue out, the way snakes do.

"Do you know about wizards?" he asked.

"They're bad," nodded the four-year-old child. "Mommy says they hide behind hoods because they do bad things."

"Well," continued the hidden dragon, "I can't tell you the story yet but it has to do with the bad wizards."

Juniper frowned her lower lip and lowered her blond eyebrows. "When can I hear the story, then?"

"Come out every night to this same place and one day soon, I will come back and tell you the story."

"Okay!" she exclaimed, "Can my brothers hear too?"

"Yes," Warthang nodded in the dark. "It will be safe then. Invite your whole family and I will tell the tale!"

"See you soon!" exclaimed Juniper. Quickly, she took her little stumpy legs and ran back into the house, leaving the red dragon in the dark. Satisfied at having met his first human and having thoroughly impressed her, Warthang crawled away and continued on his way south, his belly full and content. Once he finished his mission, he planned on returning to this small home and making admirers of this family. In his heart, he knew that they would love him, be thankful for his mission, and want to do whatever he wanted, like feeding him or polishing his scales. After this first retelling of his great feat, he would then face his father once again, meet the other dragons and be their legendary hero and leader. Everyone would love him. Everyone would look up to him, worship him and serve him.

Note 3

I was so wrong. The wizards *didn't* have it coming to them! No matter how awful a person can be, extinguishing their life is not the answer. Who am I that I should decide who lives and who doesn't? How did I ever think this would be okay? Can I ever atone for this extinction that I caused? No. Never.

Chapter 3 – Extinction

On the day of the full moon, Warthang had finally found the river. It had taken him all his strength and little sleep to make it there. Crossing the farmlands and the grass plains really had not been difficult; it was just such a great distance for a little dragon who had never gone anywhere. Unlike the adults of his kind, his small wings could not support his weight yet. Flight was definitely out of the question.

Looking across the water, the baby reptile calculated how deep and wide the river stretched. Without much hesitation, he jumped in and swam his way to the other bank the way a crocodile glides over the water, its tail languidly swishing from left to right. Although he had never submerged his body in a stream before, his body naturally took over and it was as if he had always done it.

Once he reached the other side, it took Warthang until dusk to find the rock Singe had described to him so many times. Feeling like he was running out of time, the red dragon slipped at the entrance and tumbled down the stairs, into the cave. There, in the dank underground enclosure, he spied shelves covered in books and parchments all around the walls. In the corner, a fire place sat silently, devoid of fire and heat. With a sigh, the man-sized dragon wished he had more than just puffs of smoke coming out of his mouth so that he could light that fire and see better in the dark. Alas, he was too young and the fire had not completely developed in his belly, he would have to contend with his night vision to decipher the spells.

Probing the dusty tomes, he had difficulty choosing a starting point. Most of these spells, if not all, had been written by Thangard, the high wizard, and it was hard to tell if there was any particular order to them. Looking at the titles, he found a vague one named *The book of Thangard* and decided it was as good of a place to start as any other. With much difficulty, the minute dragon stretched his stubby front legs to clutch the edges of the mammoth manuscript. After much wiggling and scratching and finally drawing the thing out with his mouth by the hard cover page, Warthang succeeded in his endeavor.

Opening the crumbling, sandy pages and flipping through them with his barely developed claws, the puffing baby noticed many possible spells to help his kin defeat the wizards. For instance, one called *The Destroying Enemies Spell* read,

> *"Enemies are a dreadful sight;*
> *When they see you, they want to fight.*
> *This spell will help you defeat them;*
> *Every utter, destroying ten."*

Warthang slicked his tiny tongue against his scaly lips, thinking. If this spell destroyed ten wizards at a time, it would not be enough to help the dragons. The sorcerers would understand what was happening and put a stop to it. With that in mind, the four-year-old figured he had to find something that would hit all of them at once.

After hours and hours, the ruby dragon finally found a perfect charm for what he required. He could not believe his luck! Not only could this spell hit all the wizards at once, but the timing of finding it seemed perfect. Already, it was getting late and the one dragon would be frozen after his attempted attack, waiting for Warthang's move.

Analyzing the spell twice to make sure he understood the directions, he finally barked out,

> *"Upon some words spoken;*
> *The air will be broken.*
> *A new spell will appear—*
> *Beyond thy doubt and fear—*
> *In the air they will be*
> *For anyone to see.*
> *So on thy brave request,*
> *This spell will be thy best.*
> *Presently speak one rhyme,*
> *And it shall be made thine..."*

Louder than ever, Warthang lifted his eyes and his front legs and screeched,

> *"All the wizard magic*
> *Upon me it will stick!"*

A tingly atmosphere built up, like when one takes a walk on a misty morning and droplets leap unto one's body at every step. From all the corners of the damp cave, mud and water swirled and collected in the air like pollen caught in a whirling draft. Suddenly, the "magic ingredients" braked in front of the scarlet dragon, structuring into words that eternally incrusted themselves into the creature's memory. Without much hesitation, for he knew time was of the essence, Warthang recited the new spell,

> *"All the wizard magic,*
> *Though it is not frolic,*
> *I take upon myself*
> *To treat well as an elf.*
> *It is now mine to weave,*
> *And it shall never leave."*

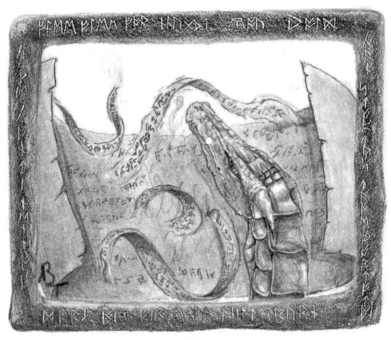

Raw magic throbbed into his crocodile head, slowly coursing through the veins of his neck and working down to his limbs. Rushing from all around him, voices and thoughts and screams and yelps shot into his mind. Deliberately, Warthang focused his psyche on the clearest and strongest mind he could hear:

'Kib can't control the dragons anymore; I have to get out of here. Wait. I can't fly!'

Looking around, the wizard caught sight of a red-headed sorceress raising her arms in vain and angrily stamping her feet. Surrounding them, the large reptiles dropped from every tree, grinning with their fangs bared. With determination, the wizard stepped forward and approached Singe, recognizing him.

'Singe, we mean you no harm. Let us know what it is you want and I am certain we can negotiate.'

'Get away!' Thangard yelled and yanked the wizard backward.

Before he had a chance to get his footing, a gust of heat enveloped the wizard's body and a smoldering sensation overtook his senses. Everything smelled of cooking flesh, burning nails and falling hair as blazing flames overtook his form. A raucous shriek poured out of his scorched lungs. Even that needed extreme strength and only caused an excruciating explosion of his charred lungs. Not able to take it anymore, the wizard thrashed around on the forest ground but found no relief; only charcoaled flesh dwindled down, sticking to the unrelinquishing pine needles. Surprisingly, the pain finally started subsiding and sensation slowly slipped from his awareness. Gradually, all consciousness left him.

Warthang's eyelids flew open and he found himself

rolled like a fetus on the cold ground of the wizard cave. By taking all their magic, he had acquired the wizard's sight, among other powers he yet knew, witnessed the beginning of the battle and felt one of the wizards' experience. A tear slid down his cheek and fell to the dirt.

"How horrible," his voice trembled.

The baby dragon shook his head, he could not believe his thoughts. Truly, he wished there could have been another way: this business of killing just did not seem right. And that was what surprised him most; he never had had a problem with the idea of ending a creature's life before, but now he felt absolutely disgusted and indignant about it. Shaking his head and picking himself off the ground, Warthang trudged his way out of the cave, wishing to erase the gruesome images from his mind. Although what had happened seemed wrong to him, the dragon still thought that in the end, he had done a great service to his kind and humanity in general, by ridding the earth of the wizard-kind.

* * *

The next night, Warthang was flying, truly flying like other dragons, but with even more freedom, the wizard magic powerfully coursing through his veins. When he saw the hut among the fields, he dropped out of the sky and graciously landed back to the same hiding spot he had used the previous time. Patiently, he waited a little over an hour while the people inside dined. When they were done, little Juniper sneaked outside, dragging her young brother with her.

"I'm telling you," she was saying, "the hero is going to come and tell us a story!"

"And I'm telling *you*," replied the brother, "that you imagined him. That's what babies do, they make up little friends to keep them company."

His heart pounding, Warthang listened to their bantering, working up the courage to speak.

"Juniper!" he called, loud enough for both children to hear him.

"See!" piped Juniper, happily. "That's my friend. He's real!"

"Are you ready for my story?" asked Warthang, tentatively.

"Wait, let me get my family!" At that, the little blond girl ran back inside.

"Hum," the boy said, hesitantly, "What's your name?"

Before the dragon could answer, the door of the house opened and out came the rest of the family: the parents, Juniper and two teenage boys.

"He has a hero story about wizards to tell us!" chimed the little four-year-old.

Uncertain, the father walked up to the boy closest to Warthang and quickly pushed him behind himself, protectively.

"Who are you to be talking to a little girl without knocking on the door and meeting the family first? We know everyone in this dump, and no one would sneak around like this. Show yourself!"

Not knowing what else to do, Warthang came out of his hiding place and stepped into the light, about two feet away from the father. Not only the parents, but the boys also, gasped and backed a step. Juniper, on the other hand, clapped her little hands and hopped up and down.

"Look, mommy! It's a little dragon!"

Stretching his hand behind him, the father signaled to his oldest boy who ran back into the house. Then, he looked squarely into Warthang's face, since they were eye to eye, and asked,

"Are you lost, creature? Your masters must be looking for you."

"My masters?" Warthang cocked his head sideways. "Do you mean the wizards? Oh, they're not looking for me, believe me. All is well, in fact! I have great tidings to share, friends!"

The mother, now walking behind her husband, frowned and pushed her children farther away, backing them behind her.

"Go back inside," she whispered to them. Then, she asked the small dragon, almost spitting at him, "What message do you bring from the wizards?"

"Why, they do not send a message, they cannot! As of this morning, they are all dead!"

"What!" both the father and mother exclaimed. Again, they pushed the children closer to the door but before they could hush them back inside, the older boy exited the house, carrying a pitchfork in his hand. Without a word, he handed it to his father, all the while staring at Warthang curiously.

Not understanding, for he had never seen a pitchfork before, the red four-year-old advanced closer to the light. When the family saw his eyes, the father dropped the pitchfork and all six of them, including little Juniper, inhaled loudly.

"It's Luya!" one of the teenage boys whispered loud

enough for everyone to hear.

"Luya's a girl," the mother harshly shushed him.

"Please forgive our insolence," the man said to Warthang, looking angrily down at his feet. "We did not know of you. Now please tell us what you wish, and then leave us alone."

The red dragon furrowed his brow. He did not understand the disdain they clearly felt toward him. Surely their demeanor would change, however, once he told them they were free of the wizards' reign.

"Listen," he said hesitantly. "I went into the wizard cave last night and chose a spell, and then the dragons took care of the wizards. But they couldn't have done it without me, you see. I was the biggest part of the plan."

By the door, Juniper whimpered. As for the rest of the family, they all trembled, something that was barely noticeable because they were trying to hide their fear, but Warthang saw everything.

"You are the only one then," understood the father. "I suppose we don't have much of a choice, and you probably still want us to stay in this place. We shall, of course, respect your laws as faithfully as we have in the past. Is there anything else?"

"I guess not..." stammered Warthang, looking around at the children and trying to fathom their reactions.

"If that is all." The mother curtsied almost rudely and led her four children back inside. After spitting on the ground, the man turned around, entered his house and shut the door firmly.

Now Warthang really did not understand. He thought the humans would be pleased to hear about the wizards' defeat and certainly proud of his accomplishment. But instead of pride, they said they respected him and seemed to fear him. Watching the ground at his feet, the young reptile had a bad feeling. He had really counted on this meeting being a prequel to his reunion with his dad; but if this was a prequel, then things did not bode well.

No matter, it had to happen sometime. Without a backwards glance, Warthang floated to the air and began heading west, toward Hall Forest. Having shortly perused through his wizard sight, he had seen that the dragons remained on the battle field, feasting on the dead bodies and boasting of their exploits to each other. It would take him another day to fly to their location, counting food and sleep, and that gave him enough time to think about what he would say.

*   *   *

When he arrived at the battle site the next night, Warthang landed in a tree and slowly worked his way down the trunk, not wanting to be seen right away. In the forest, twenty dragons lay lazily about, their bellies fat with wizard, their tails swishing contentedly back and forth. It had already been two days since their victory, and a select few of them were discussing what to do next, Singe leading the discussion.

"The ideal place," he was saying, "would be in the rocky mountains on the north of the island. There are many caves in those cliffs where we can live without being bothered."

"And how should we divide our hunting ground?" asked a purple male.

"That shouldn't be too hard," a yellow female dragon replied. "All twenty of us can just fly the land, and decide who wants what on the survey trip."

The few dragons that were discussing in a huddle approved the idea and set the trip for the morrow. Before moving on to a different matter, Singe raised his head in attention and looked in the direction where Warthang hid his human-sized bulk in the tree. Realizing he had been spotted, the small dragon slid down the trunk and shyly approached, his head bent towards the ground. Never having met the other dragons, and being considerably smaller, he did not know quite how to act or what to say.

"Well, kin," shouted Singe, bringing all the other dragons to attention, "here he is! This is Warthang, the one who made our victory possible."

All at once, the creatures in the forest cove began flapping their wings, lashing their tails up and down, belching fire into the air and roaring in triumph. The jubilation was so strong that it was a wonder the whole of Hall Forest did not get burned down that day.

A warm feeling enveloped Warthang's heart and a smile crept up on his small face. Shouts of "how did you do it?" and "tell us the story!" welcomed him as he walked slowly deeper into their throng. The farther in he went, the more his countenance changed: his back straightened, his legs walked firmly and his head he held high.

But something strange happened. Have you ever walked down a busy street to see one person looking intently at the sky? Little by little, others stop and also look up and next thing you know, everyone is doing it. Well, through the shouts and excited yelps, one dragon cut his acclamations short and stared down at little Warthang, squinting his eyes and showing his teeth in a small growl. Then another, and another, until the whole assembly had quieted to a heavy rumbling growl, staring in hate at the little red dragon.

Pushing his way through, Singe walked up to his son, towering over him like a great unmovable tree.

"What did you do, you fool?" he hissed audibly enough for everyone to hear.

Warthang cringed, bracing himself for a blow.

"What do you mean?" he asked, his voice shaking.

Singe harrumphed and turned his back on the baby dragon. As one, the other dragons backed away furious and followed the green male's lead, drawing to the edge of the clearing, all the while whispering and hissing. All alone, Warthang cowered to the ground, tears sliding down his scaly cheeks. Why was this happening? He had done everything that had been asked of him. Everything. All he wanted was for someone to tell him what a good job he had done and how proud they were of him, but not even his mother, Ferel, dared look at him. All his short life, he had had very little contact with anyone and he now longed to have company and friends. The day before, the humans had treated him with distance and fear, and now his own kind disdained him.

In their private conversations, the dragons seemed to debate over the situation and what should be done. After what seemed like hours, Singe broke from the cluster and took his time in approaching the waiting Warthang. All the others' heads had turned toward the scene, looking like cobras intently watching their prey. At last, the green leader declared without emotion to the baby dragon,

"You may live in the mountains as we do and you may roam freely as we do but you may not feed in our hunting grounds. Moreover, do not expect any pity or conversation from us, we do not wish to speak to you more than we have to. In fact, if at all possible, we would prefer not ever seeing you again, so make yourself scarce."

Having finished his sentence, Singe stared at Warthang unblinkingly. Without meaning to, the four year old's lips trembled as he whined and pleaded to the others, not daring to look at his father,

"But why?" he complained. "What have I done?"

"How about you go reflect on it in a pool?" yelled out a yellow dragon.

The others around her snickered and patted her on the shoulders.

"Good one!"

Before the chuckling turned into uncontrolled laughter, Warthang turned around and ran the other way, like a dog with its tail hanging low. For a long time, he fled in shame, tears streaming nonstop behind him. Eventually, his sobs subsided and he crumbled to the ground, energy drained out of him.

When the sun inched its way up the next morning, it found Warthang, sleepless, in the same position, breathing shallowly. Finally, once the rays fully penetrated the forest foliage, the little dragon forced himself up and found a flowing stream nearby. After dousing his head in the water and drinking deeply, he raised his head and drew back, startled. Determined, the red baby returned to the liquid surface and stared at his reflection. There, in that mirror image, he saw what caused fear, hate and disdain when others looked at him. No longer did his eyes hold a straight vertical reptile black line like snakes, crocodiles and dragons do, but the yellow of them had overtaken everything. In fact, they were completely yellow. They were opaque. They were the eyes of a wizard.

Note 4

I guess when people think of dragons, they think of these huge teethy monsters that breathe fire, hoard treasure and come down on their villages to eat them and burn their remaining houses out of a sense of evil. Well, I won't be the one to say I disagree with them because for the most part, it is true. However, the sad fact remains that there are usually exceptions to the rules and you shouldn't judge others because of their species. You see, I'm a dragon, and although I may have started out like your typical monster, I became the exception to the rule.

Chapter 4 – Friendship

When a whole species shuns one of its own and even prefers not seeing or hearing him, that outcast ends up with a lot of spare time on his hands. So, trying not to be bored and to forget his loneliness, Warthang experimented with his wizard magic and found he possessed all kinds of powers. Among other things, he could control fire, water, wind, earth, animals, and could even teleport. Once in a while, interestingly, he would awaken with a new power. The first time it happened, he found himself uncontrollably changing colors: from red, to green, to blue, then back to red. At that moment, he understood that a new wizard would have been born, but the spell he had uttered those moons ago continued stealing the magic from the humans and giving it to him.

Through all these interesting discoveries, Warthang wished he could share his knowledge and talents, but whenever he approached the other dragons, they either completely ignored him or left, not deigning to even look at him.

One day, when he was about 20, a lanky young red dragon at the time, he stumbled unto two younger dragons he had never seen before. Judging by their sizes and by the fact that they were fire target practicing on mushrooms, he guessed they were around 12 to 15 years old. He could not believe his eyes: new dragons! Maybe they knew nothing about him and he could befriend them!

"What are you doing?"

As soon as he asked, he felt stupid for having blurted out such a question since the answer was so obvious. To save face, he strengthened his shoulders and declared,

"I can do a lot better than that!"

The older of the two young dragons, a purple female, rolled her eyes at him.

"Just because you're older, doesn't mean you have to show off."

Warthang realized the conversation had already had a rough start so he decided to try again.

"Yeah, so, I've never seen you around before. What are your names?"

"I'm Flora," said the purple female. Then, she pointed to the younger blue dragon next to her with a claw. "This is my brother Brook."

"You have funny eyes," said Brook, squinting at him.

"Yeah, they're a little different..." stammered Warthang.

Brook and Flora shared a glance and their snake tongues flicked in and out, tasting the air.

"I know of a stream that cures weird eyes," offered Brook. "Our mom injured hers once in a rough landing and it cured them right away."

Warthang's yellow opaque eyes grew big. If his eyes could be cured, then he no longer would have to live like an outcast. The heaviness in his heart tightened and his breathing stopped.

"Show me," he breathed.

Without a second glance, Flora and Brook turned

50

eastward and trudged quickly between two high boulders. After a few minutes, they reached the other side and abruptly stopped by a deep bubbling stream.

"Here it is." Flora smiled, showing her sharp teeth. "You just have to soak your eyes in the water for about a minute and it does the trick."

Not believing his luck, Warthang approached the water cautiously. It looked just like any normal brook but the dragon could almost perceive magical sparkling dust following the current every which way. Seeing his reflection, he looked at his straight yellow eyes and frowned. Oh, how he hated them. They were the bane of his life.

Without much more thought, he bent his head forward so that only the top part of his head, where his eyes lay, touched the water. Slowly, he counted, making sure they remained submerged for the whole 60 seconds. Before reaching the final count, however, he felt claws at the back of his neck pushing him deeper into the water. Losing his balance, he fell on the edge of the stream and inhaled some water into his lungs as he tried to free himself from the claws holding his head under.

Their loud chuckles reached his submerged ears as he struggled to regain his footing on the shore. At their laughter, a burning anger worked its way from his core to his extremities. With his power, he blasted the two dragons backwards and jumped back to his feet, his head released from their hold.

"Who do you think you are?" he yelled at them, as they cowered against the rocks where he had shot them.

The tingling fire of rage continued coursing its way through his blood and he drew out two thin tendrils of water out of the stream. Looking at Brook and Flora, he unleashed the anger he had kept inside for the last 16 years and whipped their backs with the water.

"It's not my fault!" he cried in anguish, as he lashed at their feet, their legs and their backs.

"You didn't give me a chance! I was too young, I didn't understand enough! You should have waited!"

After his short outburst, Warthang crumbled, letting his water whips fall and splash to the ground, soaking it. He could not see anymore; tears streamed from his eyes relentlessly.

Wordlessly, Flora scuttled away and disappeared. Her little brother, on the other hand, whimpered and sniffled at the welts on his back and legs. After a few minutes, the purple female returned with a small green dragon.

"He's the one who did it, Benzady!" she hissed, hiding behind him.

"Hey, freak!" he called out to Warthang, his eyes furrowed, his shoulders hunched forward, ready for a fight.

"I've heard of you," he continued, nearing Warthang who still lay on the ground like a clump of dirt. "You're the last wizard, half dragon, half monster, and you're a coward! You don't dare attack the older ones of *our* kind, but when you see those smaller than you, you come around and beat them up! Well, we won't stand for it, coward!"

At that, Benzady lashed his tail and hit Warthang in the face. The red dragon covered his head with his clawed front hands.

"Get out of here!" commanded Benzady as he struck him in the shoulder. In shame, the outcast crawled away, enduring the tail whips from the smaller green dragon.

As soon as he turned a corner where the others could not see him, he changed into a bird and fluttered away, never looking back.

In fact, from then on he made it a point to stay away from dragons altogether, going as far as changing his form and not being himself. Whenever he did see a dragon, he laid low, as a small insignificant animal, and closed his eyes, both to forget his shame and to hide them because no matter what form he took, his eyes never changed. The next five years, he spent them secluded, living day to day without a purpose and without anyone to talk to.

*   *   *

At the age of 25, Warthang favored the human form. To him, they were such weird creatures: they could not fly or swim fast, they could not even run particularly quickly, but they seemed to dominate other animals with their cunning and dexterity. But that last part did not matter to him. All he cared about was that they were physically weak and slow, unable to defend themselves against real threats. Furthermore, because he had not yet grown into an adult, the shape he took resembled a scrawny 14 year old teenager, not yet blessed by height. To him, it was all a perfect representation of how he felt about himself.

One day, as he sat by a river in the mountains of the north throwing rocks in the water, he spied a brunette girl walking his way, clicking her tongue as she carefully traveled. Her small braided hair seemed in disarray, heading every which way as if the wind had blown it in different directions, and mud smeared her simple blue dress. Normally, Warthang would have hidden at the sight of a human, but he felt so surprised at seeing one in such a remote spot that he remained seated like a statue. As the young girl reached the opposite bank, she bent over, cupped cold water into her hands and drank. Warthang shifted uncomfortably and the girl suddenly looked up, as if she had just noticed him. She smiled mischievously.

"It's customary to greet someone when you meet them on the road, you know."

Quickly, Warthang looked away, making sure his eyes remained in the shadows. He had not spoken with anyone since the accident five years before, and certainly had not had a conversation with a human in many years. The last thing he wanted to hear were hate words about his horrible eyes, things he told himself every day.

"Hello," he said simply, quietly, barely audible over the running river.

"Hello?" Laughed the girl, shaking her head left and right. "I guess I'll have to start, then. Hi. My name is Maggie. This is my private spot. I come here every day and I have never ever heard of anyone else coming here before."

Greeted with silence, Maggie sighed.

"Do I have to do everything?" she asked, more to herself than to anyone in particular. "What's your name?" she inquired a little louder, making sure the water would not drown out her voice.

"Warthang."

"Wow. That is one gloomy name. It's no wonder you seem so down in the dumps!"

At his silence, she stumped her right foot down.

"Cross the river, WT! No one can have a decent conversation over this noise!"

Startled, Warthang scrambled to his feet and took one step backward.

"What did you call me?" he asked, hesitantly.

"WT," laughed Maggie. "Names are who we are so I thought I'd call you something more fitting and not so melodramatic."

Remembering himself, Warthang shielded his eyes from view, as if the sun had blinded him and he needed some reprieve. Frustrated, Maggie drummed her fingers on her hips.

"Are you coming or what?"

Sighing heavily, the dragon boy entered the water and forded to the other side. He knew what would happen, it was inevitable. She would see his eyes and get all weird on him or call him a freak or run away. Even though he knew this would happen, though, he felt he deserved it, so he forged ahead and reached dry ground, dripping wet drops to the ground. Content, Maggie nodded knowingly, sat down and patted the dirt next to her.

"So, what are you doing out here all by yourself?" she asked, curious.

Warthang shrugged and slowly sat down next to her, making sure he faced away where she could not quite see his face.

"I'm always alone," he admitted.

"Really?" Maggie raised an eyebrow. "Well, it's about time you make a friend, don't you think?"

Warthang shook his head and puffed air out of his cheeks. "No one will be my friend."

Turning her head toward him, the girl leaned toward

him. "Why not?" she asked, almost in his face.

The dragon scrambled to his two human feet and faced her squarely.

"Just look at me!" he shouted, looking down at her and balling his hands into fists. "I'm different and people hate me for it!"

"Someone woke up on the wrong side of the bed," Maggie said out of the corner of her mouth. Then, she clasped her hands together and looked up toward him. "You're not the only one who's different, you know. People tend to stay away from me too, and I won't necessarily say it's because of hate but more because of ignorance."

"Ignorance?" Warthang looked to the sky, partially having forgotten his anger, and sat back down next to the brunette with a plop.

"Yeah, ignorance," continued Maggie. "I'm different so I live by different rules, in a sense, and they don't understand that; in fact, it scares them."

Warthang shook his head. "How are you different? You look perfectly normal to me."

"And you, WT, sound perfectly normal to *me*." Again, she smiled, pleased at her inward joke. "You may have been too far to hear it over the water, but did you hear me doing those clicking noises when I was heading this way?"

Now that he thought back to it, he did remember her doing such a noise with her tongue, but could not see how that made her different, other than being weird, maybe.

"Yeah..." he answered.

"Well," Maggie continued, "I'm blind; I can't see a thing! But because of that, I'm learning to use my other senses in a way that others don't need. I hear really well now and I'm teaching myself to listen to the clicks I make to see how far things are from me so I can walk without stumbling. I guess people think that's really strange and they make fun of me."

"That's not so bad," Warthang shook his head then took a deep breath, preparing himself for her reaction. "I'm a wizard."

"You realize that's hardly believable, right?" Maggie looked in his direction, incredulous. "The dragons killed the wizards over twenty years ago, and strangely enough, no new ones ever rose up again."

Her soft, calm tone surprised the dragon boy but he felt convinced that when she finally understood the truth about him, her demeanor would change in a heartbeat.

"Was there ever a rumor coming out of the farmlands about a wizard who killed all the others?" he asked her.

"A rumor?" replied Maggie. "No, but there *is* a children's story meant to scare kids to eat their beets. They say that one single wizard killed all of the rest and now hides away and will come after innocent children and take them away if they don't do what they're told."

"Well, that story's a bit off but I'm sure it's about me."

Maggie burst out laughing and bent forward, rocking back and forth. "That was over 20 years ago, and you sound like a kid my age! There is no way that story is about you, but even if it *is* true, I bet you it was distorted over time. Now, since we're going to be friends, I'm only going to judge you on how you act here and now, not how a child's tale depicts you."

Warthang could not help but crook a shy smile at her continued glee. Whether she believed him or not, she was willing to give him a chance; no one had really done that before. Crossing his arms, he looked at her and nodded,

"So, as a friend, what do I need to do?"

"It's simple, WT," smiled Maggie, "Meet me at this spot every day when the sun is high and over time, we'll become good friends."

And so it was that every blissful day, Warthang met with Maggie. He told her all sorts of things he had learned about nature and animals and even let her experience some of his magic; but through it all, he never told her his deepest secret, that he really was not human, but a dragon. In turn, she taught him about how to live with others, helped him develop some social skills and explained to him the difference between good and evil. Because of these lessons, the dragon understood that what his father had done to him was not right and his hate for him grew exponentially. However, he now also knew that some of his own actions did not reflect goodness either and vowed to be kind to others, no matter how they treated him. Maggie was kind and beautiful, as much on the inside as on the outside, and he wanted to be just like her.

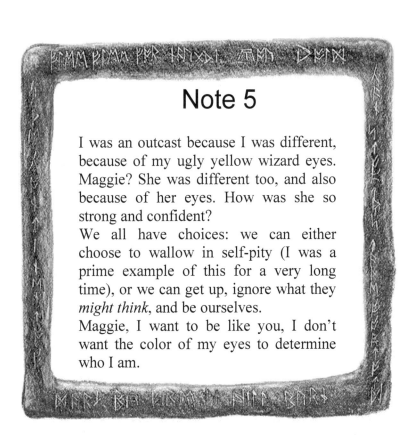

Note 5

I was an outcast because I was different, because of my ugly yellow wizard eyes. Maggie? She was different too, and also because of her eyes. How was she so strong and confident?

We all have choices: we can either choose to wallow in self-pity (I was a prime example of this for a very long time), or we can get up, ignore what they *might think*, and be ourselves.

Maggie, I want to be like you, I don't want the color of my eyes to determine who I am.

Chapter 5 – Miracles

One day, as they were walking down the river hand in hand, Maggie suddenly stopped and faced Warthang, letting his hand go. Unlike her usual self, she seemed uncomfortable, clutching her fingers together in front of her.

"Will you go to the dance with me tonight?" she blurted out.

Raising his eyebrows, the dragon boy brought his hand up to his mouth in a thinking gesture.

"Maggie? Are you talking about a social gathering...with people?"

Laughing, the blind girl pushed him lightly on the shoulder.

"Of course, silly!"

"I...I don't know," he stammered awkwardly.

"Look," Maggie started, "I know it's a lot to ask but I've thought this through. It's at night so it'll be dark and no one will really be able to see, which puts both of us at an advantage. Plus, it's about time you meet other people and see what life is like for yourself."

Slowly, Warthang shook his head. "I don't think I'm ready for that..."

Nervously, the girl bit her lip in silence, then finally sighed, resigned.

"Fine. You got me. Here's the real reason, WT, and

don't you dare embarrass me!" She shook her finger in his face. "The truth is I really want to go to this dance. I'm 16 and I've never even been to a dance! It looks bad to go by yourself and for the first time in my life, I know someone who may actually not refuse going with me!"

Warthang felt surprised, this was so out of character for her.

"Maggie," he said, perplexed, "You *never* care about what people think."

"Warthang." She never called him that unless she felt annoyed, "there are exceptions to the rules. Now, will you *please* go to this stupid dance with me?"

Not able to refuse her further, Warthang put his head in his hands and mumbled a consent. There was no going back, now.

*　　*　　*

When Warthang had agreed to go to this unknown function, he had imaged fires in the dark with dark-clad people dancing to the rhythm of music for the sake of fun; however, what he found surprised him completely. Apparently, this dance was not just a dance but an event that occurred every four years, where teenagers from the ages of 13 to 19 gathered to find their possible mate. As was tradition, a girl would come to the dance accompanied by a boy (and vice-versa, of course) to show that he/she was likeable enough, and then the meeting of potential spouses began.

But anyway, unaware of all these customs, Warthang arrived at the dance with clean black clothes and a black hat that covered his red hair, but most importantly, cast shadows over his strange yellow eyes. Already, this

62

made him feel extremely out of place because all the other boys wore nice colors, with their heads bare, showing every feature they could offer to the girls. The ladies, on the other hand, riveted on the dance floor with beautiful frilly dresses that flowed freely around their ankles. Burning torches lit the circle of people as older adults played a myriad of musical themes with wind and string instruments.

"Where did you find a loser to go with you, Maggie?" asked a tall blond boy, rudely, right behind them.

Both turning around to face the teenager, Maggie stepped forward to confront him while Warthang surreptitiously hid behind her small frame, bending his black hat forward over his face.

"And I wonder what kind of loser your mom found to have such an ugly son."

The blond boy clapped his hands, mocking. "Ugly, huh? That's a great insult from a *blind* girl!"

Behind her, Warthang closed his fists firmly, slightly trembling.

"I guess it wasn't one of my best insults," acquiesced the brunette, "not quite on my game tonight. WT," she turned to him then. "Could you take me as far from this guy as possible, please?"

Warthang released his fists and guided her away with one hand on her shoulder.

"Seriously?" The blond boy directed his attention to Warthang, prodding. "There is no way you're going to find a girl with Blindy here having to stick up for you all the time."

Ignoring him, the dragon boy grated his teeth and continued on, leading Maggie forward. After a few minutes, once they had lost themselves in the crowd, he finally asked her,

"What is that guy's problem?"

"Oh, he's just a bully," Maggie replied. "Normally, I wouldn't put too much stock in what he says but he did have a point though, WT. No offense, but you do need to stand up for yourself more."

"I don't know if that's a good idea," admitted Warthang. "I get angry really fast and I'm afraid of what I might do. I've done some bad things before and it seems better to just take it and keep it inside."

"Are you kidding me?" scoffed his friend. "That's a great recipe for blowing up later in major proportions! Here, I'll give you some advice my mom gave me when I was a little girl. Next time someone is nasty to you or calls you names, kill him with kindness."

"Kill him with kindness? I can't see what you mean, you certainly don't seem to follow that motto."

"True, true. I prefer sarcasm or jokes myself but I think that wouldn't work for you, it would just inflame your anger. No, what I'm saying is be so nice to the person that they end up feeling bad for what they did. Sometimes that doesn't really work either but you can be so nice to them to the point of making yourself laugh. It makes you feel better. Anyway, that's what my mom would say, the abridged version."

"Maggie," Warthang almost interrupted her, "there's a guy looking at you."

"Oh?" she perked up, interested. "What does he look like?"

"Well, he's got brown hair," started Warthang before she broke through his description.

"I'm blind, I don't care what he looks like. What I

mean is: what does he *look* like? Look deeper."

The dragon boy looked again, squinting his eyes and paying closer attention to the details.

"He has a serene air to him, seems like a calm kind of person and I would say even kind. His face looks like the kind that smiles all the time. He's shy and keeps to himself, his posture seems closed, like he isn't ready to talk to anyone. He observes and waits...I think."

"Mmmmm," Maggie smiled, "I like a challenge. Lead me to him; he shall wait no longer."

Firmly, Warthang grabbed his friend's hand and took her to where the young man sat. However, as they approached him, a panicked look entered the stranger's face and he melted into the darkness in a hurry.

"My lady," laughed the 25 year old dragon, "your prey has escaped!"

"Another day, then. But promise me you'll find him so I can trap him in my snare."

"I promise."

"All right!" Maggie said, abruptly. "Now what do you say we find you a pretty lady? I wouldn't want to think I brought you to this party without any end results."

"No, not interested," said Warthang firmly.

"What? You're still too young and the hormones haven't kicked in yet? Suit yourself, but be aware that this chance won't happen again for another four years!"

Maggie shrugged and together, they left the party. On his side, the dragon felt relieved, he did not want to find a lame excuse to explain his disinterest in girls; that is, in human girls.

*   *   *

The next day, as dawn beamed its light, Warthang woke up in the high branches of a tree where he slept as a squirrel. Right away, he remembered his promise to find the young man from the dance and he focused his wizard sight. Perusing through Valley City, which is where Maggie lived on the western border of the mountains, he searched everywhere but did not find the teenage boy. Refusing to give up, the dragon squirrel stretched his sight and searched further. After leaving the mountains, he finally found his quarry to the west, by the sea. There, he seemed to be casting nets, working hard to supply the city with fish and crustaceans.

Satisfied that the young man was alone, Warthang scampered down his tree, his bushy tail trailing behind him, changed into human form and teleported to the edge of the mountains, a location about a mile from the sea shore. Fifteen minutes later, after a short brisk walk, he stood behind the young stranger, wearing the black clothes and hat he had on the previous day.

"Need some help, fellow?" he asked.

The teenager, decked in simple brown shorts, his back shining from sweat, jumped and somersaulted, facing Warthang. Seeing him, he placed his right hand over his heart and smiled.

"Wow. You really scared me there; people don't usually come this way." After a brief pause, studying Warthang, he continued doubtfully. "Are you sure you want to help, with those clothes? They'll get ruined."

"Oh, I'm not concerned," shrugged Warthang. "Show me what I can do."

So the young man showed him how to cast nets, when to pull them out and what to do once they had been drawn back to shore with their catch. For hours,

66

they worked together in silence, side by side. At the end of the afternoon, the teenager stopped the work and grinned.

"You sure work hard for a scrawny kid. Think you could help me further by hauling this load back through the mountains with me?"

Warthang nodded and they set to work again, loading up two carts with fish and crabs. Once they had filled them to the brim with everything, the dragon pulled one while his companion pulled the other. On their way, they talked together to help distract their minds from the menial task.

"I'm Warthang, by the way. What's your name?"
"Willard."
After some silence, Willard smiled again and shook

his head. "I saw you last night, you know. Want to tell me the reason you're out here?"

Warthang looked sideways at the young man. He was quite a handsome fellow with his well-toned body, his short brown hair and his intelligent blue eyes. Had Maggie not been blind, he felt sure she would have liked what she saw.

"I promised my friend I'd find you. You left before she had a chance to talk to you."

"I can't talk to girls," replied Willard. "My stomach clenches, my throat dries up like I've swallowed sand and I panic."

Although Warthang had had his difficulty socializing in the past, this feeling the young man described seemed completely alien to him.

"You went to the dance," he thought out loud, "You must have wanted to meet someone."

"The intentions were there, Warthang, but not the courage."

Willard stopped pulling his cart and set it down. Looking away toward the approaching mountains, he sighed unhappily. By his side, Warthang waited for him patiently.

"I'm 18 years old and have been working for myself for a few years, now. I like my life; it's simple. But something's missing: I want a companion. Someone I can talk to, spend time with. I want a wife."

Willard sat down and put his head in his hands, pulling a bit at his short hair.

"When I saw her yesterday, I was mesmerized; she's so different from the other girls. They all seem to care about trivial things and gossip, but her? She's confident, not so concerned with physical appearances, and absolutely breath-taking. I couldn't take my eyes off her, I could hardly even breathe. Then, she started heading my way and I bolted, I just couldn't face her. Someone so perfect could only be disappointed by someone as simple as me."

"Tell you what, your unworthiness," Warthang patted him on the shoulder. "After we deliver these, you're going to meet her and let her decide for herself. Courage will have nothing to do with it because you won't have a choice in this. I made a promise to my best friend and I intend to keep it."

*　　*　　*

That evening, they arrived at Maggie's house close to the setting of the sun. Confidently, although he had never been there before, Warthang knocked on the door. Right away, as if she had heard them coming, Maggie opened the door, clicked her tongue and sniffed the air.

"I waited for you all day by the river, you dope! You could have told me you were bringing a friend!"

Warthang thumped his forehead with his right hand and crooked a smile, looking to the sky. He should have thought to send her a message but he had been so intent on his mission that he had forgotten everything else.

"Maggie, let me present to you Willard. He was the one at the party yesterday who left early. Willard, this is Maggie."

Shyly, Willard bowed his head. Obviously, the girl could not see the movement but she had the sense to understand it had been made.

"Welcome," she curtsied. Then, turning sideways, as if to invite them in, she said, "we were about to have dinner and you guys are definitely invited!"

Grabbing Willard by the arm, Warthang escorted him into the house and all three of them headed to the kitchen. There, a young woman was cutting vegetables and setting them into a simple salad.

"Leila," Maggie called to her sister as she also entered the kitchen. "Let me present to you my good friend Warthang."

Leila looked up and smiled.

"Warthang," she said, "Maggie's told me all about you. It's nice to finally meet you."

"And," continued Maggie, "this is Willard."

At his name, the young man extended his arm and shook Leila's hand in greeting. As their grip loosened, she returned to her salad, looking pleased.

"My husband won't be in until later today but we are very glad to have you over. Please, sit down," she indicated the chairs around a small table.

After a few minutes, Leila set the table and brought the salad, bread, cooked potatoes and a meat dish garnished with green herbs. The ladies sat on one side while the men sat on the other. At first, Maggie tried to spark up conversation with Willard, only to receive short, uncertain answers. After a while, she let Warthang and Leila talk while she bit her lower lip in thought. Finally, an idea crossed her mind and her whole demeanor lit up. She looked toward Warthang's direction and said,

"Warthang, take your hat off."

Doubtful and a bit afraid, the dragon boy stared at her from his plate. "Are you sure?" he asked, hesitantly.

Maggie nodded, at the same time indicating to her sister to leave the room with a small polite gesture.

Seeming to understand, Leila excused herself, saying she had to tidy up before her husband came home. Finally, once the older girl had gone, Warthang took hold of the rim of his hat and slid it over his face and into his lap. Seeing the yellow eyes for the first time, Willard sucked in his breath softly.

"Is something the matter?" Maggie asked quietly.

"His...his eyes..." Willard stuttered. Then, he strengthened up and cleared his throat, "I wasn't expecting it. Sorry for the reaction, Warthang."

Surprised, the red-headed boy shrugged, not able to say anything. He did not know what his best friend wanted by having him display his face but he certainly had never expected such a mild response to his freakishness.

"I've always wanted to know," Maggie continued, "What do they look like?"

Dragging his stare from Warthang, Willard finally looked at Maggie square in the face, as if seeing her for the first time.

"What do you mean? Can you not see...?"

The young girl shook her head, a smile growing on her face. This was the most he had talked the whole night.

"Well," he began, looking back at Warthang, "eyes usually have a black circle surrounded by a ring of color. Those colors vary from one person to the other but you can see streaks running through them outwardly. Then, around that, you have the white of your eyes and it's got red veins."

As Willard talked, Maggie smiled to herself, picturing in her mind the words he used into images.

"Warthang's eyes on the other hand are yellow. It's

71

that kind of yellow that reptile eyes have but it's also different because that's all there is. It's just yellow. Like when you look at the petals of a flower, it's yellow; it doesn't have other colors. That's how his eyes are."

At this point, Maggie's elbows rested on the table, her chin in her hands, while she absorbed Willard's description, trying to understand it.

"Wow, WT," she finally said, "that *is* different."

"Were you...were you born that way?" asked Willard carefully.

"No," Warthang answered after a brief moment of silence. "It's a condition you get from having Wizard magic coursing through your blood."

The dragon could not believe it, Willard did not seem to have any clue about wizards or magic. It seemed that time had erased the sorcerers' existence from the minds of the new human generation. Maybe with time, the same thing would happen with the new born dragons and he could integrate himself back with his own species. But maybe not: the original lizard-like reptiles would still be lurking about, spreading the word to keep away from him.

"That explains a lot," Willard nodded, "I was very impressed that a young inexperienced teenager could learn my trade so fast and not even struggle when pulling the nets in from the sea. Everything seemed so easy, like you were pulling feathers! Don't get me wrong, I'm still very impressed, just in a different way." Smiling, he patted Warthang on the back, "Even though you have all this power at your disposal, you still spent all the time doing the work. I don't know much about what you can do, but I imagine if you wanted to, you could skip a lot of menial tasks."

"I can tell you something else that's impressive about WT," Maggie said, directing her words at both of the boys, "he made a promise to me yesterday and in one day, made it come true. He's a miracle worker, and has so much potential in helping people. I know that someday he will do great things."

"A miracle worker?" chuckled the dragon boy, "I find you much more miraculous, Maggie. You're blind, which most people would consider a weakness, but you take it all in stride. You have no magical powers but you were able to make a person talk to you that thought it impossible..."

Realizing the truth, Willard turned as white as a sheet. "It's true. You got me talking like an orator when my mouth had been sealed shut, unable to utter more than one word at a time."

"Can I tell you something?" Maggie sighed, directing her inquiry toward the blue-eyed man, "I wasn't born blind and have memories of colors, of people, of nature. Your descriptions helped me remember and even create new images I had never seen before. When you were talking, it's like I wasn't blind anymore. There's another miracle for you!"

Looking at his two companions, Warthang felt happy and accepted. He was still different, but not weird anymore. Moreover, he had things in common with others, things he shared.

"We're all miracle workers," he declared, grinning.

Note 6

Loneliness. It eats you up inside so that you can't think of anything else but that heavy emptiness. I had a friend and she wasn't like me. I cherished our differences and learned much from them but in the end, it made me suffer even more. Why couldn't someone like *me* accept me too? I had to find that someone, I couldn't be alone. There had to be a friend for me in this small world of dragons.

Chapter 6 – Loneliness

From then on, Warthang met Maggie at her house every morning and together, they would travel to where Willard worked. These were changing times for the dragon and his concepts of friendship and goodness largely sprouted from the time the three of them spent together by the sea shore. Little by little, he stopped wearing hats, exhibiting his eyes proudly for anyone to see. However, as two years turned into three and it became apparent that his two friends wished to get married, Warthang began feeling left out. Partially, he felt responsible for this because even though he no longer felt ashamed of his eyes, he still had not revealed to them his true nature. These two friends of his, they shared everything, never holding back. In fact, Maggie had unveiled, one morning, the mystery of her blindness to them.

When she was a little girl of 9, she was out in the mountains with her parents, enjoying a nature walk—luckily, Leila, around 12 years old at the time, had stayed in Valley City to play with some girls from the area. On their trek, Maggie saw a beautiful butterfly that she started to follow, losing sight of anything else. After a minute, her parents noticed her absence and began calling out for her. In her desperation, her mother began making a ruckus, and she inadvertently disturbed a nearby dragon that had been fast asleep. Furious, the creature left his cave and massacred the two adults, shredding them into meaty pieces with his claws and teeth. Hearing the screeches, for she had not drifted too far, Maggie exploded out of the rocks and unto the scene, finding the dragon and the bloody remains of her loved ones, something she would never forget for as long as she lived.

When she saw the slaughter, a high pitched sound burst from her little lungs, causing the large reptile to look her way. Instead of coming after her though, the monster demonstrated his teeth in a bloody smile, amused by this little frightened thing. Maggie took her small stubby legs and ran away, blind to anything and everything, heading home, a place she knew was safe. When she had reached the edge of the mountains to enter back into Valley City, she lost her footing and roughly tumbled down the last incline, losing consciousness when her head hit a large rock at the end of her fall. Later, she awoke to complete darkness in what felt like a bed of downy. No matter how much they tried, the voices could not make her talk, nor could they make her see. However, hours later, once she recognized her sister's voice, she recovered her speech and the horror spilled out of her like a raging storm.

For a while, the two of them lived with their aunt but when Leila got married years later, the two girls moved in with her new husband and the little family had been together ever since. Maggie's eyes remained blind but she preferred it that way, afraid of what she might see if they were to ever heal.

Obviously, this whole story, when he heard it, made Warthang feel even more reticent about telling his friends that he himself was a dragon, and not a human being. So, quite some time later, when Maggie and Willard got married and even after she became pregnant, he still had not told them his secret.

Once Maggie had the child, a blue eyed little girl named Grace, their sea shore routine changed drastically. Now, every morning, Willard would go off to work while Warthang stayed with the blind woman to help her take care of the baby. Even though it was just the two of them for most of the day, the dragon felt more and more alone at seeing this new family develop. The couple seemed so happy together and especially with their little Grace, for whom they constantly seemed to bend over backwards to make happy.

Very perceptive, the new mother felt that Warthang seemed more distant and unhappy with time. At first, she had not paid much attention to him because Grace seemed to constantly need food and attention, but now the more time she spent alone with her friend, his feelings had become quite evident, and determination pushed her to confront him at last.

"WT, something's been bothering you."

Welcomed only with silence, she continued, "I don't know what it is you've refused to tell me all this time but I know some of it."

Maggie sat down and patted the ground beside her like she used to do when it had been just the two of them. Following her lead, Warthang bent his knees and sat down.

"The three of us have been friends for five years now," she went on, grabbing his hand with both of hers, "I was blind when we first met, but now Willard has been my eyes, and he's a great observer."

His other hand free, the dragon drummed his fingers against his knee, trying to cover the uneasiness he felt creeping up.

"In five years, Willard says you haven't changed and that you still look like a boy in the beginning of puberty." She frowned, shaking her head, "He also says that even if you had been 12, which neither of us believe, you would be 17 now and would have definitely grown taller. WT, is it the magic?"

After only hearing his breathing, Maggie gripped his drumming hand together with the other and squeezed. "There is nothing, *nothing*, that will keep us from being friends, you must believe that."

A tear escaped Warthang's eyes. A dragon had killed her parents and he felt partially responsible for being of the same species. Ever since hearing her story, the guilt had pressed down on his shoulders, a heavy burden he could barely keep back.

For what seemed like an eternity, heavy silence reigned between them until Warthang finally sighed, barely audible.

"I'm not human..."

"No matter what you are," Maggie began, since nothing else was coming out of his mouth, "It doesn't matter. Being blind means I can see better than others. I may not see what people look like but I see their heart and who they really are inside; I see *them*. Before I ever was blind and understood this properly, my father always told me to accept people for who they are, and then also to always give them a second chance."

"I'm a dragon!" he finally blurted out.

A sharp sting spread through the right side of his face; she had slapped him.

"Why do you hate yourself so much?" she cried, tears freely rolling down her cheeks. "You care so much about everything, you have such a beautiful and gentle heart, and yet you don't even see it. All you see are your yellow eyes, your scales. You can hide from your scales but your eyes, they follow you everywhere you go."

At that, she drew herself up, pulling him with her. With an arm, she wiped her wet eyes.

"It's time for you to get to know yourself better, WT. It's time you learn to love yourself and be yourself. You'll never be able to do much good out there until you've accomplished that. Now tell me," she took hold of his face and brought their foreheads together, "what's really bothering you?"

Without thinking, the truth spilled out of him, a truth he had hidden from himself just like he had hidden his dragon-self inside a human body.

"I'm lonely! I want a friend!"

Warthang backed away from Maggie, his eyes stinging. How those words must have hurt her!

"Yes, WT," a sad smile appeared in her face. "You need a dragon friend. Know this: we will always be your friends, but just like children leave their childhood friends eventually to find their best friend and mate, it's the same with you. You have to find someone like you, one who completes you."

The dragon boy shook his head, "It's impossible!"

"Of course it's impossible," burst the blind girl, clutching her fists, "as long as you play human! How old are you really, WT?"

"I'm 30," he replied, taken aback.

"It's time you act your age then!" She pushed him away and pointed to the mountains surrounding the valley. "Go! Be a dragon and don't you dare come back here unless you're in dragon form."

"But, Maggie..." Warthang protested.

"No!" She pushed him roughly, causing him to stumble backwards. "Go away! Next time I hear you coming, it will be with flapping wings in the wind and I'll be waiting for you so don't take too long making your mind up."

With tears in her eyes, his friend turned away, her tongue clicking, and she walked back into her house and closed the door softly. He knew she would not open it if he knocked on it; she was a stubborn one, his friend, and always kept her word to the last.

"I'm a dragon," Warthang told himself, looking up at the mountains to the east, where his kind mostly lived in their caves.

"I'm going home."

*   *   *

It had been so long since he had been himself that he had forgotten what it felt like to fly as a dragon. As he glided over the mountains, he savored the wind in his face and the currents under his red wings.

"I'm a dragon," he yelled at the wind.

Having left only hours before, he already missed Maggie and Willard and little Grace, but determination drove him forward. Maggie had commanded him not to return to her until he did so as a dragon, but he had a higher goal in mind. He would not return until he had something to tell her, a story about meeting other dragons.

After a time, he spotted a very small one in the

distance. Without hesitating, he headed that way and finally landed near the small black dragon which was sticking his head under rocks, looking for something. When the baby heard Warthang land, he shook his head out from the dirt and blinked.

"What's up with your eyes?" he asked, staring.

"Oh, enough with the eyes!" the red 30-year-old rolled his yellow eyes, exasperated. "They're yellow, they're different. Get over it, already!"

"Forget I said anything," spat the black baby, irritated. "So, are you here to help me or what?"

"Help you with what?" Warthang said, eying him and his dirty state.

"I'm playing this game, see," the little one explained, eyes sparkling. "I find any living thing I can and then see if I can kill it in a different way than the last time. I get pretty creative too!"

"No thanks," the wizard dragon answered, disgusted.

Not thinking much about this young fellow, Warthang thought he could at least get a bit of information from him.

"So...hum..."

"Dubby."

"So, Dubby," Warthang smiled, trying to be friendly. "Are there a lot of younger dragons like us?"

"Nope." Dubby looked away and burrowed his head back under the rocks. His voice now muffled was a bit hard to understand, but Warthang managed. "Counting you, there are six of us."

"Only six?" the red dragon asked, surprised. "But the dragons have been around for over 40 years now. Surely, there must be more."

The black creature popped his head out and dug into

a different rock.

"Well, they have eggs, but they won't hatch. The babies seem to come out at their own choosing and that can take years, apparently. The elders seem to think it's because we're not natural."

"Not natural?" Warthang asked, frowning.

"Yeah, not natural. I don't know what that means but you can go ask them; the elders know everything."

"Who are the elders, exactly?"

Dubby took his head out from under the rock and stared at Warthang, cocking his head sideways.

"Where have you been? Well, it must have been somewhere 'cause I've never seen you before... Anyway, the elders are the five leaders, chosen from the original 20 (that's how they describe themselves): Singe, Ferge, Star, Iric and Blog."

At hearing his father's name, goose bumps traveled through Warthang's spine. He did not want to think about that horrible, hateful monster.

"So, who are the six younger dragons?"

Dubby flicked his tongue in concentration. "There's you and me, then the brother and sister, Brook and Flora. There's Benzady. Oh yeah, and Tundra."

At the unfamiliar name, Warthang's head perked up. "Tundra? Who's that?"

"Some blue dragon Benzady likes," Dubby shrugged. "I can't see why personally; she's boring."

Suddenly, the black dragon's eyes sparkled and he dashed forward, snatching something between his small claws. Stuck there, a small mouse struggled, terrified and squealing.

"It's when you stop looking you finally find what you're looking for," purred Dubby.

Not wanting to watch what would come next, Warthang excused himself and flew on his way, in search of this boring blue dragon he had never met.

*   *   *

When he found Tundra, not too far away, hunched over like she was in great pain, Warthang immediately landed lightly by her side and bent his head over her, concerned.

"What's the matter, little one?"

Slowly, she looked up straight into his face, crocodile tears still fresh on her cheeks.

"I killed it," she whispered, pointing with a minute claw at the rocky ground. There, a delicate blue butterfly lay crumpled. Staring at it closely, the red dragon could tell it still lived, but just barely.

"It isn't dead. Look."

Gently, he blew on it a cold breath and its crumpled wings strengthened and tested the air. At first, it batted them hesitantly, but when it found the pain gone, the butterfly flew off like a feather carried by the wind. In awe, Tundra followed its fluttering, her mouth slightly open in a smile. Once she lost sight of it, her gaze turned back to Warthang and her lips curved upward.

"Thank you. No one's ever cared before."

"Have there been other injured butterflies?"

"Yes," admitted Tundra, lowering her gaze to her claws. "They seem so nice. I try to befriend them but it always ends badly."

Crouching to her level, the red dragon brought his head to the ground, meeting her downcast eyes with his own.

"They *are* very nice," he agreed, nodding, "but also very different from us. When you meet a butterfly, you have to stay still and let him come to you. Oh, look!"

As he exclaimed this, Warthang summoned a nearby yellow butterfly and let it flutter its way to the small blue dragon.

"Now," he continued, "don't move."

Tundra's eyes grew as round as stream pebbles and she trembled slightly, straining to keep her muscles motionless. Guiding the fragile creature silently, Warthang let it land on the tip of her nose and bat its wings slowly for a few seconds before he released it. Free of his influence, the butterfly remained perched for some moments and then flew away, out of sight.

"Wow," breathed the young female, "I wish I could have figured that out earlier."

"Your parents didn't want to teach you?"

Quizzically, Tundra eyed him. "Dragon parents leave their babies on their own as soon as they can survive solo, around the age of five."

"What?" Warthang exclaimed, unbelieving. "There are so many things to learn that others need to teach you. Who better than your parents?"

"Well," explained Tundra, "when we turn 20, we're allowed to attend the dragon summit where the elders tell us our history. It's every five years and the next one is tomorrow. I can't go yet 'cause I'm too young, but they teach you all sorts of things."

Tomorrow? What were the odds he would find out about such a thing on the eve of the event? Curiosity twinkled in his eyes.

"How about you and I go and see what they have to say?"

Tundra's tail twitched. "If they see me, I'll get in big trouble. Plus, I don't fly very well yet and couldn't make it there on time."

Mischievously, Warthang smiled. "Stick with me and anything is possible."

After a few explanations and directions, the two flew off together, Tundra feeling as light as a feather. To her great surprise, she hardly needed to put any effort into her flapping and gliding, the way she usually did—she did not understand that magic carried her.

Some hours later, they arrived at the mounds where the dragon council usually met and Warthang burrowed a deep hidden cave on the edge of the clearing and the two hid inside, sleeping through the night and early morning. As the sun rose high into the sky, the two sheltered dragons could glimpse others arriving and waiting at the foot of the mounds. Finally, five dragons, one being Warthang's dad, flew in and landed on five different tops that strangely resembled pedestals. Without waiting, the large yellow female began the summit.

"I, Star, begin this our fifth summit. First up, elder Singe will recount our history."

With loud whoops, the dragons greeted the green dragon, who bared his teeth, pleased. In the cave, a low growl escaped Warthang's chest.

"What's the matter?" Tundra asked him, concerned.

Quieting his growl, the wizard dragon inhaled deeply and shook his head.

"42 years ago," Singe's boisterous voice echoed through the clearing, "we awoke as we are now, fully grown dragons. We 20 originals were unnaturally made, for we were never babies, by the evils wizards. Why did they create us? All they wanted was to use us as weapons against their enemies. They trained us well, but never gave us rules, save one: Never shall we kill one of our own, lest we suffer the consequences..."

"What's a consequence?" whispered Tundra in his ear.

"I don't know," Warthang murmured back, under his breath. "I'll have to ask and find out."

"Ask who?"

Again, he shook his head, pointing to Singe, indicating they should continue listening and not miss anything. In a long rant, the green elder was listing the wizards' crimes against their kind. Finally, he reached the part of the story that Warthang knew well.

"After 12 years, Ferel and I finally succeeded in having a son, Warthang. In secret, we raised him and taught him how to read, how to think, and all about our mortal enemies. After four years, the time was ripe for our rebellion and Warthang set out to find a spell that would help us defeat the wizards. You see, because of their powers, we could not defeat them without outside magic; they could stop us at a moment's notice. On that fateful night, we lay in wait in the forest trees while all of the wizards gathered for a meeting. Star here volunteered and attacked them. As predicted, the wizards froze her in her tracks and she was helpless against them. At some point in the night, something happened and all the wizards lost their powers, releasing their hold on Star: our revolution was a success! Of course, in no time, we annihilated their sorry existences, wiping them away forever from the earth."

Quietly, Warthang lay down in the cave, curious to see how his father would describe what had happened afterward. Next to him, Tundra's small eyes peered through the crack in the entrance, cautious but curious.

"The next day," Singe continued, frowning, "my son returned to us, but he no longer was one of us. He was half dragon, half wizard, like some sick mutant!"

All around, the small group of dragons booed, calling Warthang names like *freak*, *traitor*, *half-breed*. Once they quieted down, the green elder resumed his summary,

"So we cast him out of our sight, afraid he would taint us with his sickness. To our great relief, we have not seen him much since and none at all in the last few years..."

"I wonder what a half wizard, half dragon looks

like?" pondered Tundra, releasing him from the anger that had taken hold of him.

"There's no such thing," he whispered back, patting her on the back. "Those elders speak of things they know nothing about. They cast judgment without having all the facts."

Looking up at him with her little face, the blue dragon stretched her wings and sat down. "How do you know so much about it?"

"I'm Warthang," he smiled, realizing he no longer felt ashamed or too afraid of his identity. "And I was born a dragon and am still a dragon!"

"But there *is* something different about you," thought Tundra out loud, and what she said next surprised Warthang tremendously for it had nothing to do with his strange eyes. "Good things happen when you're around, things that wouldn't happen if you weren't there. I know for a fact that butterfly was dead or at least soon to be. I also know that I can't fly that well but with you by my side, it is the easiest thing in the world. And then, the way you made this cave certainly is nothing a normal dragon could do! You didn't even touch the rock and it retreated away, taking no time at all to become this perfect hiding place."

"And what about you, Tundra?" Warthang asked her, warmth coursing through his voice. "Why are you so different? Every dragon I have met has had evil intents. The 20 originals never tried to think of a peaceful way of settling their problems with the wizards, Flora and Brook pulled a trick on me to try and hurt me, Dubby kills things for fun, and then there's you. You care about life, not just yours, but the life and beauty that surrounds you. What makes you so different?"

"I don't know," shrugged the young female, "something very strange happened to me when I hatched. I was clawing my way out of the shells of my egg when thousands of butterflies suddenly appeared, and I found myself in the middle of their whirlpool. When they flew off, my mother screamed that it was magic and she proceeded to beat me, so she could 'cast off whatever the creatures had done to me'—her words, not mine. Anyway, I don't know if that had any bearing on my being *different*, but I do think we all have choices and it's what we do with them that makes us different. A lot of the other dragons have had bad influences on them and I obviously have had my share too, but it was so unpleasant, I could never see the point of it, and so I have chosen to try something different."

"You are completely amazing," breathed Warthang, awed.

For the next few hours of the summit, the two of them ignored the elders' speech and discussed various things. Mainly, they both wanted to influence their dragon kind into being better creatures. For example, Warthang thought that if he ever had baby dragons, he would not abandon them and would teach them right from wrong. Wholeheartedly, Tundra agreed with this point but also thought it important to teach the current dragons a better, more peaceful way of living.

Before they knew it, the summit had ended and the adult dragons had flown home to their lairs. It was time for Warthang and Tundra to leave their magic-made cave and see where their friendship would take them.

Note 7

The summit was the first place I heard about consequences and once I learned what they were, I saw them everywhere afterward. They're a constant companion to all of us, whether we realize it or not. But it made me wonder. How would the consequences have been different if I had chosen a different spell to defeat the wizards? How would I have been different without the subsequent events? In the end, thinking about what could have been just gave me a headache. What I've done, I've done, and the only thing I can keep doing, is live with who I am and learn from my experiences.

Chapter 7 – Anger

After rolling away the boulder that hid the entrance to his magic-made cave, Warthang exited the lair, followed by Tundra. Although they had thought that all the other dragons had vacated the premises, they were sadly mistaken.

"If it isn't the coward and traitor," a voice sneered behind them.

Turning his head around, the red dragon looked up and saw Benzady perched on the edge of the cliff, just above where they had hidden themselves. Tundra, on the other hand, did not even turn around but simply stood frozen, afraid for having been found out.

"Hello, Benzady," Warthang replied politely, remembering what Maggie had told him about killing others with kindness.

"Tundra, Tundra," Benzady ignored the bigger dragon, focusing all his attention on the small blue female as he slithered down the side of the drop-off to the ground with a soft thud. "What kind of company are you keeping? He's not even fit to be called a dragon and he makes you break the rules!"

Uncomfortable and afraid, the small dragon looked to her feet, slightly trembling, shoulders hunched together, tail concealed under her body. At her reaction, Benzady smiled crookedly and wedged his way between her and Warthang, forcing some distance between them as he backed into her.

"If you really wanted to know what went on at the summit," he continued, "you could have just asked me. This really hurts my feelings."

He pouted in her direction, all the while staring straight on at Warthang with hate filled eyes.

"As for *you*," he spat at the older dragon, "how dare you come back to further your crimes? It's not enough that you beat up on Flora and Brook but now you try to befriend Tundra so you can get back at us?"

"That's not my intention at all," stuttered Warthang, not knowing how to respond and alarmed that Tundra would hear about what he had done those years ago.

"Get away from this monster, Tundra!" Benzady commanded her, seeming concerned. "With his unnatural magic, he beat Flora and Brook until they were almost dead! I came just in time to rescue them, they wouldn't have made it without me."

"That's not what happened!" frowned Warthang, starting to tremble from the rage that was building up inside him. But because he could barely contain his anger, he remained quiet, attempting to control it.

"You should have seen them, Tundra," goaded Benzady, "there was so much blood on them you couldn't even recognize who they were. It took them months to recuperate. And you know what the worst part is? They had been trying to play with him and become friends, looking over the fact that he was a freak. They were giving him a chance and he took advantage of them and tried to kill them!"

"No!" Warthang yelled, reaching back and striking forward with his claws at the green dragon. Benzady jumped back, barely dodging the slash that would have disfigured him.

"See what I mean?" he whispered, menacingly, "He's not safe and he's not one of us."

Ashamed of the violence and murder he felt in his heart, Warthang took flight and teleported miles away, where neither of them could see him. He could not believe what he had just done in front of Tundra, especially right after their talks of being different and showing a better way to the other dragons. Now, she would certainly hate him and refuse to talk to him, she would never be the friend he longed to have.

But he did have a friend; in fact, he had two of them: Maggie and Willard. At that thought, Warthang headed west toward Valley City, the wind easily carrying him. In a short time, he reached the valley, found their house and softly landed nearby, far enough so as not to frighten the neighbors. Since dusk approached, the dragon knew both of them were probably eating dinner, so he sent out a thought to the house, calling them by name. Without any delay, his friends exited the dwelling in a hurry, Maggie carrying Grace in her arms.

"WT!" she exclaimed in glee, yelling in the wrong direction.

"Over here!" Warthang smiled.

Hearing his voice, the blind woman ·ran in his direction, clicking away with her tongue, and abruptly stopped in front of him when she reached him. Behind her, Willard followed slowly, mesmerized by the sight of the dragon's true form.

"Wow," the young man breathed, looking up and down at his friend, "this look suits you so much better. You're magnificent!"

Without any hesitation, Maggie rested her right hand on his flank, feeling the scales tenderly, imagining what he looked like.

"What color is he?" she asked Willard.

"He's red," he replied, then continued the description for her benefit. "He's pretty big compared to us but not full grown yet. The adult dragons are as big as houses and I'd say Warthang is about half that size, but definitely big enough to make some damage!" At that, his lips curved upward and he winked at the dragon who chuckled.

"So WT," Maggie patted him on the base of the neck and smiled, "what have you been up to these past few days?"

Sighing sadly, Warthang began to tell her about his "dragon" adventures. When he got to the part about the summit, he remembered he had wanted to ask Maggie a question.

"Then, he said the wizards imposed only one rule on us: 'Never shall we kill one of our own, lest we suffer the consequences.' But I don't know what a consequence is."

"A consequence is like a reaction," Willard started thoughtfully, "and every action has a reaction."

"So if you do something nice," Maggie continued, "then normally something good will result from that. For example, if you feed a hungry cat, he might just start loving you and be your friend. On the other hand, if you do something bad, bad things will happen. At least, that's normally the way it goes. If you slap someone, you're bound to get slapped right back or worse, and that's not very pleasant."

"Are there always consequences?" Warthang asked

quizzically.

"Well," Willard answered, "sometimes you may not get caught after doing something bad so in a sense you get away with it but I think in the long run, you still suffer some consequences, although they may be of a different nature. Consequences don't have to be tangible, they can also be emotional or mental..."

"Yeah, ok," cut in Maggie impatiently, "I'm dying to know: what happened next at the summit?"

So Warthang continued on with his story, not hiding anything, all the way to his lashing out at Benzady and his fleeing the scene.

"And now," he admitted sadly, "she'll never want to be my friend."

"Really?" Maggie exclaimed, incredulous, "you're not even gonna try? Do you think that girl hasn't seen dragons do violent things before? That's probably *all* she's seen!"

"But she thought I was different and I obviously am not!" protested Warthang weakly.

"Look, no one is perfect and we all have problems," Maggie said, shaking her head. "But get this straight, you *are* different and you're going to prove it to her. You're going to go up to her and admit you have an anger problem and ask for her help. Bet you don't see your everyday dragon doing that!"

Since Maggie had set her mind on this course of action and no arguing could dissuade her from it, Warthang did not seem to have the choice but to do as she had commanded. So it was that the next day, as he flew in the mountains, he found Tundra quietly coaxing a large butterfly to her nose. Not wanting to frighten the insect away from her, he landed nearby where she could not see him and waited patiently, thinking about what he would say. When the small creature finally fluttered away, the red dragon blundered in awkwardly and declared without preamble,

"I have an anger problem!"

When she heard him, Tundra's head perked up slightly and she smiled shyly. "Maybe I can help you with it..."

Surprised, the wizard dragon forgot to close his mouth and stood there, frozen like a statue. After a few moments, he shook his head as if to wake up.

"What do you suggest?"

"Well," she began hesitantly, "If you always stay away from the problem, when the time comes and you have to face it, you won't know how to deal with it. So I think that putting you in situations that make you angry will help us find a way to deal with it better."

"You would really do this with me?"

"Of course!" she cried, astonished he would even ask, "I want to make a difference, remember?"

Approaching her slowly, Warthang sat by her side and nodded, hopeful.

"Now," she continued, "is there anything that keeps you calm or helps you focus on something else than the anger?"

"Well," Warthang said, thinking back on the previous day, "Because you were there yesterday, I was able to stop myself before I would normally have, I think. Maybe if you can stay by my side, I can focus better..."

"All right," she declared enthusiastically, "let's go find Benzady and see how it goes."

"Right now?" the red dragon asked, alarmed.

"Of course! There's no use waiting around."

At that, Tundra stretched her wings and took flight without a backwards glance, expecting him to follow. Sighing inwardly, Warthang shook his head and floated into the air behind her. Not before long, they found Benzady by a stream together with Flora and Brook. Just his luck.

Right away, the green bully spied their arrival and glared unforgivingly at Warthang. With his tail, he whacked Brook lightly on the head and pointed up to their approaching figures, whispering inaudible comments and snickering. But behind his sniggers, you could tell that seeing Tundra with the wizard dragon really displeased him.

"Tundra," he hissed, once the two of them had landed on the other side of the stream, "what gives us the pleasure of your company today?"

"I made a friend with a butterfly, earlier," she replied in her sweet, innocent way, "Warthang taught me how."

"Well whooptydoo," Benzady rolled his eyes, shaking his head, "so he came here to teach me how to tame an ant? I have a lot better things to do with my time, thank you very much."

At his remark, Flora and Brook chuckled, proud of their friend's cleverness. But no matter their reaction, the red dragon thought it as good a time as any to apologize to the brother and sister for the ill he had done to them. His heart knotting uncomfortably, he took a deep breath and interrupted their chortles.

"I wanted to apologize for hitting you that time."

The siblings sucked in air, their heads whipping back, stopping their mocking laughter short. Unsure, they both looked to Benzady for guidance.

"Dragons don't say they're sorry, you half-breed," he sneered at Warthang, "and neither do they accept apologies; we hold grudges and have a long memory." Smiling, he showed all of his pointy teeth as he said, "I am going to haunt you all the days of your life and take great pleasure in making you miserable."

"Okaaaay, I guess us becoming friends is out of the question, then?" commented the red dragon sarcastically, not in the least cowed by the other's threat. Then, looking at Tundra, he stood his ground firmly and looked square in Benzady's face. "But know this, Tundra and I *are* going to be friends, whether you like it or not."

His three opponents hissed at that and lashed their tails impatiently. Receiving only animal noises and no longer seeing the point of hanging around, Warthang shrugged his shoulders, signaled to Tundra that they should leave, and they took back to the sky. As they left the premises, the wizard dragon still heard Benzady telling the others,

"Not if I can help it..."

* * *

From that time on, Warthang spent his mornings in the dragon world with Tundra, teaching her about nature and various things, and in return, she tried to infuriate him to work on his anger. Unfortunately, she could never make him mad, her presence only brought him joy and amusement. One morning, while he slept by a stream, she abruptly woke him by splashing freezing cold water into his face, expecting his anger to flare up. Instead, the male dragon threw her into the stream and they spent the next hour wrestling, laughing, and playing in the water. Once in a while, however, they received visits from Benzady, Flora and Brook and only those harassing moments spoiled their good times. But because of his friend's presence, the young dragon did not mind these interruptions so much, and kept his cool.

In the afternoons, Warthang visited the human world, relaxing and enjoying Maggie and Willard's company. As the years rolled by, a red-headed boy named Mott and a curly haired girl named Truth followed Grace's birth. And when all three children were big enough, they spent a lot of time with the dragon. Mott's specialty was "dragon climbing," while Grace and Truth spent much of their time attempting to affix bows unto his scales. When the weather—and their mother—permitted, the three of them would play hide and seek with Warthang in the mountains for hours and make up their own creature treasure hunts. By the time he was 40, the equivalent of a human 16 year old, the red dragon could not imagine a happier, better life. He had his best friend in the morning and his human family in the evening; he felt accepted and loved.

Every morning, he would tell Tundra of his previous night's adventures—like the time Mott had pretended to be a dragon and had chased his sisters the whole afternoon. Likewise, every afternoon, he would then tell Maggie's family about his time with his kin.

That particular morning, when he woke up to the blue dragon's singing drifting down to his lair—for he had made a home for himself—he could not contain his excitement. He burst forth from his cave, running toward the melody. On the next mountain peak, Tundra sang to the sky, welcoming the rising sun. Flying quickly to her, Warthang set himself down by her, a big smile beaming in his crocodile face.

"The coolest thing happened yesterday!" he exclaimed.

Ceasing her sweet song, she looked at him and smiled. "Did Maggie catch you setting her flowers on fire again?"

"Hey! That was an accident and..." bopping himself on the head, Warthang pointed his finger at his friend. "That's not gonna work, there's no way you can make me mad! You've been trying for ten years, and never has it worked."

"You can't blame a dragon for trying," she shrugged pleasantly, then added, "So, what cool thing happened yesterday?"

"Maggie let me take Grace on a ride! Since she's ten, she said that she was finally old enough to do that kind of thing. You should have seen Mott and Truth; they were so jealous!" He laughed at the memory, thinking fondly of the kids. "Anyway, I set her inside the two spikes here between my shoulder blades and told her to hang on. She wrapped her arms around one really tight and at first I walked slowly, trying to make sure that she was okay. Then, she started to laugh and make these squeaky happy noises and telling me to go faster and faster. In the end, I was running on all fours around the house, laughing along with her. When we were done with the ride, I told her that when she was older, I would even fly her places. I said it pretty quietly but you know Maggie, she's got ears like a deer and she heard every word. And boy did I get a lecture about kids and safety and promises and waiting until they were *much* older. I thought it would never end."

"She sounds like a good mother. When I'm a mother, I'm definitely going to care about my clutch."

Warthang looked from the sunrise to Tundra, "When you went to the summit, did the elders say anything about baby dragons?"

When she had gone to the summit alone a few weeks ago, her first official one, the red dragon had not wanted to ask her about it. He remembered the insults that had been hurled at his name when they had gone to the meeting clandestinely together, and just had not desired further thought on the matter. However, he now realized the five leaders of their kind may have passed some useful information.

Tundra squinted her eyes, thinking hard. "They said that because we were unnaturally made, it's really hard for us to have babies. It's something to do with the magic in our bodies. Once we have a mate, we're able to lay eggs but the babies only hatch when they want to. Anyway, that's the explanation they gave."

"Okay," Warthang hesitated, his face turning a darker shade of red, "but at what age can a dragon find a mate and have little ones?"

"They didn't talk about that," she continued, not noticing his change in demeanor, "but I know that Benzady and Flora already have eggs together and they're in their thirties."

Turning his opaque yellow eyes to his fiddling claws, Warthang asked, barely audibly, "When do you think you want to be a mother?"

"I don't know," she shrugged her shoulders, "I think I would want to meet Maggie first and see how it's done."

"You want to meet her?" the wizard dragon asked, surprised.

"Of course! You always talk about her and her family and she seems like someone I could really admire. She's strong, determined and good; she stands up for what's right! I want to be just like that."

"Yeah, me too," agreed Warthang. "Well, that's settled! When I go see them tonight, I'll ask them about meeting you and hopefully tomorrow evening, you get to see them for the first time!"

"I can't wait!"

Tundra felt so excited that she wrapped her wings around Warthang in a hug and then jumped off the peak, gliding through the air and tasting the wind. Laughing, the red male dove off and followed her. They spent the rest of the morning flying and enjoying nature's song.

Note 8

Love and acceptance are funny things that can make you do some dumb blunders you sometimes end up regretting; I know I do. Because I was so blinded by love and my need for acceptance, my tunnel vision hid everything that was going on around me. I don't know if I'll ever be able to forgive myself. I'm so sorry.

Chapter 8 – Red

That afternoon, as promised, Warthang headed from the mountains to Maggie's house in high spirits, ready to set up the meeting. In his mind, he played different scenarios of how he would break the amazing news and how they would react. When he caught sight of their home, Tundra entered his mind and his heart began pounding harder. She had such a kind spirit, like an innocent child, and she was so beautiful. His thoughts of her drowned all his senses. So much so that once he landed at the usual spot, he did not notice right away the absence of Grace and Truth's laughter, or the wild welcoming yell of little Mott.

As he walked dreamily to the house, no one ran out to greet him and suddenly, Warthang's heart squeezed itself into a hard ball and he could no longer breathe. There, on the ground, lay Mott's tiny shoe caked with blood. Further down by the house, what looked like a small carcass ravaged by wild beasts remained motionless. The dragon recognized some of Truth's beautiful brown ringlets on one end of the corpse. Now racing, his heart pumped savagely and he panted noisily. In a panic, he ran past the small bloody body and to the back of the house. When he reached the back garden, his panting stopped, he whimpered a bit and then began wailing uncontrollably.

His best friend, the first person who had ever given him a chance, who had ever loved him, had been staked through dozens of times with something sharp. The holes still seeped red fluid everywhere, leaking and staining the damp grass, and even her face had been butchered with deep gaping gashes. Where her eyes had been, now empty sockets replaced them, mocking her blindness in her death. Around her, the rest of her family lay sprawled about in similar disrepair and what must have been Willard had an outstretched limb that seemed to be reaching for her in some sort of last attempt. Sweet Grace looked like she had been thrown around like a rag doll, the way her limbs bent backwards unnaturally and Mott...No! Not Mott too.

Unable to bear the sight any longer, Warthang squeezed his yellow eyes shut and began chanting to himself, rocking back and forth,

"This can't be happening, this can't be happening, this can't be happening..."

But no matter the darkness he saw behind his eyelids, the red color of blood seeped through, covering his mind and his heart. He thought of the river where he had met Maggie but its rustling flow turned dark red. He remembered the dance she had dragged him to, but when he saw Willard's face on the edge of the fire circle, blood oozed from the young man's eye sockets like tears and his extended hand shriveled into ashes unto the red ground. When his mind returned to the three children, Truth fell over, headless, and Grace's and Mott's arms tore from their torsos as they screamed in piercing agony. In turn, the dragon roared uncontrollably, eyes still shut tight, anguish entering his lament.

When he finally ceased his thunderous cries, he

106

cracked his eyes open to find himself in a ball on the cold, rocky ground of his lair. It had not been real, just a terrifying nightmare. Sighing deeply, Warthang shook himself, trying to dissipate the bad dream away, but the feeling of dread would not leave him. He did not remember having returned home but looking at the sky, he could tell the early evening announced itself with the slow setting of the sun. Surprisingly, he had missed most of his afternoon with Maggie and her family in what seemed like a slumbering sleep.

Without further delay, he exited his cave, only to find himself nose to nose with Tundra whose eyes grew big at seeing him there.

"I haven't seen you in three days!" she exclaimed, still in his face.

"What?" Warthang asked, disoriented, "I'm pretty sure I saw you just this morning..."

"Yeah, whatever, Warthang," sighed Tundra, irritated, "So? Did you set up the meeting with Maggie and her family?"

Bloody images of dripping red carcasses returned to Warthang's mind in a rush and a shiver ran up his spine like a bolt of electricity.

"I haven't seen them yet," he shrugged, acting as if everything was normal.

Squinting her eyes at him, her expression changed from perplexed to worried.

"Is everything okay with them?"

"Of course! Why wouldn't it be? I just feel a little bit strange and am not up to going to see them today," he said, forcing a smile on his face.

"Well then," she replied, "I guess I'll leave you to rest. You look like you need some alone time."

As she walked away from him, a thought crossed her mind and she turned her head to him and said,

"Oh yeah, I almost forgot: don't forget to stay away from Benzady!"

Before Warthang could ask her what she meant, she took to the sky and left him alone with his thoughts. Shaking his head, he slunk back into his cave and sat on his haunches. This had been the weirdest five minutes of his life: he had awoken from the worst nightmare possible, somehow had missed three days, and now Tundra told him to avoid Benzady. Normally, she pushed him towards their meeting each other, hoping he could work on his anger issues.

Not thinking too much about it, Warthang decided he would seek out the green dragon and see what mischief that annoying bully had in mind. Perusing through the mountains quickly with his wizard sight, it took him little time to find his enemy lurking about alone, a few miles away. Without further delay, he teleported to the location, surprising Benzady to the point that he jumped, lost balance, and almost fell over. Angry at his display of frailty, he bared his teeth and blew some hot fire in Warthang's direction. Then, thinking better of it, he drew himself up and smiled happily with all of his teeth. This really disconcerted the wizard dragon: he had *never* seen Benzady beam with positive energy before. Something weird was definitely going on.

"I can't believe you were friends with such whimpering losers!" he laughed.

"Excuse me?" Warthang asked, backing away.

"You know: the *humans,*" he burst out laughing, louder this time.

His heart pounding in his ears, Warthang tried to breathe slowly to calm himself. Once he felt a bit more under control, he firmly demanded,

"How do you know about them?"

Benzady lashed his tail, his chest puffed up.

"Well, you were so intent on little Tundra that you never noticed me listening in on your conversation. Mott this and Grace that. Maggie this and Maggie that. It made me *sick* to hear what looks like a dragon talk like that!"

Annoyed, Warthang growled at the green monster, turned his back to him and began walking away, saying,

"I don't care what you think about my friends. They're much better company than you are."

Ignoring the dismissal, Benzady continued on his rant,

"Having human friends is the worst example a young impressionable dragon could have! So, of course, I had to stop the problem at its source."

Warthang froze in place, a leg still in the air, ready for the next step. No. It had not been real. He refused to believe it.

"There's nothing you can do," he uttered slowly, "you don't even know where they live."

Benzady snorted.

"It really doesn't take a genius to fly by houses and notice little kids running out and waving their arms at you. All the other humans run inside when they see dragons, but these little stupid ones were well trained to do otherwise."

Warthang turned around to face the green dragon once again, his whole body shaking.

"When the parents came out," continued Benzady,

sneering, "they screamed so loud it would have made any grumpy dragon's day. And wouldn't you believe it, those screams got even better once I started chewing on their kids!"

As he declared this, he chomped his teeth in a great display and flexed his long claws, reminiscing. Warthang's trembling grew worse and his yellow eyes began turning red, as if all his blood had rushed to them. In his mind, he again saw the mutilated bodies of Truth, Grace, Mott, Maggie and Willard pierced, oozing and bloody. It had been real. He had known it but had not wanted to believe it. Before long, red blood smudged everything he could see, including that disgusting, filthy creature that stood in front of him, still laughing.

In a blind rage, Warthang rushed at Benzady and roared, blowing red hot fire in the other's face.

"Brilliant," commented the green dragon sarcastically, "don't you know that fire does nothing to our kind?"

When he had finished billowing, Warthang extended his claws and magically grew them to the length of broadswords. In front of him, Benzady watched, interested.

"I wish I would have had *those* when I speared your friends. It would have made some funny shish kabobs."

When he had finished the transformation, all Warthang could think about was his friends' blood drenching the ground and covering everything. No one had the right to do that to them, and if they thought they did, they needed to be exterminated. Those were his friends, his family!

With hate permeating his bloodied yellow eyes, Warthang struck Benzady, who immediately lifted his

110

front legs in reactive defense. Blood sprayed the angry red dragon's face and he tasted it on his tongue. It felt hot like fire, and fueled his rage further. On his end, the bully had not previously realized the seriousness of his opponent's attack, but now all snide remarks flew from his mind and he backed away awkwardly, cradling his gashed arms against his chest.

Savoring the red liquid in his panting mouth, Warthang no longer had sense of anything except the

burning feeling that wanted so desperately to explode out of him. Again, he roared fire and lashed his sword-like claws, but only to encounter air. Benzady had jumped backwards, missing the strike by a scale. As quickly as he could, he scrambled away, batted his wings with a rush of wind and lifted off the ground. But before he could get very far, Warthang jumped on him and painfully tore his left wing out of its socket with his mouth. With a loud crash, Benzady fell face first into the dirt, all the while yelling in agony, his wing and shoulder on fire with pain.

Now driven by fear for the first time in his life, the green bully turned his head toward the incoming red dragon. Tears streamed down his face and he wailed pitifully, like a poor frightened child.

"Please! I don't want to die! Please! Please! I..."

His cry stopped abruptly and was replaced by gurgling; Warthang had stabbed him through the lungs with all ten of his claws. Repeatedly, he stabbed him. Benzady was long dead and still he continued stabbing him. He stabbed him so much that the corpse began falling apart, pieces rolling away, pieces flying through the air, pieces sticking to the wizard dragon's bloody scales. After a while, the adrenaline that had driven him let off and he collapsed unconscious unto the unrecognizable remains.

When he woke the next morning, he did not quite understand what had happened, for his memory had become blurry. All around him, dry blood covered the rocks and ground, and with that blood, chunks of flesh. Directly below him, a large mass of bones and meat rested, crushed by his weight. Disgusted, Warthang moaned and carefully stepped off the massive cadaver. When he turned around, he caught his breath and stood stock still. There, close behind him, lay Tundra, crumpled in a heap, crying her eyes out.

"What have you done, Warthang?"

Speechless, the red dragon looked down at himself

112

and found his own scaly body covered with the dry blood and flesh, but especially his claws told a telling tale. Those same meaty chunks clung to them, and you could tell it was not because he had been sleeping on top of the dead, but because they had caused the surrounding massacre. In a flash, he saw images of Benzady trying to fly away, Benzady wailing in pain, Benzady torn to pieces. Benzady dead. By his own doing. Aghast, he closed his eyes and whimpered,

"I..."

"Don't!" interrupted Tundra, "I don't want to hear it. There's no excuse!"

With that, she looked away and began walking the other direction. Warthang squeezed his eyes tighter and threw himself down, not caring about the red mess under him. She was right: there was no excuse. What he had done was unpardonable. He was disgusting, the worse kind of monster. Bitterly, he wept, his tears drawing tracks through the blood still on his face.

How long did he weep? He did not know, but when he finally stopped and cracked his eyes open, he abruptly stood up, astounded. All of Benzady's remains had gone as if nothing had ever happened. However, there, in front of him, white bones, bleached by the sun, lay scattered about, a bit gnawed by smaller animals. It was as if years had passed since Warthang had killed Benzady, instead of just a night.

When he realized what this meant, hope sparkled in Warthang's yellow eyes. First, he had missed three days, and now, who knows how long? This could only mean one thing! He had recently acquired a new type of magic: time traveling. With this, he could go back and stop himself from committing this heinous crime.

Tundra would still be his friend!

Without further delay, he closed his eyes and thought of the night when he had last seen her, the day he had said he would set up a meeting with Maggie. When he opened his eyes again, the stars shown in the night and the moon announced its presence brightly. He had done it! Excited, he flew to Tundra's cave, where she would be sleeping, and whispered her name.

"Warthang?" she replied, her voice muffled from sleep.

Realizing he had not washed the blood off himself, he hurriedly whispered back, "Yeah, it's me! But there's no need to get up: I just wanted to ask you a favor, real quick."

"What is it?" she asked, now sounding more alert.

"Next time you see me," he continued, "remind me to stay away from Benzady. It's really important! Promise me you won't forget."

"I promise. If you go find Benzady, it won't be because I've forgotten to tell you."

Satisfied, Warthang thanked her and headed for a stream where he dunked himself and washed all traces of his crime away. At the end of his bath, he suddenly slapped his forehead. Why prevent his killing Benzady when he could just stop Maggie's murder and reset the whole event?

Happy at the thought of saving his friends, Warthang closed his eyes again, thought hard, and then opened them back up, only to find himself exactly when he had been. Quickly, he tried again but nothing happened.

For some time, frustrated, Warthang experimented with different times, going further and further back, and still failing to move. Finally, time shifted and he found himself in the era shortly before the creation of dragons, 60 years before his present.

Shrugging his shoulders, he figured that while he was here, he could at least find himself a wizard and see if they knew anything about how to time travel. While he searched for one with his wizard sight, Warthang transformed himself into human form, sporting his usual black outfit and hat. As a human, he now seemed about 16 years old, hopefully an age that merited his curiosity and would not arouse the sorcerers' suspicion.

Finally, in the desert area on the south of the continent, the dragon saw a group of wizards living together in a stone village. Crooking a smile, he tipped his hat forward over his eyes and teleported near the conglomeration of houses. After a few minutes, he walked up to a magic user, sitting on the ground and manipulating wind and sand in the air.

"Hello," he said to the silent wizard, tipping his hat forward, as if shielding his eyes from the desert sun.

Irritated, the mage ceased wiggling his fingers and let the sand fall to the ground. His gaze looked up at Warthang, eyes completely sky blue, and for the first time, the dragon got to see how unsettling magic eyes could be. So emotionless, so blank, yet so penetrating. Even freakier, the man's skin seemed a bit see through, transparent-like. Warthang shivered.

"How dare you talk to me?" spat the wizard, "Get out of my sight!"

Not impressed, the dragon stuck his hands in his pockets nonchalantly and walked into the village, leaving the wind wizard to his stupid play time. How rude could you get? It was no wonder everybody hated wizards. Shortly, he found another mage sitting in a chair by a hut, pouring over a book.

"Hello," Warthang tried again.

Without even looking up, the man batted his right hand sideways and the "teenager" felt a sharp sting on his cheek, as if someone had slapped him. Determined to get his information—after all, this meant his whole life—Warthang continued through the village with similar answers and reactions from each magic user.

Time after time, they continued refusing to talk to him but he just would not give up. If he could help it, there was no way he was going to live his life without his friends and as a murderer!

Suddenly, he felt someone pulling him down by the ear and dragging him away from his next target and into a nearby shack. There, the person let his ear go and he strengthened up, looked cautiously under his hat, and observed a short, back bent, old woman scowling disapprovingly at him.

"What do you think you're doing, young man?" she frowned.

"Hum, hello madam," he bent his head forward in a curtsy, "I've come a long way looking for some information that only a wizard would know..."

"Really?" She raised an eyebrow, "and how far would that be, exactly?"

"Valley City."

"You fool," she knocked his hat further down unto his head with a fist, "The wizards there are just the same as the wizards here: awful and unhelpful. You mess with them long enough and they'll throw you to the farm lands!"

"Well, if they're so horrible," Warthang retorted, "what are you doing here, hanging around them?"

At that, the old woman drew herself up proudly, grabbing the front of her vest with both her hands.

"I, young man, am making a living. No one will work for these ghastly wizards so when they find someone that will do their laundry and clean their houses, they pay them *very* well."

Letting a long breath out, the dragon shook his head.

"Are they all the same, then? Is there no wizard who will talk to me?"

"Among all of them," answered the crone, "there is one who will talk to anyone and anything. In fact, you can't get him to shut up once he's started."

"Great!" exclaimed Warthang, excited, "how can I find him?"

Rolling her eyes, the old lady shook her head slowly. "Good luck with that! That wizard flies and he loves it. That's all he does: flies, flies, flies. So much so that you can never know where he is."

"Don't worry about that, madam, I'll find him!"

And Warthang ran out of the shack, accompanied by the woman's last remark of "yeah, right!" Abruptly, he stopped short at the entrance of the rickety building and focused his wizard sight, searching avidly for the flying magician. Finally, he saw a man flying about over the forests of the east, languidly floating through the air, without a care in the world, arms crossed behind his head as if he were taking a nap.

Without further delay, the dragon teleported to a tree in the forest and proceeded to look like he was climbing to its top limb. In the distance, the tall wizard looked like he was swimming in the air, peddling his feet. The hood of his robe had flapped open from the wind and you could see the man's short brown hair. As he approached, Warthang cleared his throat, causing the wizard to somersault out of his reverie and look backwards at the teenager in the tree. When he saw him, a huge smile illuminated his face.

"Warthang!" he yelled, "I haven't seen you in a few months! Where have you been? I can't believe I was able to recognize you in all of that shade, it's so dark in that forest!"

Grinning, the flying wizard landed lightly in the same tree, on a branch across from where the dragon stood. Not sure what to say, Warthang shook his head slowly to see if he was dreaming. This man already knew him, but *he* certainly had never met him before; in fact, he was not even born yet!

"Hum," he stuttered, "I...I forgot your name. Sorry."

"What!" the wizard laughed almost uncontrollably. "You've always known my name! Even the first time I met you, you knew my name! It's Gala, Warthang. Gala. And don't ever forget it!"

"I'm sure not to forget it, Gala," the dragon responded, uncomfortable. "You sure aren't like the other wizards..."

"Bah," Gala shrugged, "they forgot they were regular humans once. I haven't forgotten, is all. Sometimes, I almost wish I could go back the way it was but when I think of not flying, those thoughts just fly out of my head. Pun intended."

The wizard chuckled at his own joke, in turn drawing a smile out of Warthang. Then, he sat down on his branch and indicated to his fellow-tree companion to do the same, becoming a bit more serious.

"So," he began, once both of them had settled uncomfortably in the tree, "have you got one of those questions for me today?"

"I do," acquiesced Warthang, surprised at how easy it was going to be to get the information he needed to change his world back to the way it was supposed to be. "Do you know anything about time travel?"

"Time travel, let's see," thought Gala aloud. "We don't have any time travelers right now but there were some in the past and I, of course, know quite a bit about it and have read extensively over the subject. You see, I've been known to spend hours in the wizard cave, reading up on whatever subject in my spare time."

Warthang drummed his fingers impatiently against the trunk of his tree. That wizard *really* could talk a lot; if only he could just get to the point!

"But if *I* could time travel," continued Gala, apparently clueless to his interlocutor's feelings, "I could become an even greater scholar. Why, I could know everything! Well, not quite, I do have a limited life expectancy and even with time traveling, there is so much you can do and..."

"What *can* you do with time travel?" interrupted Warthang, as gently as possible. "And are there things that you can't do?"

The sorcerer looked to the sky in thought and clapped his hands twice, finally resting them against his chin. After a few seconds, he looked back over at the dragon, or what he could see of him in human form, and began,

"Let me say it as simply as possible without the mechanics: time traveling is an observation tool. You go in, look around, talk to people, get information. Now mind you, it comes with some risk. You're living your life even if it is in a different time frame so you can still get hurt and die and all that fiasco."

"But wait a second," Warthang said, holding a finger up, "if you're interacting with people, aren't you changing how things are supposed to happen?"

"Time isn't linear and time doesn't change," answered Gala, knowledgeably, "when a time traveler goes to the past, he's already been there and what he does has already happened."

"No, no, no," the dragon shook his head obstinately, "Let me give you a scenario and you'll see. Let's say a girl lived through a tragic accident when she was little but lost her parents in the process. Then, later, she becomes a time traveler. Couldn't she just go back to that time and either send herself a warning or stop the event altogether?"

"It's impossible," said Gala, raising his shoulders and shaking his head, "time travelers cannot be in the same time frame twice. If they've already lived in that time, they can never return back to it."

"What? But...what if a time traveler did go back within his time?"

"The only explanation would be that he had left that time frame in the past and so it had become open for his present self. Likewise, if a time traveler goes forward in time, it kind of kicks that future self into a different time until the window is open again for him to return home. It's quite a messy business that."

Warthang thought back on the message he had told Tundra to tell him next time she saw him and realized she *had* given him that message. In fact, it was his very words of "stay away from Benzady" that had propelled him towards seeking out that blasted bully! He had not changed anything after all, and this time-hopping was completely useless to him!

Finally noticing his companion's upset demeanor, Gala leaned forward, squinting in the darkness, trying to see Warthang's face.

"Is everything okay?" he asked, concerned, "You don't really seem like your usual self today."

Vehemently, the dragon shook his head, and then buried it into his human hands. His human friends were dead. He could not do anything about it. Tundra, his only remaining friend, wanted nothing to do with him. To top it all off, he was a murderer. Not only had he killed Benzady, in a disgusting, out of control rage, but he had also caused Maggie's family's death by not being careful when he talked to Tundra and letting the other dragon overhear him. It was all his fault.

Tears began leaking silently from his eyes but as soon as they appeared, he wiped them away in shame. He had no right to feel sorry for himself. He was disgusting. He did not even deserve to live! But death would be too easy compared to these suffocating feelings. With that thought, Warthang closed his eyes and decided that he would live on alone and pay penance for his actions. He would live alone in misery, alone in guilt, alone in shame, a lone murderer.

When he opened his eyes again, he found himself back as a dragon standing over Benzady's torn up corpse, Tundra still walking away, in the distance.

Everything was as it should be. Everything was the way he had left it.

Note 9

For many years I lived in despair, barely moving from my lair and only when I needed something to eat. I looked out into the world with my wizard sight and watched it go by. I didn't really care about what they were doing, I just didn't want to look at myself and see what I had become. Finally, I don't know how long it had been, probably a couple of hundred years, she woke me up from my sleep and made me realize: It's no use feeling sorry for myself, the past is the past. I can't change it but I sure can change who I am now and who I will be, and make a difference.

Chapter 9 – Change

Due to some unknown reason, the dragons seemed to live on and never die. At first, being new creatures and not knowing their limits, they had lived carefully and peacefully, for the most part, with their human neighbors. But as time ticked on and generation after generation of man passed on, they began feeling "immortal" and doing as they pleased with the inferior races. Interestingly, some developed an obsession with beautiful shiny things and began hoarding treasure in their caves; which in turn, attracted greedy humans to them (and to their deaths). This was greatly entertaining to the rest of the dragons and so they too started raiding villages in their territory for trinkets that would eventually bring a brave (or stupid) soul with which they could play.

Through all of these changes, Warthang watched in the darkness of his depression, unsurprised, uncaring, never lifting a claw. Although his kin killed humans and acted abominably, *they* never murdered each other, and he felt ashamed of even the thought of showing his face to them. So in silence he bore his self-imposed punishment, and in gleeful screams the dragons continued their activities.

On a day just like any other, for all days seemed the same to the wizard dragon, Warthang lay in his dusty cave, watching the small village in Hall Forest with his sight. Every day, he watched a different town, alternating from site to site and keeping his mind from looking at his own disgusting self.

In the streets, the townspeople sold their wares, children ran about without restraint, and women worked hard on their various chores. In a corner, not far from all the hustle and bustle, a certain merchant displayed precious stones imbedded in earrings, bracelets and necklaces. Warthang sighed: he could never understand people's fascination with those rocks. After all, they were completely useless.

After a long morning of such mundane activities, some townsfolk sat down with their stringed instruments and began strumming and humming local tunes. With the music, a few younger teenagers and children grabbed a neighboring hand and dragged a partner into a dance. Suddenly, the whole of Hall Village had a party going with dancing, music, games and shouts. However, as it must sometimes happen that when you are having the best of times the worst of events materializes, it was at about that time that a large purple dragon flew into the throng, screeching and bursting fire into the air. What had been singing and laughing now turned into yelling as people ran with their arms in the air, trampling those that had fallen under their feet.

Chortling, the dragon set a few roofs on fire and expertly caught a small child with his claws, tossing him into the air and catching him again like a rubber ball.

"Humans!" called the beast in a deep resonant voice, "bring me food and bring me treasure and out of the goodness of my heart, I will spare this feeble boy and the rest of your children."

At the sound of the high pitched crying boy, his mother burst out of a nearby house, hysterically calling her son's name. When she saw his predicament, she crumbled to the ground, her knees having lost their strength, and begged the other villagers to oh please help and please give him what he wants. One by one, some people, not daring to leave their hiding places, threw their jewelry out of the windows at the dragon whose eyes began glittering with the shine of the stones. After a while, the treasure ceased flying in and silence reigned in the streets instead. Looking around impatiently like a snake, the purple dragon frowned and flicked his tongue.

"And my food?" he bellowed directly in the small teary boy's face.

"You can hunt your own food!" a strong female voice countered, surprising everyone.

Looking up, humans and dragon alike saw a beautiful blue dragon hovering over the scene to finally perch over one of the roofs. In his cave, Warthang sucked in a breath and clenched his claws, scraping the ground. Tundra.

He had caught some glimpses of her through the long years but had immediately looked elsewhere, punishing himself further. But this time, the sight of her heroic self flying in mesmerized him and he could not bring himself to look away.

"This is my territory," hissed the purple dragon, "and you have no right to be here."

"It may be your territory," replied Tundra lightly, "but these humans are my friends and so are mine to protect."

"Your friends?" snorted the other, "doubtful."

Then, looking around, he smiled and lowered his

toothy mouth to the boy's face. "Humans! Is this dragon your friend?"

And with that question, he flicked his tongue and licked his prisoner's cheek, causing the child to wail in fear.

"No!" the mother screamed desperately, "she is not our friend!"

Taking advantage of the purple dragon's distraction, for all his attention rested on the trembling figure in his claws, Tundra jumped off the roof and landed on the glittering pile of treasure with a thump. Without further delay, she grabbed a big chunk of the jewelry with her four clawed feet and took to the sky. Seeing most of his prize in another's possession, the purple dragon immediately dropped the boy and batted his wings after the thief. Once in the air, he followed her for a few miles with growls and threats.

"There's no place you can go with my treasure, that I can't get it back!" he continued.

Looking behind her, the female judged the distance between their location and the village's and smiled. To her opponent's dismay, she opened her claws and let all of the trinkets fall down in the forest, where you could no longer see them. With a roar, the angry beast that chased her dove in after the stones and disappeared into the foliage. As she continued flying, Tundra heard him yelling after her,

"If those humans really are your friends, then you better guard them day and night because I'm coming after them!"

Frowning, Tundra headed back to the village and found them scampering about for water to douse the flames devouring some of their houses. When she landed in the middle of the village, the people dropped their buckets and scurried away every which way, forgetting all about the devouring fire. As she approached the first burning house, Tundra continuously sucked in air, drawing the flames into her mouth and swallowing them down. Little by little, the licking tendrils entered her body and left the surrounding homes with just smoke trailing behind.

When she had finished, a few men threw some water on the coals, cooling down the whole charred mess, all the while eying her suspiciously.

"People of the village," Tundra finally broke the heavy silence, "you have to leave this town and seek shelter: the dragon will be coming back and I'm afraid of what he might do."

In a corner, a villager crossed his arms and spat on the ground.

"You just want us to leave so you can steal more of our money and jewels. Haven't you had enough already?"

Around her, the other townsfolk grunted and nodded their heads, raising their fists at her.

"That's right!" piped in a woman, "it doesn't take a genius to see you're weak and get what you want through trickery!"

From a house, someone threw a log and it bounced against Tundra's long neck with a sting. One by one, the villagers picked up rocks and sticks and threw them at her, shouting down her pleas for them to leave their homes behind for their lives. Seeing that nothing she did would get through to them, she finally batted her wings and flew high above the trees where they could no longer reach her. Eventually, she doubled back and landed into the highest tree she could find and perched herself there to watch for any oncoming attacks.

No matter how hungry or tired she got, she kept vigil through day and night, afraid to leave her post, for she felt responsible for the worse predicament of the humans. Had she not intervened, their lives would probably not be at stake. Nevertheless, she did not regret her actions and would stand for what was right to the end.

Through all of this, Warthang never left her side: he too stood vigil over her in his cave, amazed at her determination. Through adversity, she stood up for what was right and tried to make a difference, even if no one else helped her. He, on the other hand, wallowed in his own despair, disgusted by himself and afraid of what more evil he could cause if given the temptation. He was just plain pathetic.

Before Tundra could see them, the wizard magic user perceived five shapes in the distant sky, bearing straight for her position. When she finally did see them, she shook her head to strain her sleepy eyes to alertness and stretched her wings, readying herself against the onslaught.

When they finally reached Tundra, the five dragons surrounded her and landed in the trees around her, cutting any escape she might have had, had she chosen to abandon the humans. The purple dragon, the one whose territory she had infringed upon, shook his head slowly and sighed, as if disappointed.

"Tundra, Tundra. I'm apparently not the only one who has to endure your shenanigans. These fellows here tell me you've been causing them trouble too. Frankly, we're tired of it and want you out of our territories!"

With that introduction, the purple monster signaled to the other four who promptly jumped on Tundra and pinned her firmly to the tops of several trees, holding her wings and neck down against their prickly trunks. In vain, the female struggled against the bullies' weight;

four against one never are favorable odds. Grinning, the leader approached and laid his front legs in her face imperiously, blocking her sight and crushing her head uncomfortably. In his cave, a twinge pricked Warthang's heart, causing him to stir, but it was not enough to move him out of his darkness, out of his depression.

Suddenly, the three beasts holding Tundra's wings down began tearing at them, gashing gaping holes through the membranes and breaking the small bones with loud cracks. In agony, she screeched and wiggled her body under the weight of her captors, almost dislodging some of them off her elegant form. When they had finished their dirty work, all five of them jumped back into the surrounding trees and smiled approvingly. Broken and alone, Tundra gritted her teeth and blinked the tears away, trying to be brave through the pain. In the darkness, Warthang raised his head and lost the tears she would not shed.

"Now Tundra," the purple dragon declared, "you will promise to leave all of our territories alone and let us do what we want, as we always have."

"I promise," the blue female said trembling uncontrollably and biting her tongue. "I promise that though I may not fly, I will run, I will walk, and I will even crawl to your stupid territories and protect those who cannot defend themselves to the best of my abilities. I promise to be a bane, a thorn in your side, a constant reminder that your way of life is wrong."

Warthang stood up and stepped out into the sun, the light almost blinding him from the vision he held of his beautiful defending angel. There she lay in the trees, crumpled, defenseless, but still her face shone with determination and strength. With a head signal, the five dragons dropped into the woods and disappeared, annoyed but determined. After a few minutes, whimpers and yells accompanied their quick return: in their claws, they each held a trapped human, looking like mice in the clutches of eagles.

"Again I will ask," now growled the angry dragon. "Promise to stay away or these humans *will* die. We will tear them one at a time, limb from limb, right in front of you, and eat them. And we won't stop there, we will get the whole stinking village until you make that promise!"

For a second, Tundra's features contorted, her determination seeming to waver, but finally, she brought her emotions back firmly and prepared to make another declaration.

"ENOUGH!" roared Warthang by her side, suddenly appearing out of nowhere. "Let the humans go!"

Surprised, the purple dragon jumped back with his captive in tow, changing trees, leaves flying everywhere.

"Who are *you*?" he blurted.

After squinting closely at the wizard dragon's face, another one of the dragons frowned and hissed.

"It's Warthang," he growled, backing away in his tree.

Perplexed, the purple dragon cocked his head sideways.

"I thought he was dead..." Then he hunched his shoulders forward and stood firmly in the leafy limbs. "So Warthang, what brings you out of wherever you've been for the last hundreds of years?"

Sighing, the red dragon shook his head slowly. "Let the humans go, don't even lay a scratch on them, or else."

"Or else what?" snorted his opponent. "You'll kill me too, you sorry excuse for a half dragon?"

At that, a small scratch opened up on the man's face the purple dragon was holding, the poor human whimpering and holding back a cry. Like a lightning bolt, Warthang's anger flashed through his yellow opaque eyes, but dissipated just as quickly when the image of a dead Benzady flared in his mind. With a cool head, he raised a strong gust that blew out from him and burst through to the surrounding five dragons, almost dislodging them from their high perches. When the wind had ceased, the purple dragon clapped his free hands together and laughed.

"That's very impressive, but the only thing it's going to do is help me fly better."

For a few seconds, Warthang bit his lower lip. How could he convince these fiends without hurting them? Suddenly, an idea came to him and he smiled menacingly.

"Let the humans go or you *will* regret it."

With a challenge, the purple dragon again drew a claw across his captive's visage and the scratch became a deep bleeding gash. Unable to contain himself, the man yelled, but clamped up as soon as he could bear it.

"You asked for it," Warthang said, shrugging his shoulders.

As soon as he said the words, everyone heard a massive crackling and where the purple dragon had stood, now only the human remained. Well, that is not truly accurate, but it is what they thought they could see. With a sign of the wizard's hand, the gash in the man's face knit itself together and the skin glistened smoothly. Finally, he began floating like a bubble and slowly descended through the trees into the safety of the forest, obviously guided by a magical power.

"Change me back, change me back!" squeaked an extremely high-pitched voice.

Following the source of the pathetic wail, the other four dragons finally spotted their companion in the same tree, dissimulated among some branches. What had once been a massive beast was now a cute tiny dragon about the size of a household cat. Without restraint, they burst out laughing, pointing at their leader, but when Warthang glared at them, their mocking abruptly ceased.

"Drop the humans," he commanded.

Right away, all four jumped backwards, leaving their prey behind unharmed. Like the previous human, these began floating down through the trees and into the forest, joining their fellow-villager.

"Know that the humans are my friends, and whenever they are in trouble, there I will be to protect them." Warthang declared, looking in turn at each of the five dragons. "Now tell everyone what happens when you mess with me."

A crackle resounded once more and the purple dragon regained his former stature. Without a word, he took to the air, followed by his four companions, and all five of them flew away in silence, never looking back.

Satisfied, Warthang nodded and turned his attention to Tundra. Immediately, his heart clenched like a balled fist inside his chest: there she lay, crumpled and broken, her breathing marked with short, painful gasps. Not knowing what to say, he kept silent and approached her, extending his wings over her body protectively.

"Don't move," he finally whispered as his magic began coursing through her, slowly binding her body back together.

Unfortunately, the process was very painful and she sucked her breath in, squeezed her eyes shut and gnashed her teeth. After a few minutes, small whimpers escaped her lips and tears streamed down her scaly cheeks.

"I'm so sorry," she hiccupped, now crying freely, no longer holding back.

As he healed her, Tundra continued apologizing, for what, he could not fathom. After all, she had been trying to protect the humans, and her injuries were a sign of courage and determination, not a reason to feel sorry. When he had finished mending her, he spoke to her softly.

"You have nothing to feel sorry for. You did the right thing."

He turned around and prepared to leave but she stretched her right arm to his shoulder to detain him.

"I abandoned you!" she blurted out.

Shaking his head, Warthang looked to the ground below the trees and sighed.

"You only did what I deserved. I'm a murderer."

Again, he tried to leave but Tundra desperately jumped in his path to block him.

"All the time we spent together and the talks we had about trying to make our society better, being a good example to influence the others, do you remember that?"

When he nodded, she frowned, looking down at herself.

"No matter how many dragons I tried to influence, even giving them second chances time and time again, I didn't even lift a claw to give my own best friend that second chance. When I saw what you had done to Benzady, I was so scared and disgusted that I ran away. Over time, I was able to somewhat get over my aversion but even though I felt convicted to help make other dragons better, I was too ashamed of the way I acted to face you. I'm a complete coward and I am so very sorry."

Tears appeared in Warthang's eyes. She was sorry for having shunned him? Well, he was sorry that she was sorry: he certainly did not deserve her sympathy or help.

"No matter how terrible and hateful Benzady was,"

Warthang started in a shaky voice, "I am far worse for having ended him. There must have been some other form of punishment I could have enacted on him, but instead of justice, I threw vengeance at him in a blind rage. I certainly am not worth your consideration."

"Vengeance?" asked Tundra, perplexed. "Vengeance for what?"

Warthang shook his head, either refusing to answer her question or unable to utter the words.

"No matter," she sighed, "you are the only dragon who will give goodness a chance and the only one who can help me defend the weak. Will you help me?"

Her question surprised him so much that he stumbled where he stood in the tree, almost falling to the ground. When he had righted himself, he looked at her sincere eyes then batted the water from his own and stopped his trembling lower jaw by shaking his head.

"You really want me to help?" he asked shakily, hopeful. He had realized in that moment how much time he had wasted wallowing in his cave, when he could have tried to make amends for his terrible sin.

"I wouldn't ask if I didn't mean it, you dope!" Tundra laughed. Then, pensively, she asked him, "what you did to Slug, making him so itty bitty, why don't you do it to all of them permanently? It seems that would make our job easier and the humans could defend themselves and not rely so much on us two."

"Didn't you want to try to show them a better way and help change them?" Warthang avoided the question, not wanting to disappoint her.

"Pft!" she exclaimed, "That was a child's dream. I tried that for centuries and the others really never cared. In fact, over time, they've gotten worse! I have a new plan now: try to stop them from doing bad things and if I'm too late on that, then try to undo what they did, somehow."

Warthang nodded in understanding. Even though he had wanted her "child's dream" to come true, he had never really believed it possible.

"So?" Tundra persisted, "are you going to change them all into smaller little dragons so the humans can kick their butts around a bit?"

Sighing, the red dragon shook his head. "I can't," he admitted sadly, "the way the magic works is it flows out of me into whatever I'm doing, but when I'm done, it comes right back to me and doesn't stay. I can do things that are natural that will stick because that is the way it should be, like healing or maybe moving things, but if it's unnatural, as soon as I'm gone, so is my magic."

The blue female looked at him, perplexed, the wheels turning in her head.

"That doesn't make any sense," she declared. "If that's the case, then how did the wizards make us dragons? The elders say they changed us from two different animals and molded them together, morphing them into us. If what you say is true, then that magic should have stopped as soon as the mages did and we could not exist without them."

"I don't know, Tundra," Warthang shrugged, "they must have had some tricks I don't know about."

"It's too bad you can't go ask them," she pondered, quietly.

"Oh!" Warthang exclaimed. But he could go ask them: he had the power!

Without a backward thought, the wizard dragon jumped time and arrived sometime before he had met

136

Gala in the trees. Quickly, he morphed his form into a human, scanned the continent with his wizard's eye and teleported himself a safe distance from where he found the flying man. This time, the wizard was taking a nap in the long grasses of the plains, his arms crossed behind his head and his legs wide open in abandon. Walking nonchalantly toward him, Warthang smiled at Gala's funny pose and stopped by his head, casting a shadow over the man.

"Hum, hum" he grunted.

At the sound, the startled Gala jumped twenty feet into the sky (no joke) and landed roughly in a pile at Warthang's feet. Like a shriveled claw, his hand grabbed at his heart while he desperately tried to control his accelerated breathing. When he had calmed himself down, he looked up from his position on the ground and saw the figure of a man looking down at him with a smile. Recognizing him, he returned the smile and laughed boisterously.

"Well, you sure gave me a scare there!" he exclaimed between guffaws.

Jovially, he accepted Warthang's extended hand and drew himself to his feet. Brushing off the grass from his robes, Gala cocked his head sideways and looked at the young man.

"It's really strange meeting you in the middle of nowhere like this," he started, looking around. "I thought no one walked these parts. But what am I talking about? Every time I see you, it's never in the same place. It's like you follow me around. Are you following me?" he asked, one eyebrow arched.

"I must be." Warthang replied, mysteriously. Then without delay, he veered the conversation away from the wizard's constant babble. "I have a question for you."

"Of course you do, Warthang," Gala smiled again and then raised his arms into the air, "Question away!"

"How does magic work?"

The wizard's eyebrows lowered themselves over his eyes. "What do you mean exactly?"

"Well," the dragon began, crossing his arms over his chest, "when a wizard does magic, like let's say he changes a sheep into a cow, how does he make it stay a cow and not revert back to its true nature?"

"What kind of a question is that? I have never heard anything so weird," Gala mumbled to himself, "why would anyone change a sheep into a cow? Goodness, gracious. But I guess Pita is pompous enough that he would do something like that. I think I remember him one time..."

"It's an example," Warthang interrupted, a bit exasperated.

"Well sure, sure," the mage patted the man on the back three times, as if humoring him. "So what was your question again?"

Warthang squeezed his eyes shut and covered them with one hand. He did not remember the wizard having been this scatter brained when he met him the first time; perhaps, he had not fully awakened from his nap.

"How does magic work?" he repeated, pronouncing every word pointedly.

"Oh that's right!" remembered the wizard, "well, there are different kinds of magic but with the example you were talking about," at that, he snickered a bit, "the power flows out of the wizard and then permanently stays with the animal. So, in a sense, it's now a magical cow."

Uncontrollably, Gala burst into laughter over his joke and slapped his thighs, imagining his magical cow eating grass, maybe braying instead of mooing. Warthang, on the other hand, pondered over the information. This was not how the magic worked for him: it never stayed behind like that. Again, he thought back on how he had acquired his powers and remembered the last line of the spell he had uttered: *All magic to me it will stick*. There was the answer: even the magic he used came right back to him and so some of his spells could not be permanent because of that. What a bother!

Over the next few hours, the two walked together amiably, discussing various topics on magic. At first, not wanting to be rude, Warthang had accompanied the magician; but with time, he began enjoying Gala's company. Although he talked to himself a lot, the wizard was positive and funny, an interesting show in himself. Without a doubt, the dragon knew he would come in the future—or the past, really—to see this strange character, and not just to ask him questions.

As the sun found its way down, the two friends, for they had become so in Warthang's mind, went their separate ways. When he felt sure Gala could no longer see him, he changed himself back into his real form and time traveled to the exact moment he had left Tundra behind. To her, it only seemed like he had flickered for a moment, and she blinked her eyes, trying to dispel the strange hallucination she thought she had had.

"Oh what?" she said, continuing their conversation.

"Oh what what?" Warthang asked, having forgotten what had happened before he left.

"I don't know," she shrugged, "you just all of a

sudden exclaimed 'Oh!' Well never mind that, let's go to my cave and talk for a while, we've got a lot to discuss."

And so they left Hall's forest and headed back to the mountains. That night, they did not sleep a wink but talked and talked until the birds began singing and the sun peeked its rays between the peaks. Life would start again for Warthang, no longer would he remain cooped up in his dank home of loneliness.

Note 10

Have you ever done something without realizing what the consequences would be? I thought I had already suffered them and in a sense, I had. Self-hate. Depression. Exile. Rejection. But apparently I was still missing one consequence that would plague me until my death: vengeance.

Chapter 10 – Worms

The next few years were some of the happiest for Warthang. He had his best friend back; and over time, their relationship became more—but that really is none of our business, so we will skip that part of the story. Together, they defended the humans from dragon attacks. Tundra was permanently posted at Valley City, it being the biggest town on the continent, while the wizard dragon kept vigil with his magic sight and teleported to the other locations as needed. Although this system worked well enough, the dragons at times still succeeded in ransacking areas whenever poor Warthang slept. Their ire for him even pushed them into working together in each other's territories; they would mount synchronized attacks so that some of them would get away with treasure and food. Warthang did not know how to be at more than one place at a time, unfortunately.

All over the continent, the humans came to recognize the pair of them as benevolent, and cheered them on whenever they flew in to the rescue. But even with their grateful thanks, they still acted aloof and refused to converse with them more than necessary.

One morning, while the two dragons slumbered in their cave, Warthang abruptly woke to the sound of falling pebbles. Sliding uncontrollably down the hill, a small green dragon, for he must have been very young indeed, struggled to regain control of his limbs, only to plant himself face first at the bottom of the slope. A smile creeping up on his face, Warthang nudged Tundra awake. She blinked several times and then focused on the small baby who was at this point rolling himself to his feet. When he had stood up, he shook himself, dust flying everywhere, and suddenly stopped to stare straight at Warthang. Upon seeing the adult dragon awake, the young one slashed his tail, furrowed his brows, showed his teeth and hissed loudly.

"Well, aren't we a feisty one!" laughed the wizard dragon.

At the sound of Warthang's voice, the green baby began scuttling toward the entrance of the lair, all the while hissing and sputtering. Once at the opening of the cave, he proceeded to slash his claws and bite at Warthang's legs, for he could not reach anything else.

"Whoa, there!" exclaimed Tundra, "that's enough!"

But the young one ignored her; he only had eyes for the red male dragon.

Perplexed, Warthang smashed the baby down with his two front legs, as gently as he could, preventing him from continuing his attack.

"What are you so mad about?" he asked gently.

Without answer, the small creature struggled to set himself free, to no avail. When he had tired himself, he sighed noisily and lay still under Warthang's large claws.

"There, there, now. Isn't that better?" he asked.

The captive harrumphed and glared at his jailer, still silent. Tundra bent down to look at him, shrugged her shoulders and exited the cave.

"Since we're up, we might as well get going," she declared. "See any activity this morning?"

"Not yet," Warthang answered, "but I wouldn't mind flying around and getting some fresh air."

And so the two took to the sky, leaving the strange green baby behind, figuring he would go on his not-so-merry way once they were gone. But that was not the case; in fact, he was there when they returned that night, his energy recuperated and ready for a fight. No matter how much they tried talking to him, the little one refused to calm down and just kept clawing and biting. Finally, tired of this charade, Warthang grabbed him, flew a long distance with the little one in his clutches, and deposited him far away, to the edge of the mountain slopes. Once rid of his load, he teleported back home and rested for the night.

Unfortunately, this became a routine for the two dragons: a morning wakeup call with hissings and growlings and a night flight to distance the creature. This became so unbearable that one morning Tundra lost her patience and shook the baby, demanding his name and what he wanted. For the first time, he looked at her, surprised at her presence. Apparently, his rage had been so blinding that he had never noticed her, in all of this time. Staring at her, his lower lip began quivering and he burst into tears, wailing uncontrollably. Feeling awful, the blue female let go of his shoulders and wrapped him up in her arms, rocking him back and forth. After some minutes, his wail subsided into a whimper and he calmed down.

"What's your name?" Tundra whispered gently into his ear.

"Gurb," he sniffled, wiping at his face with one

small clawed hand.

"Ah!" exclaimed Warthang, "now we're getting somewhere!"

But as soon as he heard the dragon wizard's voice, Gurb's subdued demeanor reverted to his hostile self and he proceeded to continue his usual attack.

"Warthang," Tundra said, "how about you go on alone today? I'll see if I can get any answers out of our young…friend."

Warthang nodded and left for a tiring day of protecting. All day long, he wondered about what she would find out and the minutes could not have crawled any slower to evening. Before arriving home that night, Tundra met him in the air and indicated that they should sleep elsewhere. When they had settled themselves into a new dark hole the wizard had built within minutes, he noticed the worry lines in her brow and the sad set of her mouth.

"What's going on?" he asked, concerned.

"Gurb is just a few months old and barely knows how to talk he's so young," Tundra rattled on, not needing prompting. "It was hard to get anything out of him because of that but here's what I gathered: he doesn't understand it, but he has this driving force to find you and kill you."

Warthang drew back, surprised. Before he could get a word in however, Tundra continued.

"Whenever he sees you, it's like a spirit controls him to attack. He can't stop himself, and he doesn't even want to stop. When he thinks about you dead, he gets the biggest grin; it's the creepiest thing I've ever seen."

She shook her head at that and a shiver ran down her spine.

146

"One more thing," she said, staring intently at Warthang, gauging his reaction. "He's Flora and Benzady's offspring."

The red dragon stood up abruptly, hitting his head on the ceiling of the cave. He rubbed the sore spot and frowned.

"Does Gurb know I killed his…his father?" he asked quietly.

"That's the weird thing," the blue female answered. "He doesn't. He acts like he wants revenge, he hates you so much, but he doesn't know why."

"I hate to state the obvious," Warthang sighed, "but something abnormal is definitely going on."

"What are you going to do about it?"

"Nothing for now," he answered, shaking his head. "Let's just sleep somewhere different every night so he can't find us and we can just avoid the situation."

"Okay," Tundra agreed.

And so that's what they did: they slept in a different place every night. Over time, they developed a system of homes and managed to never encounter little Gurb. In fact, decades passed without seeing the hate-filled dragon and the two began forgetting about the reason why they had so many lairs.

All this time, Gurb searched for Warthang without any luck. When he reached thirty, he finally decided to change his tactic, and from what he had learned by questioning the others, his new strategy was a sure way to gain a confrontation with the object of his hate.

That first day, Warthang and Tundra stopped a few attacks. However, while the female protected Valley City, the red magic-user arrived too late at a farm where he found crops burning, dark smoke billowing into the sky. When he had doused the flames with conjured-up rain, he found the fire had left behind infesting worms. Warthang had never seen such a sight and found it highly unusual, but he dismissed it as some kind of fluke. Quickly, he grew the crops back up for the farmer and teleported back to Tundra.

The next day, Warthang found Hall forest destroyed, once again by flames, and littered with those same white wiggly worms. Confused, he grew the trees back and set out to search for some eye witnesses: he needed some answers. Back in Hall's village, people milled around as usual: selling, buying, and working on chores. A small child playing in the street with pebbles looked up and suddenly screamed a piercing screech. Following his frightened gaze, the people recognized the red dragon descending upon them as the protector and patted the scared lad on the head reassuringly. When Warthang had landed in the middle of the town, the humans gave him a strange look; he had never come into the town before.

"Is something amiss?" the mayor asked, sitting on a chair on the side of the street, right next to where the giant creature sat.

"Maybe. I don't know," answered Warthang. "Do any of you know anything about the burning of the forest?"

The mayor stood up, tapped his right foot on the ground impatiently and regarded Warthang suspiciously.

"What's your name, protector dragon?"

"Warthang."

Not surprised one bit, the mayor nodded and pointed a finger at the red dragon.

"He left you a message." Taking a piece of paper out of his shirt pocket, he proceeded to read it: "Stop

148

running, you coward, and face me. I will be waiting for you in the hills where the sheep herds graze, tomorrow morning. If you don't come, I will burn them all."

The mayor crumpled the message, threw it in the street, spat on it and ground it in the dirt with his heel.

"Who gave you that message?" sighed Warthang, already knowing the answer.

"Some green dragon who thought well of himself, but he's obviously young and inexperienced."

At Warthang's silence, the mayor frowned and squinted his eyes.

"You will go, won't you? I don't think he'll stop otherwise."

"What good will it do?" breathed the dragon, exasperated. "I just don't see the point of it all."

"You *will* go!" ordered the man, pointing his grubby finger at Warthang's nose. "That monster won't stop burning things and eventually he'll move beyond animals and start killing *us*!"

Surprised and annoyed at the human's tone, Warthang shrugged his shoulders and stood up.

"I'll see what I can do."

* * *

The next day, as early as sunup, Warthang paced the same hills he had crossed when he had been four to find a way to defeat the wizards. It felt strange being in the same place and again having an enemy with no known defense. His stomach writhed inside him but suddenly clenched when he perceived the shape of a small green dragon in the distance. When the dragon in turn saw him, his calm soaring was replaced by an enraged flapping. Warthang took to the air, refusing to have his enemy on higher ground, and was welcomed by scorching fire. Surprised, the red wizard frowned. Dragons were immune to fire, what was the point of that?

Suddenly, as the flames that enveloped him burned out, white festering worms appeared on his scales, burrowing between them to reach his hide. Warthang

bellowed and fell to the ground on his back, his legs flaying every which way. Without thinking, he caused a torrent wind to explode out of his body, sending the grubs to the ground, a few feet away. In the air, Gurb descended upon him with an evil grin. Again, he opened his mouth and new flames rolled out, ready to infest

Warthang with new maggots but before they could reach him, the wizard dragon teleported to the air just above his attacker. Without delay, he brought his heavier bulk upon the teenage dragon and threw him to the ground, pinning his wings and front legs.

"Where did those maggots come from?" he asked his captive shakily.

"I may be small now," sputtered Gurb, wiggling and struggling, "but someday I'll be just as big as you and you won't be able to stop me. My worms will get you then!"

Warthang grabbed Gurb by the neck with his teeth and ground him deeper in the dirt. He yelled louder, his voice now muffled with the flesh inside his mouth.

"Where did those maggots come from!"

In the dirt, Gurb began laughing hysterically. "I'm special! I'm the only one who can do it. My worms are the only thing that can kill you!"

"Kill me??" Warthang let go of the green dragon's neck and spat.

"I don't think anything can kill me, so you might as well give up. And for that matter, leave the poor people and their things alone."

"Of course they can kill you!" retorted Gurb, stubbornly. "Singe told me so."

"My father told you so?" Warthang's heart clenched inside his chest, threatening to block his breathing. Where did these worms come from and what did his father know about them? He had to find out, but there was no way he was going to talk to that awful dragon who abandoned him!

"Meet me here in two weeks, Gurb," sighed Warthang. "If you promise to not attack anyone or anything, I will be here."

"You're here right now, what do I care about setting up a meeting for later?"

"Promise me or I'll tear out your wings and you'll never fly again," whispered Warthang in the green dragon's ear.

"Fine!" consented Gurb, grudgingly. "I promise. I won't hurt anyone or anything and I'll see you here in two weeks."

As soon as the last words left Gurb's mouth, Warthang disappeared as if he had never been there.

*   *   *

In human form, a dark hat obscuring his eyes as usual, Warthang entered the fortress where a large group of wizards had assembled to train dragons. In the courtyard, several mages discussed various strategies on boards while smiths worked on armor and women cooked on fires. Seated in a corner, Gala twiddled his thumbs, looking outside the walls through a small window at a couple of black dragons napping. Quietly and calmly, Warthang walked across the courtyard looking like he had every right to be there. When he reached the flying sorcerer, he stood before him and cleared his throat. Broken out of his reverie, Gala looked around and frowned when he saw his friend standing there.

"I thought I'd never see you again." Slowly he stood up, patted the dust from his robes and squinted at Warthang. "I can't believe you've called yourself my friend when you've been lying to me all this time. Did you take me for a fool or think I wouldn't figure it out?"

Speechless, Warthang opened his mouth, closed it and repeated the motion two more times. Before he could think of anything to say, Gala continued,

"Let me guess: you have a question for me, right? I'll answer this question of yours but only if you answer mine first. What happens to me? What happens to all the wizards?"

Frowning, Warthang shook his head.

"What do you mean?"

"Are we really going to play this game?" returned Gala angrily and with one quick swoop, he tore Warthang's hat off and threw it on the ground. Automatically, the dragon covered his eyes, hiding them from sight.

"Who do you think you're fooling?" Gala ranted on, "there's no use hiding your eyes: I already know! You're a wizard and a time traveler at that. You gave me a few clues along the way like knowing my name the first time I met you. And this whole time: all these years, you've looked the same! Except last time, that was ten years ago now. You didn't know my name. I couldn't see very well in the dark that time so I hadn't noticed, but you were quite a bit younger and definitely immature. And then, you disappeared right in front of my eyes. I tried to explain your disappearance away but when we created the dragons, that's when I was sure. So I repeat: what happens to us wizards?"

Warthang shook his head uncomfortably, "What do you mean?"

Gala punched him in the face, leaving a red welt on Warthang's cheek.

"What happens to us? You don't know anything! You keep coming to me with questions about us. That must mean we don't exist anymore, or maybe that we've gone elsewhere. What happens to us! Answer me!"

Warthang withdrew his hands from his face but not before closing his eyes, letting a tear trickle down his cheek. *What happens?* He thought to himself. *Very soon, a small red dragon with yellow eyes will be born who will be taught to hate the wizards. At four years old, he will find a spell that will steal all of their magic, leaving them vulnerable to the dragons. In a frenzy of revenge, all the wizards will die. Gala will die. All because of him. He is going to kill his friend, and all he gets is a punch in the face?*

Tears still falling, Warthang looked straight at Gala with his yellow opaque eyes.

"I'm sorry, my friend. I'm so sorry."

Gala's expression softened and he nodded.

"So I guess we all die…"

But Warthang never heard him, he had returned to his own time.

*　　*　　*

"Thank you for meeting with me on such short notice," said Tundra, eyeing the elders cautiously.

"Of course," answered Singe calmly. "We'd rather talk to you than that half breed freak."

"Why do you hate him so much?" blurted the she-dragon, unable to restrain herself. "He's your own son!"

"Silence, you fool, before we throw you out of our presence," growled Warthang's father. "He is no son of mine, but a wizard. He is all of them. He is everything and everyone we hate. The only reason he lives is because we cannot kill him."

At that remark, Singe showed his teeth in a large smile.

"But there is now one who can," he said triumphantly.

"Gurb? And his worms?" asked Tundra. "What do you know about it?"

"Let me tell you a story, little one," smiled Singe, winking at the other four elders as if sharing a joke.

"In the beginning of time—that is, at our creation—our territorial instinct drove us to kill each other. Displeased by our fighting spirit, the head wizard Thangard laid a curse on us. It went like this:

> *"When your kin you kill,*
> *On earth his blood spill,*
> *A curse on your head:*
> *Return will the dead!*
> *With worms to follow,*
> *His path he will show.*
> *To break this here spell,*
> *You must die as well.*

"And so at that time we understood that we could never kill one of our kind or else we ourselves would die. For that reason, we never dared touch the half breed; but one beautiful day, as you well know, all those centuries ago, he killed Benzady in a fit of rage. When that happened, Benzady's spirit of vengeance rested upon one of his eggs that finally hatched a few years ago. Those worms that protrude from Gurb's fire? They are from Benzady's decaying spirit and until that wizard dies, they will continually try to kill him."

Tundra stood silently for a minute, thinking it over.

155

"You gathered all that from that curse?" she finally asked.

"It is only logical," nodded Singe. Then, looking down at her, he added, "Do you want anything else, little one? I believe I gave you the information you needed."

Far away, Warthang shook his head and returned his sight to his own location. Singe, though a horrible father, was right about the curse. In order for Gurb's death worms to cease, Warthang had to die. But that was not a solution he was willing to accept. If he died and Benzady's vengeful spirit disappeared, evil, egotistical dragons would still litter the world. He had to not only die, but take them all down with him.

Note 11

What happens when you die? Does it hurt? Do you just cease existing? I really can't see the point of living a life if in the end you are just snuffed out; there has to be something more to it than that. Unfortunately, I didn't have time to explore those venues, I knew I had to kill the bad dragons to protect the humans and I knew I had to die along with them or bad dragons would always exist because of that curse.

So the search was on. I needed to find something to destroy us. Kill a few, save millions.

Chapter 11 – YingLong

Exhausted, for Warthang had been flying for several hours without rest, he had finally dived into the ocean and changed his shape to help him float better: he now resembled a red sea serpent with an elongated body and fins at the end of his legs and tail. After swimming for a while, he felt warm with the sun beating down on him and he closed his eyes to the bright light. In his mind's eye, he saw again his last conversation with Tundra.

"You're going to what?" she had asked, cocking her blue head sideways.

"I'm going to find a way to destroy all the bad dragons," he had repeated, chewing his lower lip. "I have to give the humans a way to kill them because I can't do it myself."

"Or else you'll have more evil spirits coming after you," she had interrupted. "But won't you have to die too?"

With downcast eyes, he had nodded. "Yes, and then there will be no more bad dragons left."

"But I will be left alone," she had argued. "What kind of a life is that? And I'm not a bad dragon, what if there are more good ones to be born in the future?"

"Look," he had hugged her and closed his eyes to listen better to her breathing, "I've thought about this a lot and I think it's the right thing to do. Dragon's aren't natural and if they're bad anyways, we shouldn't keep them around."

"What did you tell Gurb?" she asked as they broke their hug.

"Just that I was going away a while and would be back when he was big enough to defeat me," he answered, shrugging his shoulders.

Tundra snorted. "I imagine he didn't take it too well."

Warthang shook his head and swished his tail.

"No. He told me I would regret leaving and that there would be dire consequences."

"And that's not going to stop you from going?" she raised an eyebrow.

"Whether I leave or stay," he answered, dismayed, "Gurb will do bad things. There will always be consequences: I can't second guess myself and wonder which decision will reap the worst results. I'll never make up my mind!"

Looking concerned, the blue creature laid her clawed hand on his. "You sound so frustrated," she murmured.

"I just wish the wizards had never made us! This stupid act of theirs has caused nothing but..."

Warthang abruptly looked up; an idea had interrupted his thoughts.

"What is it?" inquired Tundra, curious.

"I can't undo what they've done," he replied slowly, "but maybe Gala has an idea on how to end it."

She shook her head, "how is he ever going to talk to you again after what happened last time? He knows all the wizards going to die!"

"I'm going to go earlier than that," nodded Warthang. "That conversation will not have happened yet and he will be none the wiser."

Their goodbyes lasted a few hours; after all, it is difficult to leave loved ones without knowing the time of reunion. But in the end, he jumped back in time and once again found the flying sorcerer. This time, he was in Hall's Forest, hiding in the night behind a tree, of all places. Directly behind him, Warthang smiled and crossed his arms. He knew exactly how Gala would react.

"Hey Gala," he whispered right behind the mage's ear.

The wizard in question summersaulted as high as a kangaroo and landed on his behind, facing Warthang, and his back to the tree. Since it was dark, all the magician could see was a dark shape in the night. But with his wizard eyes, the dragon saw that his friend looked angry.

"Subaru, is that you?" he whispered, sharply.

Warthang backed a step, a bit surprised.

"No," he said, keeping his voice low, "it's me: Warthang."

Relaxing, Gala exhaled and stood up. "Warthang? I've never heard of you. Did...did Subaru send you?"

In response, Warthang shook his head. So, this was the famous first meeting between the two of them. Well, it had already happened so he could do no wrong.

"If he didn't send you," continued Gala, "then what do you want with me?"

"Well," answered the human dragon, shrugging his shoulders in the dark, "I've seen you flying, and I thought you might be able to give me some explanations on wizard things."

"You've seen me what?" sputtered the young man,

flabbergasted. Then, he squinted at Warthang in the dark, trying to see him better. "You can't tell anyone."

"Oh, please," responded the dragon a bit sarcastically under his breath. Then louder, "the people will see you as more likeable if they know you can fly. They really hate the wizards but you, they'll tolerate."

"For flying?" shot back the young man, incredulous.

"Sure," continued Warthang, as if stating the obvious. "But not just that. You'll talk to them as if they're people and they'll appreciate that somewhat. The flying will add a 'flightiness' to your personality which will make you seem harmless."

"Harmless..." repeated Gala, now deep in thought.

"Gala!" a gruff voice interrupted them as a large man surged from the other side of the enormous tree. Immediately, the wizard straightened himself, squared his shoulders and tightened his fists.

"How did you expect me to find you behind that tree anyway?" grumbled the man a bit angrily.

"My apologies," Gala replied with clenched teeth and a fake smile. "I was having a conversation with my friend here and forgot the time."

"I'm not surprised," the man raised his nose condescendingly. "All you scum wizards think about is yourselves. Why did you want to meet with me anyway?"

"Why," the sorcerer jovially answered without missing a beat, "I wanted you to meet my friend here. His name's Warthang. He's a wizard."

Confused, for the dragon knew the darkness hid his eyes perfectly and no one should be able to tell of the magic that coursed in them, Warthang raised his hand amicably, but the man completely ignored him.

"Is he as much of a flop in wizardry as you are?" he taunted. "You think two of you will make me go away?"

The dragon's brows furrowed over his eyes. Apparently, this guy was causing his friend some trouble. Well, he could definitely help Gala in getting rid of him.

"And who might this lowly *boy* be, Gala?" Warthang asked, assuming an air of superiority.

"This is Subaru, my sister's...friend."

"You scum bag!" Subaru spat, drawing back his fist as if to hit Gala in the face. "I'm her lover. And she isn't your sister!"

Before the situation escalated any further, Warthang stepped between the two to intervene, facing the large man.

"You don't have much respect for a wizard with as much power as I. I will demonstrate: on the count of three, I will cause Gala to fly up in the air so high that he will disappear."

"Go ahead," Subaru countered, undaunted. "That's not going to impress me."

Warthang counted to three and as predicted, Gala went flying. Of course, this was of the mage's own power and not the dragon's. And as soon as he was far out of sight, Warthang turned himself into his original form, a monstrous red dragon with completely yellow eyes. Not knowing what kind of beast appeared before him, Subaru yelped and made to dash, only to be blocked by gigantic claws.

"Hear me, puny human," Warthang rumbled in a voice much deeper than his usual one. "You will leave this town and you will run away from Gala. Got it?"

"Yes! Yes!" yelled Subaru, completely frightened

out of his wits.

At that, Warthang let him go and reverted back to human form. Without delay, the large man noisily scampered away, screaming about magic and demons. Chuckling to himself, Warthang looked up just as Gala floated down through the trees. Once he had landed, he brushed some leaves off his clothes and heavily exhaled.

"I thought I heard some screaming..." he commented.

"Yep," chuckled Warthang, "that flying of yours may have impressed him after all. I do believe he's going to skip town."

Thoughtfully, Gala scratched his chin for a moment and then nodded.

"All right. Thanks for the help, I guess. I'm gonna go now."

"Hold up!" Warthang interjected, raising a hand. "I came to find you because I have a question for you."

Gala's shoulders seemed to tense but he turned around and watched intently the dark human shape he saw facing him in the night.

"What is it?"

"Well," Warthang said thoughtfully. "Here goes: if a wizard were to make a monster impervious to water and fire, covered in...hard skin and full of magic...how could a normal human being kill such a creature?"

"What?" Gala chuckled uneasily, "that is the most ridiculous question I have ever heard! Are you pulling my leg?"

"Well, you know," stammered the dragon, "hypothetically speaking..."

"Well, hypothetically answering, I don't think there's anything the humans of this time or continent could possibly possess to destroy such a creature. One would definitely have to be able to travel great distances and time to find the answer to that."

Disappointed but not surprised, Warthang sighed heavily and began to try to end their conversation.

"Gala, I'm very curious about magic so you should be expecting to see me from time to time with new questions."

"What?" sputtered the wizard. "Why ask *me*? I hardly know anything! You should ask some more experienced wizard."

"Because," Warthang answered nonchalantly, "you're the first wizard who has even talked to me. The others were all mean and just ignored me."

"Typical," grumbled Gala.

"You should expect me in a week," smiled Warthang.

The wizard put his hands on his hips. "How do you already know you'll have a question by then?"

"I won't have one," the dragon shook his head. "I'm just going to make sure that Subaru has left town, as promised."

Gala cocked his head sideways, then turned away heading to town.

"See you then," he waved calmly.

"How strange," commented Warthang to himself once the wizard had disappeared. "He seemed so...dark. Not lighthearted like his usual self."

Shrugging his shoulders, the dragon made a hat appear to cover his wizard eyes properly and jumped to a week later.

"Nice," he murmured as a beautiful sunny day welcomed him. Quickly, he found Hall's Village and entered the clearing of the town, being careful to tip his hat over his face. But the people paid him no mind and went on their business.

When he had reached a house on the edge of town, the one he knew Gala inhabited, he abruptly stopped in front of it to watch a girl storm out and bang the door shut behind her. As she passed him, she understood he was heading to the same house and she turned that way, making sure her voice was loud enough.

"Don't trust anything he says!"

Warthang watched her stomping away, long blond hair flying every direction, muttering to herself under her breath. Once she had disappeared behind a house, the dragon shook his head and knocked on the door. Receiving no answer, he entered without hesitation. In our human world, this is considered extremely rude in most cases, but Warthang was a dragon and had very little knowledge of our social rules. The time he had spent as a human had mainly been with Maggie who had had no social decorum.

In the first room of the house, disarray reigned: broken plates littered the floor of the kitchen and feathers floated down into the living room. Frowning, Warthang went deeper into the house and reached a bedroom. On the bed in the far corner, Gala lay, facing the wall as if studying it.

"There's a reason I didn't answer the door, you know," he said quietly.

"Sorry," answered the intruder, shrugging his shoulders. "I came to check on you, as promised, I just didn't know it was going to be such a bad day for you. Who was that girl?"

Gala rolled over and sat up on the bed. Quickly, he

166

ruffled his short brown hair and rubbed his eyes, as if to wake himself up, but behind that tired look, Warthang could see a red tinge to the gray opaque eyes.

"That was my sister," he explained. "She's blaming me for Subaru's disappearance. I keep telling her he left town but she keeps saying he never would have left her behind. Well, whatever. He's gone, so thanks for the help."

"Sure, sure..." Warthang patted Gala on the shoulder and not knowing what else to say, he headed to the door.

"I asked around," continued the wizard, "and no one's ever heard of you."

Warthang snorted and turned to look at Gala.

"Of course they haven't," he smiled. "My parents had me secretly in the mountains; no one knew about me."

"Why is that?" asked the young man, crossing his arms.

"They were forbidden to have children."

"Really?" he retorted, skeptical. "And where are they now?"

Sighing, Warthang turned around to head back out. "You won't find them: they still live in the mountains."

"But," Gala prattled on, following him out. "Why aren't you with them if you're such a *secret*?"

Stopping at the outside door, Warthang clenched his fists.

"They hate me."

At that, he relaxed his hands again and headed toward the forest. At his doorstep, Gala kept silent and watched him leave. Deep in thought, he stood there a long time, even until the sun set.

Breathing deeply, Warthang opened his eyes and

immediately felt disoriented. It was night and he was floating on the sea, without any land in sight. Finally, he realized he had fallen asleep and had been dreaming about the events preceding his voyage to find a way to kill his kin. Now fully awake, he began swimming again, hoping he would soon see some kind of continent.

*　　*　　*

Unfortunately, he did not see that continent until a few weeks later. For days on end, he swam and swam, always searching and never finding. It seemed that his island, the continent of Atlantis, was far removed from the rest of the world. But once he did find land, would it just be some small insignificant rock? Could his island be the only one on earth? Of course, his fears were unfounded and completely appeased once he caught sight of a huge landmass at the end of those weeks of traveling. Right away, he spread his wings and left the ocean to occupy the sky with his long serpentine body. In no time, he was soaring over grass, mountains, trees and flowers. With the wind, his heart soared and sang: o beautiful, blessed, luscious land!

After a few minutes of aimlessly enjoying the new smells that did not include salt and seaweed, Warthang remembered his true mission. Somewhere, somehow, he had to find a weapon of some kind to destroy the others and…himself. Not seeing any sign of human life even though he was now deep inland and following a brownish-yellowish river, he decided to jump time frames. At first, he only flew through a few years at a time but when he found this fruitless, he began jumping decades and then centuries. Finally, signs of civilization appeared below him but things did not look so good. That river he had been following through the mountains now was majorly flooding the plains in the distance where the humans lived. Everywhere, the water seemed to have decimated crops and even destroyed some of the

homes. Without thinking too much, he flew closer to see men desperately trying to fix the dikes that had been overrun. One man in particular, taller than the rest, seemed to be issuing orders and pointing at different places. These men looked different than the ones on Warthang's continent: their skin almost shined with its paleness and even reflected a yellow hue and upon closer inspection, their dark eyes seemed longer, reaching closer to their black hair and more squinted.

When he had no one left to command, the taller man

suddenly looked up and saw Warthang flying in the sky. Right away, he began waving his arms back and forth, as if calling the dragon. Not one to ignore even a stranger's summons, the red serpent dove down and landed soundlessly on the raging yellow river that continued pumping its liquids into the inhabited land. Reaching the shore, he let his body sink just to have his head protrude from the water, his snout very near the commanding man.

"YingLong," breathed the human as he prostrated himself face to the ground before the submerged beast.

For a second, Warthang said nothing because of his surprise. The man spoke a different language,—which he understood, probably because of his wizard magic— but this was not what astounded him. Rather, it was the meaning of that word YingLong: responding dragon. Apparently, hundreds of years into the future, people still knew what dragons were. Had he failed his mission? Sighing inwardly, he put the thought aside and focused on the situation at hand.

"YingLong is it?" he asked quietly. "I suppose that fits me perfectly. And you are?"

"O great one," the man declared with his forehead still down on the soggy ground, "I thank you for answering my call of distress, and I am forever honored. My name is Yu, your humble indebted servant."

So respectful and so nice: Warthang could definitely get used to this kind of treatment!

"All right, I'll help you," the dragon said as he surfaced his body out of the depths of the water. "In turn, you can help me later but for now, climb on my back."

As Yu entered the shallows to mount the creature,

Warthang looked around and realized all the workers had ceased their labor to prostrate themselves in the same way their master had done, but some of them were peeking between their arms, trying to see what their leader would do. Looking back at Yu now climbing on his front leg to reach his back, the dragon saw that the man had completely lost his humble demeanor in his excitement and boldly grabbed a hold of him. Once he had somewhat secured himself, he stared ahead and noticed Warthang watching him. Right away, he laid himself forward along the dragon's back, feigning fear. Shaking his head and frowning, Warthang jumped, spread his wings and let the wind carry his serpentine form upward. With the sudden movement, Yu yelped and held on tightly, now truly afraid.

Chuckling to himself, Warthang ceased his assent and leveled off. Once Yu had realized the dragon was not going to flip over or do anything crazy, he straightened up, gritting his teeth in an attempt to bear the cooler wind.

"Can you see the ocean from here?" yelled Warthang back at the human.

"Of course not!" he shouted into the wind. "It is very far away from here!"

"Well, the only way to let the water flow on," the dragon explained, "is to dig deep trenches that will empty into the sea. That's the only place it can go."

Shaking his head vehemently, Yu slapped his hands on the creature's scales. "That's impossible! We would not know the best way to go as there are many mountains to the east and this would take such a long time…"

"I will show you the way!" exclaimed Warthang

as he descended to land where he had found the human.

Once on wet land, Yu dismounted and the red serpent dug his tail deep into the ground and walked forward, forming a deep ditch that followed the side of the yellow river.

"I will dig these all the way to the sea," he said, looking back at Yu and stopping for a minute, "so that it will be less easy to flood this basin region. All you have to do is take your men to make them deeper."

"Oh, is that all?" Yu retorted sarcastically.

Warthang raised an eyebrow and growled at the human who immediately prostrated himself once again. Under his bow, the dragon could tell that the man hid an unhappy scowl. With all his show of servitude and humbleness, he truly had none of it in him and seemed to just want to make others believe he was a humble servant, and not the proud man he truly was in his heart. Shaking his head, the red serpent continued boring his ditches with his tail and before he knew it, he had spent the whole day at the task. Once in a while, he would fly to make sure he had chosen the best path for the water but mostly, he stuck to the soggy ground by the river and continued his trek. This he did the next day, and the next and so on, for hundreds and hundreds of miles until on the thirteenth day, he reached the salty ocean. However, because of fatigue, he then spent the next two days resting on the beach, catching fish and bathing in the sun.

So, fifteen days after having left Yu to work with his men, he returned to the settlement in the basin to see what information he could glean from these strange slanted eyed humans. He had skipped so many years that he felt sure humanity had invented some kind of impressive weapon! At the inhabited area, workers were indeed laboring and striving to expand the ditch he had formed by the river but the task seemed insurmountable and grand. Ahead of them, Yu dug tirelessly, setting the example to the others of perseverance and courage. However, when he saw the dragon flying in his direction, he planted his shovel down and leaned on it, waiting for news.

"It is done," declared Warthang once he had landed by Yu.

Noncommittally, the man bent himself forward slightly, in a quick bow of respect.

"Now," said the dragon, "it is your turn to help me."

Without much enthusiasm, Yu nodded, still not saying anything.

"I'm trying to find out if your people have any powerful weapons," he continued, not beating around the bush.

"Ah!" exclaimed the human, pleased, as he let his shovel fall to the ground with a splat and rubbed his fists together. "For that, you will need to see the yellow emperor. I will take you."

Note 12

Huang Di was the first emperor I had ever met, well the only one I have ever met, and he made a really good impression on me. Imagine, to have a leader who actually wants to make things better for his people! Nothing like the wizards. Well, maybe that's a bit prejudiced of me. I was only 4 when we killed them and I wasn't the wisest back then. But anyway, it was such a breath of fresh air to find someone good in charge of so many people. Regrettably, as it seems the way of the world, when good is done, evil always comes out to try and undo it. Even so, I would do my best and fight for justice, fight for Huang Di.

Chapter 12 – Battle

On their flight to the Yellow Emperor's dwelling, Yu told Warthang a bit of the people's history. Apparently, they had been nomadic tribes as long as they could remember, traveling from place to place, gathering and hunting. One day, one of the tribal leaders named Xuanyuan Gongsun began to make extraordinary changes for the people. With his great inventive mind, he taught them how to build houses made of wood, he figured out that certain plants possessed medicinal properties that could help the sick and he also showed them how to grow various grains and other nutritional plants. This changed the tribe greatly and for the first time, they stayed in one place and settled down in warm houses, growing rice, barley, beans, oats, soybeans and all sorts of greenery to help sustain their new way of life. Before they knew it, another tribe had joined them and then another, until they started calling Xuanyuan *Huang Di*, the Yellow Emperor. When the tribes had merged, Huang Di wrote laws to form what he called the ideal country, filled with just and moral citizens. Even his wife contributed in this new country when she showed the women how to breed silkworms and weave fabrics of silk to create these beautiful shiny, soft robes.

However, no matter how ideal and beautiful Huang Di's state had become, an enemy had arisen to steal and take what he had built. This man, Chiyou, felt extremely jealous and wanted all the power the Yellow Emperor had acquired. Because of this, the two tribes waged war off and on, and Huang Di continued inventing to give himself the advantage. First, he had his men forge weapons out of bronze, this hard metal that lasted longer than stone and broke less easily. Finally, he also constructed large boats that could float up the yellow river and silently bring armies to their destinations without much effort. Also, whenever the battles subsided, they used these same boats for fishing in the deep sea.

"Turn north from here," indicated Yu as they reached the point where the yellow river emptied itself into the sea. "The central city is a short way from here."

When they could see the city in the distance, Warthang was blown away by its beauty and orderliness: never in his life had he seen such a clean human settlement. The wooden houses were made of these reed-like round sticks that Yu called bamboo and throughout the dwellings, simple gardens beautified each corner street, adding a quaint personality to the whole area. But in the middle of all of this stood a large palace, the largest structure the dragon had ever seen.

"Huang Di will be in there," pointed Yu. "I will have to get him, you are too large to enter."

"Too large?" laughed Warthang. "I can make myself smaller. I would definitely love to go in there!"

Squinting his eyes against the sun, his passenger squeezed his hands tighter on the dragon's spikes.

"Could you be small enough to perch on my shoulder?" he asked.

Pensively, Warthang nodded and began circling

downward toward the simple palace. As soon as they had landed, the people going about their daily business prostrated themselves to the ground in the same manner that Yu had done when they had first met. When the man slid off the dragon's back, Warthang hovered in the air a bit and shrank his serpentine form to the size of a cat to finally rest on Yu's right shoulder. Throughout all this, the people never moved. They remained bowed, now looking as if they were showing their respect to Yu instead of to Warthang.

At the entrance of the palace, two guards stood on each side of the door with their arms crossed. As Yu approached, they only watched him and the creature on his shoulder, not saying a word, not moving a muscle. Once inside, a great hall filled with tapestries welcomed them. At every door they passed through, a guard silently watched them without ever stopping them. Reaching the end of a long hallway, they stopped at an unguarded doorframe draped with red silk. Before it, Yu bowed to the floor as Warthang balanced himself on the human's back to not fall off.

"Huang Di," he called out, "your servant Yu requests the permission to enter into your presence."

"Enter," came the reply from inside the room.

Yu rose—Warthang climbing back to the man's shoulder—and walked through the silk fabric to find Huang Di sitting on the floor, playing with a couple of black rocks.

"Come sit with me," the emperor invited him without looking up.

Obediently, Yu sat in front of him, intently looking at his leader but not saying anything. On his shoulder, Warthang sat and watched Huang Di pick up a rock.

"Look at this," he told Yu, and as he approached the rock in his hand to the one on the floor, they stuck together with a click. Patiently, he separated them again and put the pebble back on the floor.

"Now watch when I turn the piece around."

In his hand, he flipped the object over, neared the other one and this time, instead of sticking together, the rock on the floor moved away, as if repelled. Chuckling to himself, Huang Di rested his hands on his knees.

"So, who is your friend?" he asked, finally looking up.

"This is YingLong," answered Yu, bowing slightly.

Huang Di nodded his head once in greeting and then addressed Yu again.

"I do believe you have much work to do, digging some deep trenches."

Yu looked up abruptly, surprised, and then slowly stood up.

"Yes, thank you, master," he said as he bowed to the emperor, turned around and headed to the door.

"Take one of the boats," ordered Huang Di, "it will be faster."

Once Yu had left, the emperor studied Warthang, who now stood on his four legs, a diminutive image of a legged serpent.

"Yu seems to look up to you," the dragon began as he laid himself down like a feline.

"I am glad," admitted Huang Di, stroking his long dark mustaches. "My father killed his father and left him orphaned at a very young age…"

Taking a step forward, the dragon raised himself and rested his front clawed feet on one of the Yellow Emperor's knees.

"How did he come to respect you?" he asked as he peered into the great man's face.

"Yu is a good man," Huang Di replied, "he sees and he understands; so much so, that I have made him my successor."

"Your successor?" Warthang inquired, now sitting on the emperor's knee. "Why is he working so far away then?"

"It is a learning period." Huang Di pointed southwest, "There, he learns leadership and hardship. It makes him strong and hopefully humble. One day, when he rules in my stead, he will understand the people because of it and will be a good leader."

"Huang Di," a voice called from behind the red silk curtains at the door, "your servant Yandi requests the permission to enter into your presence."

The Yellow Emperor stood up, letting Warthang climb to his shoulder, and put his hands inside his long sleeves in a serene pose.

"Enter," he commanded.

"Brother!" exclaimed Yandi as he rushed into the room, his long black hair streaming behind him. One could tell they were brothers, they had the same long black hair and the same long thin mustaches that went down to their chins on each side of their mouths. But mostly, the way their eyes slanted gave it away the most.

When Yandi burst into the room, in his distress he had missed Warthang but as soon as he caught sight of him, he fell facedown before him.

"This is YingLong," explained Huang Di calmly.

"Your presence here could not be at a better time, YingLong!" exclaimed the emperor's brother. "This must be a sign, a boon."

Without a word, Warthang sized up the man prostrated on the ground, instantly disliking him. He was not sure what it was, but something made him distrust the man.

"What news do you bring?" asked the Yellow Emperor, as he picked up the rock from the ground and placed both pieces into a pocket.

"It is Chiyou," spat Yandi, "he is attacking my tribes! I need your help: he is too powerful and wild."

"Where is he?" asked Huang Di, a frown forming on his face.

"By two days' time, he will be in the Zhuolu plains."

The emperor sighed.

"Come back tomorrow, I will see what I can do."

Yandi stood up, bowed slightly and exited the room without a backward glance.

"Your brother is not of your domain?" inquired Warthang, trying to understand the situation.

"He is leader of two other joined tribes," answered Huang Di. "I must help him. Not only is he my brother, but if Chiyou defeats him, he will then come for my people next."

Descending to the floor, Warthang sat on his haunches in front of the emperor to see him better. He could tell the ruler needed to take action but something made him hesitant.

"What's the problem?"

"The flood," answered he. "The majority of my men are trying to rebuild homes, save our crops and empty the water from everything. That leaves a quarter of my army to fight. It is not enough."

"You have me," declared the dragon, "I can fight for you."

"No," he shook his head, "if the enemy sees you fighting for me, he will attribute the victory to you,—if there indeed is one—and not to me. Once you are gone, he will come again and at full force."

"Then," Warthang announced, "I will build you a secondary army. I will teach them to listen to you and they will be under your command."

For an hour, the emperor and the dragon discussed their strategy and when they had decided on everything, Warthang left the palace on a special mission, to return within two days. On his end, Huang Di had extra swords and halberds forged for the men he had with him. Furthermore, he continued his experiments of his attracting and repelling rocks and found that if he put them on a pivoting point and turned different directions, they kept on pointing south. From this deduction, he found a bigger piece of the metal and carved it into an arrow. Somehow, he knew this would be useful in the battle.

*   *   *

By early evening, Warthang had flown far to the North East to a mountainous area where he had detected several animals of prey he thought he could enlist to help Huang Di. Back home, on the continent of Atlantis, he had adopted the shapes of many animals and had a pretty good idea how the different species thought and what they desired. Spotting a large striped cat swimming in a river, the kind we know as a tiger, the dragon landed nearby and spread his wings wide to impress the carnivore.

"I am the king of the jungle!" he declared, "and I

181

need the strongest to help me in a territorial war!"

From his bath, the 700lb cat looked up at the dragon and then languidly swam up to shore, taking his sweet time. Once on dry ground, he shook the water out of his fur and stretched his large claws over the dirt, making sure Warthang could see their long sharp points. On the right side his face, a large serrated scar stretched from his ear to his muzzle.

"I am Scar Face and I *am* the strongest," he stated matter-of-factly, "I will help you if you do something in return for me."

"What is your desire?"

"Young Paws is almost large enough to challenge me and I grow weary of him and his uppity ways," the large animal began as he lay down on the ground. "If I help you win your territory, then find him a new place to live so I don't have to deal with him."

"Granted. Bring Young Paws on our hunt against the human enemies and I will find him a new home."

"Against the what?" Scar Face asked, swishing his tail impatiently.

"The humans…they are creatures that walk on their hind legs, have a long mane on their heads but otherwise are hairless. They wear things of the forest to cover their bodies."

"Bipeds!" Scar Face hissed as he jumped to his paws, the fur on his back slightly standing on end. "Because of them, I have been named Scar Face for the rest of my life! If our goal is to kill them, then I shall also bring Young Paws' mother and two sisters. We will decimate their kind!"

"There is a catch," Warthang said, his wings now laying naturally on his sides, "you will have to listen to a biped who will tell you when to kill the enemy."

"I refuse!" the tiger spat and began to amble away, the discussion being over in his mind.

"You don't need that coward," a gruff voice said from the forest.

Without missing a beat, Scar Face turned back toward Warthang.

"Don't listen to that brown bear, I am not a coward!"

"Why should it matter if a biped tells you when to kill other bipeds, as long as you get some revenge?" the bear continued, as he wobbled out from the darkness of the foliage toward the two other predators. "As it is now, your territory doesn't get much biped action and you're not likely to get your teeth into one of them anytime soon."

"Fine!" harrumphed the angry tiger at Warthang, "I'll go get the others of my kind, as we agreed."

Having dismissed himself, Scar Face left the two large animals and disappeared behind the dark leaves of the forest.

"Good evening, King of the jungle!" laughed the brown bear amiably, "my name is Boulder, and I can find you some more help."

Raising his eyebrows, Warthang brought his head down to look at the brown bear eye to eye.

"Is there also something you want?"

"I'm getting old and have never seen one of your kind before; surely you must have strange powers…"

"Perhaps…"

"I wish for an easy life, where I no longer need to hunt for my food," said Boulder, staring expectantly at the dragon.

"I'm guessing you don't mind the bipeds?"

"They're a clever sort," nodded the bear, "and they have never bothered me."

"The only way for you to have a life devoid of hunting would be to work for Huang Di, the lord of the bipeds."

"Work?" sighed the furry creature.

"I imagine he would want to have you to scare his enemies; in exchange, he could feed you whatever you wish. I can have it arranged."

"Deal," Boulder smiled and then left the same way Scar Face had, indicating he would get a few young adolescent comrades he knew who spent their time fishing salmon upstream.

After a few hours of waiting, Warthang had his small army: 5 tigers and 7 bears. Satisfied this number would suffice to help defeat Chiyou, he nodded at the predators each in turn.

"We have quite a distance to cover," he told them, "and going on foot is out of the question."

"We could swim," Scar Face suggested.

"No," the dragon continued, "we shall fly."

At that declaration, large wings began sprouting behind all of the animals' shoulder blades. The six adolescent bears began cheering as they stretched their new appendages and tested their new muscles, while the tigers looked at each other in silence. In the midst of them, Boulder laughed deeply, then dashed out from the group, jumped to the air and took flight. Of course, never has a flying bear been seen before, for this is the only time in history such a thing ever happened, but what a sight it was! Immense brown wings stretched out behind the colossal bear, and the animal in the air flailed his feet like he was swimming; it was all so comical.

"Don't leave us behind!" new voices yelled in unison from the trees.

And out jumped three large female cats from high up in the trees, their white and orange fur populated with black circles—she-leopards! While Warthang had been recruiting his fanged army, these three had been watching the proceedings, curious of its outcome. Once the wings had appeared on the tigers and the bears, they no longer had been able to contain themselves and had jumped on the chance of taking part in these strange happenings.

The army of now 15 ready, the group flew off into the air in the direction of the Zhuolu plains. On the way, Warthang explained to them the plan he and Huang Di had concocted and their part in it. Hours later, they had arrived at their destination with a whole day to spare, so the dragon—after having removed their wings—left them to rest and prepare themselves for the bloody battle. He, on the other hand, returned to the Yellow Emperor's palace, as he had agreed he would.

*   *   *

Back at Huang Di's palace, on the day of the battle, a small Warthang paced back and forth, trying to appease his clenching heart. He could not breathe right, and staying behind out of the action felt alien to him. In his mind's eye, he was following the Yellow Emperor's human army closely, now deep within the Zhuolu plains. Every step they took, he mimicked, albeit in a closed room.

There! In the distance: some kind of movement rustled the bushes! Once Huang Di's men approached the area, Chiyou and his larger army burst forth like wild animals. And what a sight! Whereas Huang Di's men advanced in straight lines, their weapons raised to eye level, shields held before their breasts and wearing hard bamboo suits for protection, Chiyou's army ran at them like a pack of rabid dogs. They wore dark brown leather over their bodies, mud covered every surface of available skin and caked their long hair, and a savage look of lust and exultation sparkled in their eyes. Almost, one could imagine long fangs growing out of their mouths and foam frothing around their lips to complete the perfect picture of "crazy."

In a second's time, the two groups had clashed in a roar of shouts and a clang of weapons. Fiercely, Chiyou's men, who outnumbered their enemy three to one, slashed through the defenses and opened deep bloody gashes on their opponents' arms and legs. After a few of his men lost their heads in a spray of red viscous liquid, the Yellow Emperor ordered a retreat and a mad race ensued. Around fifty men, now holding their fear in check, dashed the opposite direction followed by a hoard of twitching demons that thirsted for death and blood.

After quite a distance, Huang Di abruptly stopped and faced the enemy while his group continued on its way. Looking straight at Chiyou, he smiled, raised his arms to the sky and chanted a three note wail that could have been described as some sort of scream of defiance. At the signal, for that is what it was, Boulder and his adolescent bears, Scar Face with the other four tigers, and the three she-leopards emerged out of their hiding places and leaped upon the incoming army. Animal met animal in a frenzy of bronze, teeth and claws. Without discrimination, Huang Di's animal army tore the enemy's throats out with their jaws and disemboweled others with a swipe of their massive claws. At a command from their leader, the Yellow Emperor's men

charged back into the fray, slowly overpowering Chiyou and his brutes.

When he saw that the battle was lost, Chiyou's face darkened and he ordered a retreat. As his men slipped on their comrades' intestines and guts to flee, they threw down small rectangular objects that spewed smoke and created an impenetrable fog.

"Warthang!" a voice squeaked out of surprise.

The dragon's sight returned to the palace where he had been standing vigil just in time to jump backwards and see a long knife plant itself into the floor where he had been moments before. Abruptly, his head snapped up to see Yandi, the emperor's own brother, standing in the doorway, his hand still stretched outward from the knife throw.

Well, thought Warthang, *this is as good a time to find out if this bronze stuff can hurt a dragon.*

Before Yandi had a chance to draw another knife out, Warthang slid between the man's legs into the hallway, gained his footing and dashed toward the exit with the click of his claws. Without a thought, the human chased him desperately, banging into the walls at every corner. Once he burst outside the palace, he stopped suddenly and stared at a full sized serpent-like Warthang. Clenching his fists tightly upon his sword, he raised it high and ran at the monstrous beast with a battle cry. The dragon shook his head slowly and swatted the man aside like he was a fly. Unfortunately, Yandi did not have wings and he landed unceremoniously in the mud face first.

"A small weapon like that will never reach a dragon," commented Warthang.

Yandi slurped himself out of the mud and grabbed a halberd from his back. Again, he came at the reptile and when the dragon brought his clawed hand to swat him once more, the man managed to stab it. Warthang looked at his hand and sighed: the weapon had barely pricked him. For a final test, he jumped into the sky to expose his belly and when Yandi threw the halberd at his bare flank, it ricocheted harmlessly against the scales and fell onto the wet ground.

"All right," Warthang declared, "I'm done playing now."

And suddenly, the roots from two nearby trees surfaced out of the ground and grabbed Yandi to hug him into the mud in a tangled mess. Vainly, the man wiggled to free himself but at every move, the roots only seemed to tighten on him.

"I better tell your brother of this treason," Warthang told him.

And without further ado, he disappeared to reappear high over the Zhuolu plains. Before all of this had begun, the emperor and the dragon had agreed that Warthang would never join the battle. If for some reason Huang Di needed to return to defend his people, for he had left no one to guard the city but the dragon, then Warthang would let the leader see him without his army catching a glimpse.

The moment the wizard-dragon arrived over the plains, he could not see anything because Chiyou's fog still permeated the air. With his wizard eyes he found Huang Di and then he created a bright light that flowed from him straight to the emperor. Surprised at this sudden brightness, Huang Di looked up, saw the dragon and nodded in answer to the summons. Before disappearing back into the fog, Warthang saw the Yellow Emperor pointing and issuing orders to his men. Satisfied, the dragon appeared back at the palace and frowned unhappily at what he discovered. Where he had left Yandi tied up, he now only found cut and disentangled roots. He had only been gone for a couple of minutes and the man had managed to escape!

A few hours later, Huang Di entered his room and found the small Warthang sitting in the middle of the room, quietly waiting for him.

"I thought I was going to find everything burned down!" exclaimed the emperor with relief.

"I guess I overreacted," replied the dragon as he stood up on all fours.

Huang Di crossed the room and sat in front of the creature.

"What happened?" he asked.

"Your brother Yandi happened," responded the dragon. "I don't know what he was doing here but he was surprised by my presence and he tried to kill me."

"My brother tried to kill you?!" shouted the emperor, his face reddening.

"Son of Heaven," interrupted a female voice outside the room, "your servant requests the permission to inquire about the bear. All the other surviving animals have left except this one."

"I will come for him later, thank you."

At his dismissal, silk rustled and then silence reigned once again in the hallway. Warthang sat back down and watched the emperor, perplexed.

"Son of Heaven?" he asked.

The emperor grunted and smiled.

"The word spread fast," he laughed. "It all has to do with the battle."

"Yes, the battle!" remembered Warthang. "I watched up to when Chiyou created the fog. What happened after that?"

"Well," Huang Di began, his hands in his lap, "Chiyou thought the fog would let him escape free but I had two weapons to help me. First, the animals followed his men and slaughtered the majority of them. Unfortunately, most of them were killed in turn and only a few bears, a leopard and two tigers survived. But second, I used the arrow I carved out of my black rocks and placed it as a pivotal finger on a wooden figure so that as long as the arrow finger pointed straight, it meant we were heading south. Because of that, the fog did not confuse us and we were able to catch the rest of the enemy and kill them. Just as I had finished slaying Chiyou myself, a beam from heaven lit me. Everyone saw it and was awed! They now call me the Son of Heaven and believe the gods are on my side."

At the end of his tale, Huang Di stood up and sighed.

"Although we won this battle, I suppose the war is not over: I have Yandi to deal with now."

"Son of Heaven," Warthang said sadly as he thought of the tigers, bears and leopards he had led to their deaths. "I'm sure you will succeed in doing what is right and taking care of your people, but I must now bid you farewell."

"Are you leaving so soon, YingLong?" asked the emperor, saddened.

"Yes," nodded the dragon, "I didn't find what I sought and I must look elsewhere."

"Very well," accepted Huang Di, "we shall forever honor you and I will never forget your help. But if what you seek is not here, then look to the west. The land is grand and who knows what you could find there!"

Warthang followed the emperor out and when they reached the exit of the palace, he looked around at the beautiful city.

"Take care of these people," he said in farewell, "and take care of that big old bear: he will forever be loyal to you as long as you feed him!"

And that was the last he ever saw of the Son of Heaven and his people. He flew away, back on his quest to find another land that maybe had some way of killing his kind. But before completely leaving the kingdom, he stopped in a nearby region where two tigers, a leopard and three bears walked together.

"Greetings, king of the jungle," said the younger of the two tigers, the one named Young Paws.

"Good day," Warthang said and inclined his head. "Did Scar Face survive? I had a promise to uphold."

"He perished," the leopard stated.

"I regret his demise," the dragon said, feeling guilty.

"Don't," Young Paws shrugged, "his last moments were the happiest of his life."

After a few moments of silence as Warthang and the large animals stared at each other, the dragon finally asked,

"May I help in bringing you home?"

"No, king of the jungle," one of the adolescent bears replied for the group, "we are enjoying this country and may explore it a while."

"Very well," Warthang acquiesced and flew off, leaving his small decimated army behind, his heart as heavy as ever.

Note 13

From the Yellow Emperor, I learned justice and unity. From a princess, I learned about getting what you want through trickery and deceit. In the end, I find that those tactics just bring about unnecessary work and hard feelings. It is so much better to be true to yourself and go for the direct approach. Lesson learned! I hope.

Chapter 13 – Sacrifices

Oftentimes, the beginning of a journey is fun, fresh, new and easy; however, the more time passes and the longer the road drags on, the more the traveler feels tired and sick to the bones of traveling. Now imagine poor Warthang. Already, he had spent five weeks away from home and now four more weeks had added themselves to the number: weeks of flying overland, weeks of seeing only blips of civilization, nothing significant, nothing useful. Not only did he miss his home, but he was bored out of his mind!

Tired of flying, the dragon let himself glide downward and then crash through trees and into a stuffy marsh with an explosion of water. As the liquid fell like rain over him, he laughed and sat there, in his original form, thinking nothing, just feeling the slime trickle down his body. After a good ten minutes of staying as still as a snake, Warthang stood up and determinedly flew back into the sky high enough to see the sea to the north. When he had done that, he jumped time, thousands of years at a time, and immediately stopped the transition when he saw a huge city surrounding a gray stoned castle. If they could build such an interesting structure that seemed so defensible, then surely they had to defend themselves against some formidable weapon!

He flew down to the tallest tower of the castle and groped the sides of the structure to climb it, a bit like a lizard. Since dark clouds reigned the night sky, no prying eyes saw the reptile scaling the tall structure. At one window, Warthang peered in and saw a girl with brown hair to the small of her back holding her face in her hands and kneeling on the floor, rocking back and forth. The dragon knew what it was like to be sad and could not stand to see others in that same state.

"What's the matter, child?" he asked making sure that his body and face could not be seen from the window, so as not to scare her.

She abruptly stood up, wiped the tears from her eyes and sniffled. Slowly, she approached the window and peered into the darkness.

"Who's there?" she whispered in the night. "There is no way a normal human being could climb this fortress! Are you…are you a sorcerer?"

Warthang's heart stopped in his chest. She knew what wizards were! If that were the case, then he must have died and magic must have come back to man. As the thoughts flew through his mind, the girl misunderstood his silence and drew herself back into the tower, clutching her hands to her heart.

"Are you here to kidnap me?" she said, her voice shaking.

"No! Of course not!" interjected the dragon hurriedly.

"Then why are you hiding? Show yourself at once!" she demanded, a frown creeping up on her face.

Warthang plopped himself on the window sill in human form and tried to look nonthreatening with a bright green outfit and a black hat.

"Sorry," he apologized, "I was in dragon form and thought it might have scared you."

The girl harrumphed, drew her chin up bravely and crossed her arms.

"I am a princess. A princess never fears."

Warthang raised an eyebrow and did not comment on the fact that she had seemed scared when she had thought he had come to kidnap her. Instead, he focused on the whole reason why he had started this conversation in the first place.

"But they *can* be sad," he said, quietly.

"Yes, well," the princess patted her dress uncomfortably, "at times, circumstances merit a few tears. So, what brings a sorcerer to my window?"

"I was just passing through…while on my quest to

find a powerful weapon," Warthang said, a small smile perking at one corner of his lips.

"Oh!" the girl exclaimed, barely containing her excitement, "and for what purpose, exactly?"

"If you tell me why you're sad," he pointed at her mischievously, "then I'll tell you why I need this weapon."

"Very well," she nodded decidedly and headed to her desk to finally sit at a cushiony chair in the corner of the large room. "I am princess Sadra and my father the king owns this whole great land. He has many riches and in fact has everything and plenty of it!"

"Sounds like a nice situation," commented the human dragon.

"For *him*!" retorted Sadra with as much attitude as she could muster. "But he doesn't think so. He wants more and even wants to strengthen his position by marrying me off to the prince of Egypt."

At the mention of this last news, her face contorted in an effort to hold her tears back. Warthang approached and lowered himself so they could look at each other eye to eye. His earlier reasoning of wizards having returned to the world was further strengthened by the lack of reaction the princess had to his yellow opaque eyes.

"What's so bad about the prince of Egypt?"

Sadra rolled her eyes and uttered a loud sigh. "You are kidding, right? Where are you from anyway? A sorcerer, of all people, should know these things!"

"Humor me."

Looking away from him, she exhaled loudly again. "Egypt was powerful and important a long time ago. Now, they are not much but they still think they are. The prince of Egypt is arrogant, insufferable and to top it off, extremely ugly! I cannot believe I have to marry him! I begged my father but he would not listen!"

Sadra hid her face in her hands and cried loudly, a bit too loudly in fact. The whole castle could probably hear her.

"I want to marry a knight, a brave man, a strong man, not some Egyptian pampered prince!"

Warthang was starting to regret having struck a conversation with this young girl. Although her situation did seem a bit unfair, he could not help but wonder if the princess did not exaggerate a bit or overly dramatize her situation. As if to confirm his weary feelings of her, she suddenly stood up, her face perfectly clear and unblemished.

"You surely are a powerful sorcerer," she said in a breathy voice that a human male would have understood as flirtatious. This, of course, only confused the dragon who now took steps back as she advanced on him. All he could think was that she had been supposedly crying and now she was completely fine! What was wrong with this human?

As his back found a wall, she trapped him there with one of her hands against the wall and the other twirling a brown curl.

"What do you need a weapon for?"

Uncomfortable by her proximity, he tried to glue himself to the wall as much as possible.

"I'm looking for something that can kill a dragon."

Sadra squinted at him and bit her lower lip. Then, she smiled and let go of the wall, giving a thankful Warthang some breathing space.

"I have the perfect plan to help us both!" she declared confidently.

Then, she headed back to the chair and once again sat in it. Cautiously, Warthang walked that way but kept some distance.

"Here is what you will do," she told him, not leaving any room for discussion, "you will turn yourself into a dragon and terrorize this city. In fact, you will scare it so much that no one will be brave enough to face you. To help spur a hero to come forward, my father will have to offer my hand in marriage to whoever defeats the monster! Some gorgeous, courageous and strong knight will come at you with the strongest weapons possible and voilà! I get my husband and you get to find out about all the marvelous weapons we have here."

Warthang raised his eyebrows incredulously and folded his arms over his chest.

"I see two problems with this scheme," he said. "Number one, how can you guarantee your father will offer you up as a reward? And number two, for you to get married, doesn't that mean the hero has to kill me? Personally, I'm not quite ready to die."

On the chair, the princess rolled her eyes and shook her head.

"Number one, sir sorcerer," she replied sarcastically, "I'm a princess and I can take care of my father on this side of things. Number two, you are a powerful sorcerer: I am certain you can figure out how to fake your own death."

In silence, the dragon contemplated the plan and tried to think of reasons why he should not go through with it. He would destroy people's homes and ravage the country? No matter, he could fix it all in the end. The princess would get to marry a strong man…but what about that man? Could Warthang wish Sadra on a knight? But then again, that hero would inherit wealth and fame; maybe it would not be so bad for him. So, it seemed, everyone would get something out of this and he could maybe find what he needed in this time and place.

Finally, the wizard dragon nodded.

"Very well," he told the princess, "I will start tomorrow."

At that declaration, he climbed unto the window sill, jumped off into the air and transformed midair back into his original form to fly away into the night. Before long, he had crossed the marshes and found a cave on its outskirts big enough to accommodate him. Restless, he finally fell into a fitful slumber after a few hours of tossing and turning.

The next morning, he waited until midday and when the sun reached its zenith, he flew to the countryside by the large city, spitting fire and roaring like a crazed beast. On the ground below, farm folk began to run for cover while the people in the city pointed up at the sky. Not satisfied with the reactions of the townsfolk, Warthang dived low and scraped some roofs and set other houses on fire. Unbeknownst to the terrorized populace, he made sure to go after the empty homes so that no one would be in danger and watched every movement the humans made with his wizard eyes to ensure no one would come to harm. Chaos ensued and women and men began screaming and running every which way. To make sure he had made his point, he continued this activity for an hour before retiring to his temporary home by the marsh.

The following day, at the same hour as the previous day, he appeared again in the skies with his fires and screams. To spice things up, he landed in the middle of the crops and set those ablaze, again this activity lasting for an hour before he would stop. In his mind, he cringed at the loss of the poor hard working farmers but told himself he would miraculously regrow all of the plants to a healthier, bigger size later to make up for everything.

This one hour of terrorizing the city at midday lasted for eight days before a change finally occurred. On that day, as Warthang burst in the sky, he saw a boat in the middle of the large lake that supplied the people with drinkable water. On that small boat, two sheep bleated unhappily, not daring to move a muscle on this unsafe, moving ground, and shaking like leaves in the wind. Up in the heavens, Warthang chuckled. The people had offered a gift to appease him! Without further delay, he swooped down and scooped the two sacrifices up in his claws and carried them home without attacking anyone or anything.

Once at the cave, he gently laid the sheep down at the entrance and wondered what to do with them. Should he eat them? No, that did not feel right. Tundra and he had always hunted for their own food, never stealing from others, and in a pinch, Warthang would change himself into a small herbivore and fill up his stomach with grass. Luckily, the digestive system of a dragon was much like a snake's in that they only had to eat once every week or so and at this time, hunger did not plague him.

Already, the fluffy animals had lost their fright and they were grazing the grass just outside the cave. Pleased, Warthang lay down by them and began telling his two little friends about his long life and what had led him to them this day. He hoped they did not mind too much and promised them they would return home in the end.

The next day, when he visited the city at noontime, two more sheep awaited him in the boat on the lake. And the following days, the same gifts greeted him, so much so that before he knew it, he had a nice little herd of 14 fluffy, bleating sheep. In his spare time, he had begun naming them: his favorite was Maggie and the ugliest, Benzady. Even though he did not like that last sheep, he took better care of it than the rest and apologized to it repeatedly for the predicament in which it found itself. Not too concerned, Benzady ate his grass with the others and followed them wherever they went.

That whole week, with his growing herd, Warthang had felt at peace with himself and really regretted having to die because of the curse. Life was such a gift! Could he not live it to its fullest? At this point in his quest, he doubted a human weapon could do the job of killing a dragon and thought that maybe he ought to look into other kinds of possibilities: maybe some other magic or power he did not know about. But first, he really had to finish with the plan so that princess Sadra could escape her arranged marriage.

So the next day, as he flew over the large lake by the city, he ignored the two white fluffy animals in the rickety boat and crashed into the city wall, blowing it apart with his sheer mass. Instead of setting fire to things from the air, he ran through the streets, bashing everything behind him with his tail and scraping the ground with his large claws, bypassing all alleys where any living being breathed. At a corner, he surprised a dog feverishly eating something on the ground and he grabbed him with his mouth, shook him for good measure, in case anyone was watching, and flew back home with the canine in tow. Once at the cave, he laid the animal by the sheep to recover and sat himself in the musty dark to watch the princess with his wizard sight. It was time he found out what was happening in town so he could predict what actions he needed to take.

In the center of town, the citizens had grouped around the king, the princess and some kind of counsel to listen to what they had to say. Throughout the crowd, some people cried and whimpered, some yelled angrily while others stood silently staring. When the king raised his arms, the tumult hushed, one could only hear the strong wind's howl and an occasional sniffle.

From the small cluster of the counsel, a tall bearded man stood and addressed the sovereign.

"The sheep no longer appease the dragon, my king. What shall we do now?"

Before the king could answer, Sadra stood up and suddenly collapsed to the ground, her eyes rolling in her head and her limbs shaking. The crowd gasped as the counsel and the king rushed to her side, smothering her in a circle of fabric. Before long, her fit subsided and she opened her eyes, a panicked look darting from her father to the men and back again.

"I had a vision!" she murmured breathlessly.

Helping her up, the king stared at her, concerned, while the people leaned forward to hear her better.

"I saw..." a soft sob escaped her and she shut her eyes tightly. "I cannot tell it," she shook her head and looked at everyone, horrified, "it was too terrible. But know this: the dragon hungers for human flesh."

Chaos broke through the mob as the people cursed

the monster and held on to each other in desperation. Why was this happening to them? Had they done something to anger the gods, the voices cried. As the moans and yells babbled on, the king and his counsel deliberated until they reached a decision. Again, the ruler raised his arms and the crowd silenced itself. A heavy cloud of grief seemed to press down on everyone.

"Times are difficult, with everything having been destroyed and burned," the king said to break that stifling silence, "and we need every skilled hand at work for our survival. Because of this, we will offer to the beast," at this, he paused and clenched his fists, "our children."

I am certain one can imagine what kind of reaction the people had to this declaration of their offspring's deaths; however, they were highly superstitious and could not see any other way out of this. The truth is, as soon as they had heard Sadra's doomsday message, they had come to the same conclusion and so they only objected halfheartedly. How desperate they felt!

The next few hours, the council had determined to set up a lottery that would determine each day's sacrifice. Children from the age of 11 and under had had their names thrown in. Against the king's wishes but to the people's admiration, Sadra herself had placed her name in the lottery to show everyone that the king cared dearly.

So, early in the morning, Warthang watched the drawing of the name, the cries and the goodbyes, the tying of his sacrifice in the boat, and the lonely float rocking in the water, patiently waiting for him. He really felt all of this as very distasteful but supposed the children might enjoy spending time with his sheep and his dog. Without a fuss, he showed up at his usual time, scooped up the young boy from the boat and headed home again. Once at the cave, the child scrambled away and ran deep within the cave to find Warthang's herd sleeping the hot day off. As long as he stayed with the animals, Warthang lay still at the entrance, but as soon as the boy would take a peep or walk his way, a low growl scared him deeper into the depths.

From that day on, the dragon, to his regret, no longer had his long talks with his bleating companions; instead, he had to assure himself that the amassing children kept cowering into the cave. Unbeknownst to them, dangerous creatures lived in the forest and in the marsh and Warthang refused to have them run out there and get injured or worse while he was gone to "eat" more kids. After a while, however, his home no longer had enough room to accommodate more people and the lottery—of course, he watched it: what else was he going to do with his time—never fell on the princess. So, it seemed, he had to intercede and cheat on the next morning's drawing!

The following morning, he caused boulders to fall before the entrance of the cave and trapped the 14 sheep, the one dog and the 29 children inside. Every day, while he left for the daily offering the city left him, his large famished crowd of children had mysteriously found food and water at the mouth of the cave and had forgotten all thought of escape to fill their hungry bellies. This day, since Warthang could possibly be gone more than an hour, he had blocked any outside route in case his captives were to develop ideas of fleeing. Promptly, he changed himself into a mangy brown dog and teleported himself into a deserted street, paralleling the town square. Nonchalantly, he padded his way to the center and sat at the back of the whispering crowd.

In his mind's eye, he searched the box of names and did not find Sadra's name! Outraged, he looked everywhere and finally found the slip of paper safely tucked away into the king's robes, where it probably had resided since day one of the drawing. He uttered a growl and a man in front of him turned around surprised and kicked him in the ribs. Meekly, tail tucked between his legs, Warthang limped away to sit in the street, away from the people. The nerve of that man! What kind of a person would treat a dog, or any animal for that matter, like that?

Trying to concentrate, Warthang healed his bruises and looked again into the box. Using the ink embedded into the papers, he made the substance on each slip change position until all of them read the princess' name. What a surprise the poor king would receive this morning!

Finally, the time came and an old man stuck his hand into the box while the people bit their nails and wrung their hands. He drew the slip out, looked at it and his face turned a greenish white. For a second, nothing came out of his mouth, but finally he croaked,

"Princess Sadra is today's sacrifice."

The king jumped from his seat and ran to the old man, tearing the paper from his hand and bringing it to reading distance.

"No..." he trailed off, his eyes ogling and his hand covering his nose and mouth.

Although the people seemed relieved the lot had not fallen on one of their own, they felt the king's grief as their own and they bitterly wept with him. But after a few minutes, the king fell to his knees and prostrated himself before them, begging them to spare Sadra's life. He would give them all his silver, all his gold, even up to half his kingdom if they would just let her go! But no, the people would have none of it. Already they had lost many of their children and no amount of money could buy their family one less day from their precious ones.

In the corner where she sat, Sadra adopted a determined look. She stood up, clenching her teeth and forming fists, and walked to her father. There, on the ground, she knelt by him and began to whisper in his ear. Her father looked at her, blinked away his tears and stood up. Talking to his council members, but loud enough to be overheard by everyone, he declared,

"Send edicts throughout the land! Whoever slays this monster before noon today will receive as a reward my daughter's hand in marriage!"

At his command, everyone official scrambled away to gather paper, writing materials and messenger pigeons. As for the crowd, it dispersed in excited chatter. Surely the reward would spur some courageous man to take arms and end their suffering. To marry the princess was better than material gain for not only did one gain a beautiful damsel as a wife, but also one stood to win a title, riches, and authority over the land.

Four hours before the sun had reached its zenith, the princess already sat in the boat in the middle of the lake, wearing a beautiful, adorned white dress. Red flowers rested in her hair, completing the picture of a perfect sacrifice. By the water, Warthang, still a brown dog, lay down watching the tranquil surface of the lake. This was the day he could finally move on to something and somewhere else. This scheme that had lasted over a month, would now end with his "death."

Time dragged on by the peaceful water and the tired dog took a nap. In his mind, he dreamed of Tundra playing with his 14 sheep, Huang Di having a conversation with the dog and the 29 children chasing Sadra in bursts of giggles. Some say that dreams recall our subconscious thoughts and organize them but whatever they are, sometimes they can be a nice reprieve from everyday life.

Around an hour before noon, a rugged man, plated with armor arrived at the lake and followed its bank to get as close to the boat as possible. The clip clop of his black mount woke Warthang, who stared at the animal, never having seen a horse before. When the knight realized a beautiful lady lay in the boat, he thought she had lost her oars and had no way to return to shore. Quickly, he dismounted his dark steed, ripped off his armor, dove into the water and swam to the princess. Amused, Warthang barked at the man, jumped into the water and followed him to the center of the lake.

Surprised at the splashes she heard, Sadra opened her eyes and sat up to see hands grabbing the side of her float. At this point, the young man was dragging the boat to shore and did not see the princess smiling triumphantly at him. Without shame, she appraised his dark hair, callused hands and muscled arms and liked what she saw. Noticing the dog paddling with her hero, she caught a glimpse of the yellow eyes of the animal and she winked at him knowingly.

Once at the bank of the lake, the man hoisted himself out of the water, slightly panting, turned around and offered his hand to the princess.

"My lady," he said, breathlessly.

Sadra took his hand, jumped graciously to shore and lingered a few seconds before releasing his hand.

"What brings you to our town, fair knight?" she asked innocently.

"I have heard of rumors for weeks of a dragon devastating the land and the people of this city," he answered. "I have now come to find out where it lives and slay it."

Sadra bit her lower lip and looked away in the distance.

"You did not come to save me, then," she said, disappointed.

"I..." the knight shook his head, trying to understand. "What do you mean, fair lady?" he finally asked.

As if faint, the princess slowly sat on the ground and drew her hand to her temple.

"In less than an hour," she began, "the dragon shall come and devour me."

Outraged, the young man bent down on his knees and took her hands into his, looking deeply into her eyes. But before he could say anything, she continued,

"I am the sacrifice of the town. To appease the monster, I am forced to give my life in hope that it may leave my people at peace."

"No, my lady," interjected the rider, "this will not come to pass. I shall slay the dragon as I have set out to do. Point me the way to his lair and I shall accomplish the task."

"The king has issued a reward..."

"I need no reward," he interrupted, "but God's protection and love."

Seemingly shy, Sadra took her hands out of his and wrung them together in her lap.

"What is your name, sir knight?"

"I am called George," he smiled.

"The reward is my hand in marriage, Sir George," continued the princess softly, "and even were it not so, you have saved my life and I will not leave your side."

Sir George closed his eyes and stood up. After a moment's silence, he nodded, opened his eyes and helped the beautiful lady to her feet.

"Then it must be God's will. Now, fair lady, point the way and I shall seek the dragon out."

Sadra pointed, the knight adorned his armor over his wet clothes, mounted his steed and left at a gallop to the general direction of the marshes. By the lake, the wet dog watched the princess smile at her future husband, admiring him as long as she could see him. Once he had disappeared, she planted her hands on her hips and squinted at the mangy canine.

"Don't you have somewhere to be?" she asked rhetorically.

Warthang sighed and shook his head. If only she knew how close she came to her plan failing because of a cheating, but loving, father. Had the dragon not intervened this day, Sir George would have come anyway and she would not have been the reward for a dragon's death. But no matter, there was no time to spare!

"I suppose I do," he said out of the mouth of the dog and vanished into thin air.

At his cave, he returned to his true form and removed the rocks he had placed at the entrance to block the animals and children from escaping. When all seemed ready,—everyone cowered at the back of the cave—he laid down inside the cave, his nose poking out into the sun, feigning sleep.

Before long, Sir George and his black horse broke through the trees, brandishing a long spear. For a second, Warthang really doubted that any kind of metal could penetrate his scaly hide and he almost threw caution to the wind. However, upon further thought, if such a weapon could wound him, he had to be careful to not be knocked unconscious by some ill fate and thus be killed.

Only a second had passed between the time he saw the knight through the trees and these thoughts had crossed his mind, and he immediately burst forth from the cave roaring like thunder and spewing flames like a volcano. A bit terrified, the horse's nostrils flared and his eyes rolled into his head; luckily, even through the fear, he ran forward when his rider dug his heels into his flanks. Dodging the fire by a hair, the knight hit Warthang's side with his spear as he passed by, but the weapon shattered into thousands of pieces on the monster and the momentum threw Sir George off his animal. As he clattered to the ground, he managed to roll himself under a low branched orange tree.

Displeased at the flimsiness of the attack, Warthang looked around the tree, playing the dumb animal that has no sense of smell. After a few moments, he returned to his cave as if he had forgotten all about the failed attack. Under his orange tree, Sir George panted quietly, trying to figure out his next move. Maybe if he waited long enough, the dragon would let his guard down and he could wound it with his sharp broadsword. While he thought about this, he grabbed an orange that had fallen to the ground, peeled it and ate it. Looking at the skin that now littered the ground, it gave him an idea on how to injure the beast. An orange is but a part of a tree, like the scales are but a part of the animal. The orange falls from the tree from its stem so if he could hit the monster at one of its "stems," then he could puncture through and peel him out through that first wound, if need be.

Determined, Sir George rolled out from under his tree, brandishing his sword, and struck Warthang at the base of one of his legs. The sword stung a bit but did not inflict any damage; however, the dragon reacted by bellowing some fire at his persecutor, knowing the man would easily dodge the blast. The knight rolled sideways but his armor cracked from the heat. Not paying attention to the prickles of his armor, he took his chances and dove unto the monster with his sword pointed downward. Before Warthang could jump out of the way, the weapon punctured the base of his wing and Sir George drove it to the hilt into him, inflicting a major wound.

Warthang fell to the ground and tried not to move for the pain on his back: it felt like burning lava slowly working its way inward. Seeing that he had debilitated his foe, Sir George looked around and found his horse missing. He shook his head, grabbed his sword hilt, swiftly drew it out of the moaning Warthang and set out to find his mount. Not sure of what the knight was up to, the magic user did not question it but took advantage of the man's absence. Quickly, he healed himself with a sigh, changed himself into a human and ran into the cave. Not too deep in, he found Maggie and Benzady quietly standing. Without much thought, Warthang scooped up the ugly sheep, Benzady of course, and brought him outside. There, he laid him down and transformed him into a perfect replica of his dragon self.

"Oh no..." he said, realizing what he had just done.

He was about to take Benzady back in when Sir George returned with his horse. Stealthily, Warthang tiptoed back into the cave and walked all the way to the back to find the rest of his herd and the kids. At the sight of an adult, the children surrounded him and held on to him, sniffling and crying.

"Children," he told them quietly, "I'm here to take you home."

Before they could cheer, he shushed them with a finger to his lips and everyone filed behind him and walked after him like students following their teacher to school. With his wizard eyes, Warthang saw the "dragon" Benzady meekly walking behind his captor to town, like a sheep following his shepherd. Apparently, Sir George had taken some rope from his saddle pack, had tied it around the beast's neck and now led him back to the people Warthang had terrorized for so long. What was he up to?

Carefully, the dragon made sure that his group had plenty of distance with the knight. He had to time this just right for maximum effect.

Once at the gate of the town, after a long, slow walk, Sir George cried out to the people,

"Come out! It is noon and the dragon has come."

Heads peered out above the wall, then disappeared again to tell others of what they had seen. Truth be told, the whole city had come to the gate an hour ago, once princess Sadra had told them a deliverer had arrived.

"It is not dead!" yelled a mother behind the wall.

Sir George smiled and then pointed to the lake.

"There is a lake behind me," he said loudly. "If all of you repent of your sins, get baptized and receive Jesus

214

Christ as your Lord, then in His name I shall end this demon for you."

Without hesitation, the people began pouring out of the gates, once they had been opened, and rushing to the lake. In that body of water, all baptized each other, even the king and the princess. When Sir George felt satisfied, he took his sword out of its scabbard accompanied by a resounding metal sound, and brought it down on Benzady's neck, severing his head from his body. In the trees, not too far off, Warthang once again felt weighed down by the guilt: he had killed Benzady. Again. Was this cruel fate trying to remind him of his sin?

With these thoughts in mind, Warthang pushed the children and sheep to run home. As they emerged without him and the townspeople cried out in joyous disbelief, he also caused all the crops he had destroyed to grow back and every structure he had burned to be as good as new. Beside themselves, the people cried and embraced their children after a long frantic run. It was a miracle, they all cried, sir George is a saint. God sent him to save them!

Looking sadly at the dead Benzady, a thought suddenly struck Warthang. The dog! Where was the dog? He had not come with the rest of the herd and children. Without further thought of the dead sheep, the conniving princess, the rejoicing people or the strange knight, Warthang teleported to the cave and ran inside.

"Dog!" he called out.

Suddenly, he stopped short in his tracks and tried to control his heavy breathing. There, sitting by the mangy canine, an old man calmly petted the dog. His smile seemed playful enough, his bright white hair long and flowing down past his shoulders, his hands and face wrinkled by old age. But what caused Warthang to panic was his eyes, his light blue eyes. They were wizard eyes.

Note 14

I've been a good dragon. I've saved people's lives, I've helped others, and I've done my best at being good. But still, I killed Benzady, one of my own kind, and although I've done all these good things, this one bad act seems to haunt me wherever I go. But I'm good. Doesn't that count for anything?

Chapter 14 – Bush

As soon as he saw those light blue wizard eyes in that dank cave, Warthang forgot about the dog, forgot about his mission, forgot about everything. His mind just froze and he ran the best way he could: by jumping a thousand years into the future. There, he stumbled into two humans who seemed to be struggling on the ground. Not liking fights, he grabbed the one who had domineered the other and threw him backwards off his opponent.

"Hey!" cried the female Warthang had just saved, "what are you doing?

"I'm..."

"Yeah, you perv!" interrupted the male who had gotten back on his feet. "Go get your own cave!"

"Were you married, you yourselves would not be using this cave," said a deep rich voice, behind the three of them.

Warthang and the boy turned toward the voice, while the girl sat up to catch a better view of the new interlocutor. Impossible! The old wizard had followed him into the future; he was a time traveler too!

"Now scram!" the wizard commanded the young couple who had not been fighting but had been engaged in other activities.

Angrily but without comment, the boy grabbed the

girl by the hand, helped her up, and together they ran out of the dark cave and out of sight. Once they had gone, the old man's serious demeanor melted away and a large smile took over his features. In excitement, he clapped his hands a couple of times and then jumped on

Warthang, embracing him into a tight hug.

"I found you!" he exclaimed, elated. "After all this time, I finally found you!"

"What" asked Warthang, disentangling himself from the waving arms. "You couldn't have been searching for *me*."

The wizard burst out laughing and pointed at Warthang. "You're the dragon aren't you?"

"Why yes," nodded Warthang, now completely

confused, "but how did you know?"

"You have dragon eyes, like mine," explained the old man while he tussled his long crazy white hair.

At his declaration, many thoughts and possibilities crossed Warthang's mind that made him both sad and happy. Welcomed by this silence, the old man looked around the cave and squinted his eyes.

"Strange," he commented, "this is the same cave, yet not. What kind of magic did we do to get here?"

"We traveled a thousand years into the future," replied Warthang, shrugging his shoulders.

"No" groaned the blue eyed man, "I can travel in time? I spent my whole life in the slow path to find you and I could have traveled in time! Bah," he smiled to himself, "I had many adventures. I suppose it's not a big deal."

"So," began Warthang, now wanting some answers, "you're a dragon, then. What's your name and...where do you come from?"

"Sounds like I need to tell you my story," winked the blue eyed dragon. "Let's fly and I'll tell you on the way."

Without further explanation, the old dragon headed outside, closely followed by the younger one. Once there, he turned himself into the biggest green reptile Warthang had ever seen. Apparently, as they grew older, dragons continued to get bigger, which would make this one incredibly ancient, judging by his size. Warthang seemed like a child once again by his side but nonetheless felt like he had the upper hand in knowledge. Dragon eyes? These were wizard eyes! Which must mean that this old one was the only dragon left in existence and had never seen wizard eyes but for his own, thus assuming they belonged to his species. Another thing: the only one with such eyes was himself, meaning that this ancient one must be one of his own descendants...

Already, they were flying north, heading towards water when the old dragon began his story.

*   *   *

The first memory I have is of cracking through my egg shell only to find more darkness in the outside world. I was so sick of the black that out of my desire, I formed a fireball that lit my surroundings. Behind me, four more eggs rested like dead, and all around us, rock shone red with the light of the flames. I didn't understand anything, had no thoughts of my own until I saw this: an inscription on the wall in bright white letters. It said, *You are not the only dragon.* My father or mother must have left it behind as a message of hope to me, but to this day, I don't know for sure. Anyway, it let me know what I was, a dragon, and that I should look for others like myself.

So, tentatively, I exited that tiny cave and set out in the night. Boy, was I hungry, and I tried all sorts of green things but everything upset my little stomach. At some point, I figured out about grubs and bugs and those satisfied me for a long while.

One night, I don't know how long I had been out on my own, I saw a fire in the distance and I knew in my heart I had found the dragons! After all, I had made fire and all the other animals I had discovered so far could not do such a feat. So, I ran on those little legs of mine as fast as I could and burst in on a human camp, yelling

"Dragons! Dragons!" I definitely had no idea what those creatures were and they were three times my size at this point so when they ran out of their shelters, they frightened me out of my wits. I turned into the first thing I knew best: a bush. That's where I found my food, that's where I slept at night, it meant comfort and shelter; it's what I knew.

At seeing a bush by their fire that had not been there before, they thought some sort of god had planted it there and they offered me/it some meat, all the while repeating the name *bush*. When they returned to their shelters, I devoured that meat and it was the best thing I had ever eaten in my life. I had to have more! So, for a few nights, I ran in yelling "dragons," they offered their food to the bush and I feasted. After a while, however, I found I had lost my goal in finding the other dragons for the comfort of a full belly and I promised myself I would ask these humans for their help.

That night, I stood by their fire and announced my presence with my usual call. When they came out and saw me instead of the bush, they fell to the ground and groveled before me. They called me god but I explained to them that I was the bush and not their god. I don't think they bought it, but they called me Bush and that name has stuck ever since.

Through my connections with these humans, I sent out the word to be on the lookout for dragons. Whenever they met new groups, they asked about my kind and when they met blank stares, they taught others about me. Before I knew it, everyone I encountered knew about dragons, but had never seen one in person except for me.

When I had lived about 300 years, I found my first sign of another one of my kind: a red dragon with yellow eyes—quite like you in fact but—with a longer shape, more like a snake with fins. He had appeared in what is now China and had been there for a short period. I had just missed him by a few decades! But no matter, that gave me the proof that I needed to keep searching and never give up. After China, I spent most of my time as a human, I traveled all over the place and had all sorts of fun adventures. Five thousand years later, give or take a few, I was just north of this body of water we're crossing right now when I heard a rumor of another yellow eyed red dragon terrorizing a town in north Africa. I had found a dragon; but this time, I wasn't too late!

I arrived at that cave just in time to see you transforming a sheep into a dragon. Since you seemed busy with important business, I let you do your own thing—I've had plenty of schemes myself and know how vital it is to finish them—and watched you leave with your big group of people and sheep. Quite a procession, by the way. I called the dog back with my mind, who you'd be proud to know was following you like a champ, and we waited for you in the cave. You know the rest!

*   *   *

"Here we are!" pointed Bush with his nose at a landmass, fast approaching.

Warthang looked at the older dragon sideways. Why had he led them here? They had been flying over this water for over an hour, now.

"If you don't mind," apologized the green giant, "I have some unfinished business in these parts. The first rumors I heard of your activities, I ran out of there without doing what I needed to do. But no matter, I could use your help anyways."

As they landed on the beach and both transformed back into human form, Bush looked around, a bit confused.

"Things seem a bit different..." he trailed off.

Behind him, Warthang hid a smile with a hand.

"We're still a thousand years into the future," he explained.

"Oh, right, I forgot," Bush said, slapping his forehead. "Well, lead the way, I'm not exactly sure how I did it last time: I just followed your magic."

"No," disagreed Warthang, "I have things to do and I did not find what I needed during your time period."

Disappointed, the old one crossed his arms, then uncrossed them and rested a hand on one of his companion's shoulders.

"I can help you find what you're looking for, I bet. And then, if you're up for it, you can help me solve a mystery."

Warthang sighed. How much should he tell Bush? After all, the poor guy had been searching his whole life for dragons and he himself sought to annihilate the lot of them. Would he really help him, or try and stop him?

"I'm looking for a powerful weapon," he finally said.

"For what purpose?" asked Bush.

"To protect some people from a terrible fate."

"Well," the old dragon shrugged his shoulders, "that's not terribly specific but I have an idea of where we can find the information. Follow me!"

And he began running inland on his two human legs, away from the beach. Without comment, Warthang followed him, a bit surprised at how spry Bush could be for his age. After a good ten minute run, they found a road covered by a dark gray surface and they followed it, figuring it led to some sort of civilization.

"I have never seen such a perfect road as this in my life!" commented Bush, mesmerized.

A loud beep sounded behind the two companions and they jumped on the rocky side of the road, just in time to avoid getting hit by a rectangular shape on wheels speeding by.

"What is that!" exclaimed the old man, holding a hand over his heart.

"I saw a person inside of it," answered Warthang, "I bet it's the new and improved horseless chariot."

Together, the two dragons laughed and marveled at how much things had changed, sharing their various experiences with humans and their gadgets. Before they knew it, they had reached a large cluster of houses. On the side of the large road, pedestrians walked on a smaller path, some running with wires in their ears, others walking their dogs. As a runner made to pass by them, Bush waved him down and he stopped to see what was up.

"Is there some place where we can read books?" Bush asked him.

The runner nodded, staring at the old man's light blue wizard eyes with distaste. Then, he looked at Warthang's yellow eyes and rolled his own at them.

"Continue on this road and look to your right for the library."

Without further comment, he ran past them and never looked back. The two dragons raised their eyebrows at each other questioningly, sighed and continued on their way. Once they found the library a bit down the road, they entered the little white building and found at the entrance a girl constantly chewing what looked like a piece of bright pink sap.

"Excuse me," Bush said to her, catching her attention, "we're looking for books on weapons."

The brunette looked up and when she saw their eyes, a big grin lit her face.

"*Those* are the coolest contacts I have ever seen!" she exclaimed, "Where can I get a pair?"

Bush smiled at her and crossed his arms.

"There is no way we're going to share our secret."

Laughing, the girl nodded knowingly and pointed inside.

"Just check our database on the computer by subject and it'll point you to what you need. Weapons away, blue eyes!"

He nodded and the two of them headed to where the girl had pointed.

"Hum," said Warthang, "I understood nothing of what she just said. For that matter, what are contacts?

"I have no idea," laughed the ancient dragon, "but as for the other stuff, I do believe she meant these machines here."

Bush sat himself in front of a flat black framed screen accompanied by a rectangle pad filled with lettered keys. On the flat surface, it had different categories written on a white background: title, author, subject, etc. Following his lead, Warthang sat by the white haired man and waited. Nothing happened.

"What now?" he asked, a bit impatiently.

Bush turned to him and looked straight at his eyes. "Be specific now," he told him, "do you need something to target one object at a time or would you rather a weapon that can destroy a whole area?"

Thinking quickly, Warthang remembered the thought he had had while he had waited those long weeks for Sadra's plan to come to fruition. Maybe a weapon was not necessary; maybe there was another way.

"Bush, you and I, we have magic," he told him seriously. "Is there some other kind of power that can trump our own?"

The old dragon brought a hand to his temple and scrutinized his companion.

"Yes," he finally answered, "wait here."

Without an explanation, he stood up, talked to the brunette at the entrance, who in turn walked to a row of nearby books, grabbed a large tome and handed it to him with a smile and a wink. When he returned to Warthang, he gave him the massive volume and pointed to it.

"Read it," he said, "this book has many answers about life and it holds the biggest power of this world."

"Okay," nodded Warthang, a bit skeptical, "but it'll take me a couple of hours to read it."

"In the meantime," Bush smiled and stretched his arms out, "I'm going to play with this computer and see what weapons this time period holds."

And so both of them set out to accomplish their tasks: Warthang read as fast as he could turn the pages and Bush controlled the machine with his magic, never once touching it. After five minutes, the younger magic user pushed the book away, frustrated at its content.

"What's the matter?" asked Bush, not looking away from the screen.

Tapping his fingers on the table, Warthang glared at him.

"I'm angry, that's what."

"Yep," nodded the old one, "there are lots of reasons to be angry when reading that book, but what's yours?"

"Oh I'm not angry for myself," he answered quickly, "just for the unfairness of things."

"You sure are good at not answering a question," observed Bush, "now spit it out and stop making me have to ask you over and over again."

"All right," he nodded, joining his hands together and taking a deep breath. "Here goes: Moses did everything God told him to and then he makes one tiny mistake and because of that, he doesn't get to go to the Promised Land."

"Wait until you get to David!" Bush raised his eyebrows, "he's said to be a man after God's own heart and yet because of a *mistake*, thousands and thousands of people died."

"What?" exclaimed Warthang, "how does that make any sense?"

"Ever heard of consequences?" interrupted Bush, "God made the world with consequences and boy am I glad he did! They help us understand better the difference between right and wrong. But if not that, at least they can give some fear to those who would do bad things."

"But what about those who are good, like Moses, and do one bad thing?"

A man at another computer shushed at them, feeling Warthang's tone a bit too loud for the library.

"They don't deserve to be punished," continued the young dragon in a lower voice.

"And who are we to decide who deserves punishment and who doesn't?" retorted his companion, finally looking away from his computer, "we certainly cannot tell the true motivations behind a man's evil action. Before a sin is committed, a thought *must* be made..."

"Still," Warthang persisted, "a good person can't be expected to be perfect all the time and they should be forgiven for one bad act."

"What if the bad act is murder, or adultery, or theft, or lying? At what point is a sin not too bad that it should not have a consequence? Being forgiven doesn't mean you don't have to pay for what you've done."

Not finding a good retort to that line of logic and feeling uncomfortable, the younger dragon raised his shoulders and shook his head as answer. Then, he looked back down at the book and began again reading and turning the pages. Another five minutes passed this way and he finally stood up and gestured to his companion that they were leaving.

"But you're not done reading it. I'm sure you haven't even gotten to the best part," protested Bush.

"I got what I needed," answered Warthang as he headed out of the library. "I'm going to meet the prophet Elijah and he's going to talk to God for me."

"What, you're going there *now*? What about helping me with my problem from my present?"

Warthang stopped in the street, surprising Bush who ran into him.

"Don't worry," he smiled reassuringly at the worried, lonely dragon, "I'll be right back."

And he disappeared.

Note 15

It's weird how we can deceive ourselves. We tell everyone around us, including our inner minds, that we're doing something and going toward a certain goal; when in reality, we're really subconsciously aiming for something completely different. And imagine, even though I am a few hundred years old, I was deceiving myself! Well, you're never too old to learn something new and wisen up.

Chapter 15 – Revelations

Finding the prophet Elijah was no easy task: not only did Warthang have to find the right time, but he also had to look for a location he had never visited. Luckily, the book he had been reading had had tentative dates and maps detailed enough to point him the right way. However, because the search was far and long, this gave the dragon time to think and to feel guilty. Poor Bush. After 5000 years, he had finally completed his search for another of his kind, but this one not only did not tell him anything, he also left him behind without an explanation. Moreover, he had not shown him how time travel worked and the poor old dragon could possibly panic at the thought of being stuck in the future. This feeling certainly would have intensified when he would have tried to follow Warthang like the previous time but miserably failed. One could never go back to a time he had already lived! But Bush did not know that, of course. To make up for this disappearing act, Warthang promised himself he would tell the old dragon everything. He would tell him all about the origin of their species, their evil, what he himself had done, and his plans for the future of their species. He would tell him everything! When the time was right, obviously.

Time passed quickly while he searched for the prophet Elijah, his thoughts running along like the high current of a river. At one point, to his great surprise, he appeared and scattered a small flock of crows carrying various foods in their beaks. When he saw them, he remembered what the book had said about the black birds bringing food to the prophet and he could not believe his luck at having found them. But maybe it was not luck but the hand of God guiding him.

Quickly, as the crows banded back together, the dragon took their bird form and followed them a ways. For a while, they glided over a river, not paying him any mind, and then began to fly lower and lower. At a bend of the water, they landed by an olive tree, dropped their load in a pile and chattered at each other noisily, seeming to boast at each other of their great feat. Quietly, Warthang reached the ground a small distance from them and waited to see what would happen next. When one of the crows noticed him, it stopped its chattering and before long, the rest of the crew had gone silent. With their beady yellow eyes, they glared at him menacingly. Not intimidated in the least, the dragon-bird stared back in challenge. Let them try! They won't stand a chance!

Suddenly, the crows squawked and flew off in a rush of black feathers. Behind them, to Warthang's satisfaction, a middle-aged man stumbled and calmly knelt by the food. Before touching it, he bowed down, whispered some words, looked up to the sky and nodded. Finally, he sat down, grabbed a flat piece of bread, broke it and began to eat it.

Not sure how he should approach the man, Warthang hopped closer to him. Right away, Elijah spotted him. He stopped chewing, put the rest of the flat bread back on the pile, stood up and patted the dust off his clothes.

Then, he stretched both arms towards Warthang.

"Little black bird!" his rich voice rang out, "I have a message from the Lord."

At that, the prophet quickly glanced up to the sky and put his hands back down to his thighs.

"What you are seeking, you will not find. What you need, the Lord will provide."

With that short message, he nodded at the bird, grabbed his flat bread and sat back down to eat it. On his little legs, Warthang shook, furious: he had come to talk to God and now, apparently, he was only going to get a one sided conversation. What he was seeking, he would not find: so, no way out of the curse. But why not, pray tell? Was not God supposed to be all powerful?

"Little black bird," Elijah interrupted his thoughts, "the Lord hears you and he has made a decision. Now fly home and He will take care of the rest."

The Lord will provide? He will take care of the rest? So this was it: he was meant to die after all, because that was what he needed—or what the world needed. And maybe it was right for him to die and suffer the consequences of his actions. He had been cursed because he had killed Benzady. He had killed Benzady because of a blind rage. He had developed this incredible rage from being hated and shunned by his whole race. His whole race had hated him because he had stolen the wizard magic for himself and they hated the wizards above all else. And finally, he had stolen the magic for himself. Why had he done it in the first place? Why had he not just spelled for magic to disappear altogether? In the core of it, in the beginning, he must have had some sinister motives himself: he had been evil after all, just like the rest of them.

"Little black bird," Elijah impatiently burst out, causing Warthang to jump back, "I am not feeling particularly like having company right now so please fly home before I smite you."

Surprised, Warthang jumped place and time back to where he had left Bush in front of that library where he had learned about God and Elijah and all the rest. Although he still had the appearance of a crow, Bush was frowning down at him and tapping his foot impatiently, knowing perfectly well who it was that had appeared before him out of nowhere.

"That wasn't very dragony of you, Warthang," he said in a low voice.

In a flash, the bird disappeared and reappeared as the young redheaded man with the yellow opaque eyes.

"What do you mean?" Warthang asked, completely lost.

"Dragons are good, noble creatures, and what you just did was quite rude."

"Ah..." Warthang started then just stood there in silence, not sure which statement to address first. Finally, after a few awkward moments of silence where the two dragons watched each other uncomfortably, Warthang interlaced an arm with one of Bush's—the way Maggie used to with him—and led him away from the library to follow the sidewalk back out of town.

"Let me tell you about dragons," he began, a bit sad. "They are not good and they certainly are *not* noble; in fact, they are just plain evil."

"Nonsense!" protested Bush as he freed himself of Warthang's lead to face him. "From the time I came out of my egg, I had a sense of right and wrong and always wanted to help others and make life worthwhile for

236

everyone! And you yourself certainly don't seem evil to me!"

Sighing, the younger dragon closed his eyes for a moment and when he opened them again, he put his hands on his companion's shoulders.

"You and I, we're different from the rest of them. Normally, dragons only care about their own pleasure, their hunger or their power: they're incredibly selfish. They do nothing good for others, unless it's for their own gain."

"If that's the case," Bush said shaking his head, hardly believing what he was hearing, "then why are *we* different?"

"When I was four," Warthang explained as he let go of the old man's shoulders, "I stole all of the wizards' magic. When that happened, something inside me changed and I no longer was like the rest of them. The truth is, for me, it didn't happen right away. I still had the evil in me but overtime, I've been able to fight it."

Putting one hand to his temple, the old dragon frowned, then nodded slowly.

"So then, I was born with this *wizard magic*...which means that we are related by blood..."

At that understanding, Bush's face burst into a terrific smile and he jumped on Warthang, squeezing him tight.

"In one day," he yelled excitedly as he jumped around with Warthang in tow, "not only did I find another dragon, but I found one of my own ancestors!"

Finally releasing his parent, he patted his face several times and grinned widely like a poor man who wins the lottery.

"So!" he exclaimed, "how are we related?"

Warthang raised and lowered his shoulders, chuckling a bit at Bush's elated reaction.

"The truth is," he answered, "I'm not really sure. I don't even have eggs yet."

"Hold up!" Bush said as he raised a hand up. "Don't tell me you're going to make babies with some evil dragoness!"

"Certainly not!" Warthang defended himself, "I have a mate and she is a much better dragon than I have ever been."

"But you said we're different because we have wizard magic. She has it too then? How many of us are there?"

Warthang looked up at the sky in thought and then shook his head.

"She isn't like us. I don't know why she's different: it's an anomaly. I guess she's..." he smiled at the thought, "she's a gift from God."

"Oh!" exclaimed Bush, "speaking of God, what did He tell you?"

"He told me to go home," answered the ancestor, "He told me He would take care of my problem."

"Can I come?" Bush asked, worried.

"Of course you can! Why couldn't you?"

"Well," continued the old dragon, "I tried to follow you to Elijah but I wasn't able to."

"That's because of the rules of time traveling," said Warthang, remembering that awful day when he had first discovered this new gift of time traveling. "You can only go where you haven't been. And since my time is before your birth, you won't have any problems in following me there."

"Well, that's a relief," sighed Bush, "but first, there's

still that thing I have to finish up in my own time and I would greatly appreciate your help."

"Sure thing, lead on!" Warthang patted him on the back.

*   *   *

Bush knocked on the door of a small house that stood by itself, surrounded by a large garden of herbs. Inside, pots and pans clattered and footsteps hurriedly drew closer. The door opened a crack, an eyeball peered at the old man and when she recognized him, the old lady threw the door wide open with a grin and gestured for him to enter.

"Back so soon you old geezer?"

As Bush came into her home, she noticed Warthang standing outside and liking what she saw, she attempted to fix her disheveled short gray hair by passing her fingers through it, and she winked at him knowingly.

"Oh my, you found a nice young apprentice, then? I have never seen another wizard before."

"No," Bush yelled from inside the house, "he's not my apprentice but a relative of mine. He's come to help."

"Well, come on in then, young man," the old woman smiled, showing him a few crooked teeth.

Warthang nodded and entered the house to find a room brimming with herbs drying from the ceiling, swaying with the wind from the windows, several glass containers filled with different liquids littered the tables and a fire in the corner crackled under a large cauldron. Once everyone had sat down at the messy table, Bush made the introductions.

"Warthang, this is Francesca, the local healer and wise woman of the village. Francesca, this is Warthang."

"Interesting name, that. Where are you from exactly?" the old woman eyed him, curious.

"It's from an island far, far away. You wouldn't have heard of it."

Seeing as Warthang was not going to say anything else, Francesca turned to the other wizard and bent forward confidentially.

"Father Fernando came to see me while you were gone," she rasped as she raised her eyebrows.

"That can't be good," frowned Bush.

"He blamed me for the disappearances!" she exclaimed, exasperated, "accused me of being a witch."

Bush hissed, shaking his head. By his side,

Warthang set his hands on the table and looked from his companion to the woman.

"What's a witch?" he asked, "and most importantly, what's going on in this town?"

"A witch," Francesca spat on the ground, "is a person who consorts with demons. They call on them to get power and to obtain what they want. Nothing good ever comes of it."

"Okay," Warthang nodded, taking the new information into consideration, "so what would a witch have to do with these disappearances you spoke of and why would this Father Fernando accuse you of being one?"

"Francesca here," Bush said, putting his hands over hers, "is wise in herbs and in their healing properties. Father Fernando who is from the church does not understand how she is helping the people and calls it demon's work. It's really too bad he feels that way because both of them want the same thing: to take care of the people."

"I keep telling him God created these plants for the purpose of healing," raged Francesca, "but he doesn't want to hear any of it! Anything the church doesn't know about can't be from God, he says! Sometimes, I just want to strangle the man!"

"Francesca!" Bush reprimanded.

Surprised at her angry outburst, the old woman made a sign of the cross on her shoulders and then kissed a cross she wore on her right hand.

"Forgive me," she said, subdued, "I have been quite upset since his visit. I got carried away."

With a smile, Bush patted her hands and then turned to Warthang.

"Here's the situation: for one month now, men disappear one at a time for a couple of nights only to return with no recollection of having been gone in the first place."

"Are they hurt in any way?" inquired the young dragon.

"No."

"Are they missing anything other than time?"

"No."

"Are they different after the experience?"

"No."

"Then why does it matter so much?"

Francesca burst out laughing at this exchange, slapping her knees.

"He really didn't tell you anything, did he?" she managed to croak out between guffaws.

"There really wasn't time for explanations," Bush defended himself, almost offended.

"This great old wizard here," she continued laughing as she pointed at poor Bush, "was one of the first disappearances!"

Warthang hid a smile behind his hand and feigned a cough to cover up the bit of laughter that escaped his throat. After a moment, he recovered his composure, placed his hand back into his lap and adopted a serious look.

"What have you done to discover the kidnapper?" he asked.

"I walked around town, asked around, but no one seemed to know anything," answered Bush, raising his shoulders.

"What about using wizard sight?"

When Bush gave him a blank stare, the younger

wizard understood that the lone dragon had a few more things he needed to learn about his powers. After an explanation, some practice and some jubilant exclamations, the old dragon was up to Warthang's level.

"Perfect!" announced Bush, "now I'll show you who I talked to, where I went and hopefully the abductor will notice you and take you."

"Ha!" laughed Warthang, "so I'm the guinea pig, here. Please make sure to watch over me because I don't want us to have to find some other person to watch."

"Sure thing," the older dragon smiled, "now, follow me!"

The two dragons got up from the table, left Francesca to her work and headed to town. In the fields and vineyards, they talked to every worker. Some of them offered them some produce and at one point, a disgruntled owner chased them away. After that adventure, they reached the village and began knocking at each door. Mostly, women and children answered but all were too busy to talk to them long. In the streets, various artists and venders attempted to sell their wares but the two had no money or interest in human things. Throughout their walk, a few beggars fawned over them, grabbing their clothes or their hands for a scrap of anything. This shocked Warthang because some of them seemed awfully sick, were missing limbs or were even blind, from children to elderly people. After visiting all the houses and the streets, they entered into the bar and talked to the drunks loitering at the tables. Once they left that establishment, Bush turned to Warthang and smiled.

"We've talked to everyone now except the clergymen. All we've got to do now is wait and see."

"Where will we wait?" asked Warthang.

"At Francesca's," grinned the other dragon, "not only is she a good friend of mine, she's also a great cook!"

So the dragons left for Francesca's house to wait for Warthang's abduction to take place.

Note 16

Bush told me once about people who sometimes get so drunk that the next day they wake up with no recollection of what they did the night before. I have never been drunk in my life, I don't think that's even possible for a dragon, but I had that experience of not remembering what I did and it is one of the worse things to gnaw at someone's soul. What terrible act did I commit when I wasn't myself? Why can't I remember? Do I even want to remember! I try not to dwell on it too much but once in a while, that feeling of helplessness just comes back to me and I can't stop it from plaguing me.

Chapter 16 – Bewitched

In the middle of the night, a few weeks later, Warthang woke to the sound of a screaming girl. Without much thought, he slowly rose from the floor where he had been sleeping and dragged himself out of the house in a daze. As he walked toward the hysterical high pitched screams, he tried shaking his head to help him think better, but to no avail. Also, he could barely open his eyes, like when the sun keeps shining in one's eyes so that everything feels too bright—but at night. Finally, he gave up on fighting whatever feeling had overcome him and he blindly followed the call for help.

He passed the vineyards and the fields, he trudged through the town, went through some more countryside until he finally reached an old abandoned wooden structure. Without hesitation, he stumbled through the broken door and the continuous cries suddenly ceased. At the sound of nothing, Warthang stood in the entrance a bit dizzy but conscious enough to notice the little girl sitting in the middle of the floor, tears streaming down her cheeks. His heart felt a sharp pang and his stomach plummeted: how sad this little girl seemed. She wore a small tattered dress that once must have been white but now was caked with mud, her long dark hair seemed matted and out of control and her bare feet and hands were covered in blisters and scratches. When she opened her eyes, something seemed wrong with them but the dragon could not pinpoint the problem.

"What's the matter, little girl?" he asked, sad.

"I'm lost and alone," she managed to hiccup. "My mom abandoned me and I can't find my father."

"I know I can help you, I'm certain of it," stuttered Warthang, confused at knowing this but having forgotten how he knew it.

"Are you my father?" she asked, drying her tears with an arm and adopting a pout.

"No...Don't you know who your father is?"

"How could I?" she almost shouted, "My mother's a prostitute! My father could be anyone, he could be *you*!"

"Now *that's* impossible," Warthang laughed uncomfortably.

"We'll see," she declared.

Suddenly, she stood up, walked up to the dragon and slapped his forehead with the palm of her hand. At her touch, Warthang crumbled to the floor, conscious but unable to twitch a muscle. Carefully, she spread his arms and legs out, like preparing a sacrifice, all the while stumbling all over him. When she felt satisfied, she sat on his stomach and drew a large knife out from under her dress. Although he could not move, Warthang's heart began to pound like a drum within his chest and he attempted to say something but only gurgling bubbled out of his mouth. Not paying him any mind, the little girl slid the knife across her palm and with her blood quickly dripping, she drew a red circle around his head and finally let some of the red liquid fall into his mouth, forcing him to swallow. With a pang of guilt, Warthang enjoyed the warm taste of blood—he *was* a dragon, after all—and closed his eyes to battle the mixed emotions raging within him.

A few seconds later, he felt the weight on his stomach leave and he opened his eyes to see the little girl holding the hand of a wondrous creature. It looked like a human but it had enormous beautiful feathered wings on its back and its whole being shone pure white. Never in his life had Warthang seen such a wonderful sight.

"Is he my father?" the little girl asked it as she pointed at Warthang sprawled on the floor.

"No," it answered, shaking its head sadly.

Then, it let go of her hand and reached for Warthang's instead. When their fingers touched, warmth coursed through the dragon's body and he felt good and as light as a feather. Staring at the creature, he sat up and sighed.

"You are so beautiful," he murmured, mesmerized.

The white being smiled and nodded.

"So are you, Warthang," it told him, touching his human face. "Shed your disguise and let us fly together."

Like in a dream, Warthang floated to his feet and the two of them walked into the perfect starry night. Smiling, the creature spread its great white wings and took to the sky. It was so graceful that Warthang took it all in for a few moments before he jumped after it with his own natural form. Looking at his scaly red wings, he felt disgusted and he looked back to the white feathers to erase the negative feeling.

"You are very beautiful, Warthang," repeated the shining creature as they soared into the sky, "but something dark shadows you."

Saddened, the red dragon looked at the being's face and saw it crying.

"Death follows you," it continued, "you, who should be immortal."

Now, tears slid down both of their cheeks. This beautiful angel cared so much for his sorry fate, it was just too much not to be touched.

"Come little dragon," it beckoned, "rest a while on me."

So Warthang let himself fall and the next thing he knew, he was back in human form, resting on the creature's back as its soft wings spread on either side of him. For hours, it flew for them in silence, sharing a very intimate experience. When the dragon felt completely at peace, a peace he had never known before, the creature spoke again.

"There is a way to rid yourself of the darkness," it said.

"No," Warthang replied, holding on tighter to the flying being. "God told me I could not find a cure."

The creature looked back at him and gave him a pitying smile.

"That is because it is not to be found," it explained, "it is something that has to be made."

"But I don't know how to make it," answered the dragon with renewed hope.

"You see that church over there?" pointed the creature to the beautiful building with the cross, in the middle of town. "Bring me Father Fernando and I can take care of the rest for you."

"Will you wait for me outside the church?" asked Warthang.

"No," the creature shook its head, "once you have the priest, find Paulita and she can call me again."

With that, the beautiful being disappeared, leaving the wizard alone in front of the great building. Without its presence, Warthang felt empty inside and he could not wait to see it again. He knew what he had to do but his ears still buzzed and bothered him at every step, confusing him and leaving his head heavy and dizzy.

On the large door of the church, a simple knocker adorned the middle part of it and it made quite a racket when Warthang used it. Not long after, a slim middle aged man going completely bald and wearing simple brown robes opened a small wooden door to the right of where Warthang stood.

"Can I help you, my son?" the man asked kindly.

"Yes!" exclaimed the wizard dragon excitedly, "I'm looking for Father Fernando."

"It's cold out here in the dark," the man said, then he indicated the inside of the church, "come on in and we can talk."

Feeling like he did not have much time, Warthang hurried into the building but as soon as he reached the light inside, the one who had invited him in gasped.

"Demon!" he hissed, then he quickly grabbed a flask from his robe, opened it and threw its wet contents at Warthang's face, all the while saying in a commanding voice, "In the name of the Father, The Son and the Holy Ghost, I cast thee out!"

When nothing happened, he stared a while at the yellow eyed demon with his mouth wide open and the empty flask still clutched in his hand.

"Nothing happened," he told himself surprised. After a few more seconds, he looked at the dragon and covered his mouth with his right hand.

"I'm terribly sorry," he apologized, "I must have made a mistake. But I was terribly sure...but your eyes? Are you sick? Is that why you're looking for me? You need me to pray over you or anoint you?"

"Ah!" shouted Warthang in triumph now that he knew he had found Father Fernando, "there's a shadow hanging over me,—it's death,—and I need you to help me stop it."

Quizzically, Father Fernando stared at the dragon.

"Son," he began, "we all have to die at some point, but there is hope of eternal life after death."

"No, no, no!" replied the wizard, impatiently, "you have to come with me right away! I need your help!"

"And where shall we go?"

"We need to go see Paulita."

At her name, the priest took a step backward and shook his head slowly. His countenance had changed from concern to worry, but Warthang had not noticed anything.

"Who sent you?" Father Fernando asked shakily.

The dragon opened his mouth, closed it again, blinked, scrunched his face and finally lifted his shoulders.

"Honestly, I can't remember."

"That's what I thought," replied the priest, backing up some more, "I shall not be following you this night, my son."

Calmly, Father Fernando turned around and began walking to the altar at the other end of the church. Knowing he had to have his cure to rid himself of the curse, Warthang grabbed a nearby candle stick and swung it at the priest's head. It hit the man with a clunk and he fell to the ground unconscious. Carefully, the wizard picked up the clergyman, set him across his shoulders and started the long walk back to the abandoned house. Never once did it occur to him to use magic or to wonder at his strange actions. Cotton balls seemed to fill his head and only a few thoughts could pass through: the cure, Father Fernando, Paulita, hurry.

Although he walked as fast as he could, the dead weight on his shoulders slowed him down remarkably and it took him at least half an hour to reach the broken down shack. Once inside the building, Warthang deposited his load on the ground and watched Paulita jump from the floor to her feet. She had obviously been sleeping in the dust and the hushed sound of Father Fernando's body hitting the ground had awakened her.

"Who is it?" she screeched, trying to fend off attackers with her arms.

"I brought him," muffled Warthang as he sat by the unconscious mass on the ground, "he's the cure."

Paulita's face lit up and she carefully walked toward the priest, feeling every step with her feet. Finding him with the tip of her toes, she knelt down and began spreading his limbs out the way she had Warthang's. However, when she felt the cross that hung at the churchman's neck, she backed away and frowned.

"Remove that thing," she ordered Warthang.

Without questioning, the dragon unclasped the chain that hung around the man's neck and placed it and its cross on a table at the back of the room. On the ground, Father Fernando groaned and placed a hand on the back of his head. Immediately, Paulita's take charge manner disappeared and she broke down in tears, falling on her face. Hearing this, the priest squinted an eye open, looked around confused, and then focused on the little girl.

"I've seen you before," he croaked out in recognition, "you're that blind girl that begs in the street."

"Are you my father?" she cried out in despair.

"Certainly, my child," answered the priest, puzzled.

A creepy smile grew in the young girl's face as a tear slid down her cheek and she crawled to the priest and sat on his stomach.

"You really *have* brought the cure," she told Warthang who still stood at the back of the room, watching in a daze.

Then, like before, the long knife appeared in her

254

hand and she paused to feel that its edges were still quite sharp. Father Fernando looked at her and frowned.

"Child," he told her, calmly, "you are much too young to be threatening me with that knife."

Gritting her teeth, Paulita slid the blade over her previous wound and the blood began pouring in torrents. As before, she drew the circle around the man's head and finished with some drops on his lips. Disgusted, the priest wiped it off with the back of his hand but Paulita, hearing the sound, punched him in the face with her good fist and slapped her other bleeding hand into the man's mouth. He gurgled and sputtered but in the end, he was unable to stop from drinking some of her blood.

Throughout this ordeal, the middle aged man had remained calm; however, when he saw the great creature appear by the little girl, his face lost all its color and he froze to the ground.

"It is time, as you promised," Paulita told it, pointing at Father Fernando's face. "Gouge his eyes out!"

The beautiful shining creature's features darkened and it laughed in a low growl. Still, Warthang teetered by the table not far away, feeling like he was either going to pass out or throw up. No matter how hard he tried, he could not help but feel that something was terribly wrong, but he just could not see or understand what he could do about it. It all just seemed like a terrible nightmare where one watches something horrendous happen and can hardly move or even make a sound, like a helpless, newborn baby.

Suddenly, an old man with light blue eyes appeared out of nowhere and grabbed the cross Warthang had laid on the table. Quickly, he winked at the confused dragon with a teethy smile and jumped at the beautiful creature in the middle of the room, brandishing the silver cross like a sword. Afraid of the little piece of jewelry, it shifted backward and hissed at the old man with an ugly black snaky tongue.

"Don't step any closer," warned the elder with the cross firmly in hand.

Paulita, still holding the knife, made to stab the newcomer where she heard his voice but her weapon dissolved into dust and flew into her face, causing her to cough uncontrollably.

"Nice trick, don't you think?" the old man directed the comment at Warthang who stood there with his mouth open.

Then, before the creature or anyone else could react, the blue eyed old man grabbed Father Fernando from the ground like he was a light child and ran out of there so fast that Warthang doubted he had even been there in the first place.

"Paulita," hissed the creature menacingly, "you were discovered."

"We have to get him back!" she squeaked between coughs, desperate.

"It is impossible now," it answered angrily. "Clean up this mess and we shall move on to another town and find   another."

"But how can I have another father?" she protested.

In answer, the beautiful white creature slapped her across the face and she landed hard on the ground, sobbing from the force of it. When her cries subsided, she understood it had left her and she turned to the helpless dragon.

"Sleep now," she commanded quietly, "sleep."

* * *

Warthang woke up in Francesca's house with a stabbing headache, feeling like he had barely slept. Stumbling from the room to the main area of the house, he found Bush and Francesca sitting at the table, speaking in hushed tones.

"Good morning," Warthang greeted them with a raised hand.

Without a word, Bush brought a finger up to his lips and then pointed at a cot by the fire. In it, a middle aged man slept, quite at peace. Tiptoeing to the table, Warthang leaned closer to his two friends and whispered,

"Who's that?"

Francesca looked at him like she had just swallowed a bug and Bush silently laughed at her.

"Told you he wouldn't remember!" he chuckled quietly, then he pointed to the sleeping man, "This, my friend, is Father Fernando."

"You mean the one who called Francesca a witch?" asked Warthang, not able to believe his ears.

"The very same," acquiesced Bush with a knowing smile. "But he certainly won't be calling her that anymore!"

In the corner by the fire, Father Fernando stirred and Bush stood up right away to push Warthang back into the room where he had been sleeping.

"We can't let him see you," he whispered, "but you can definitely listen in. The last piece of the puzzle is about to be placed."

Completely confused and irked at not knowing what was going on, Warthang watched Bush wink at him and close the door, making sure Father Fernando would not see the younger wizard. Sighing, the red dragon sat on the ground and focused on the next room. He supposed he had been abducted, his memory erased and Bush had solved the mystery all in a day's time. How frustrating not to remember! But wait, if Father Fernando would help clarify what was going on, did that mean he had been the cause of it all? No use in wondering, Warthang finally told himself, one had only to watch and listen.

In the next room, Bush knelt by the priest who now held the back of his head in wonder.

"Strange," he murmured, "I would have thought it would have hurt more than this."

"That's because it would have," Francesca popped her head behind the old wizard's to look at the squinting man of God. "I used some of my plants to help you on your way. Although I dare say you sure didn't deserve it."

"Oh, I'm so sorry Francesca," apologized Father Fernando, "I let fear rule me. I had no right in accusing you of witchcraft."

For an answer, the old lady harrumphed and pushed a wooden cup into the priest's hand. Without hesitation, he drank the green viscous liquid in one shot and gave her the cup back. Francesca at that moment felt quite impressed because she knew that the drink tasted and smelled like wet socks taken off sweaty feet, but the man had neither flinched nor grimaced at drinking it.

"What made you so afraid?" Bush asked as he helped the man sit up on the side of the cot.

"I'm sure you've heard of the disappearances?" Father Fernando questioned rhetorically, "well, even though those people didn't remember anything, many of

258

them had visited me, then the next day claimed they had not done so when I asked them about it."

"And what did your forgetting guests want?" probed Bush.

"All sorts of things and only one thing. Some wanted a cure to a disease or another, others asked for forgiveness or help in overcoming a sin. In the end, they all demanded I come with them to see *Paulita* and none of them knew who she was or who had sent them."

"Did you have any theories?"

"Demons," the priest nodded, "enemies of the Lord. I knew that if I went to see this Paulita, the demons would ensnare me somehow and they would be free to take over our town without God protecting it through me."

"What did you do with the visitors whenever they came?" Bush asked, staring intently at Father Fernando.

"Well," he answered with a shrug, "I would always pray for their deliverance and then sprinkle some holy water on them. They would fall asleep on a pew and the next morning, they would be gone."

"Tell me about last night," Bush said as he sat on the floor.

"It was different that time," the priest frowned. "My visitor had eyes just like yours, but yellow. At first, I thought he was a demon but I quickly determined that wasn't the case. Really, it all scared me quite a bit because the holy water didn't put him to sleep like the others. I don't know what he was, or what you are for that matter, but it's certainly not human."

Bush smiled but remained silent; this conversation had been a highly repetitive one over the centuries.

"So you were not able to subdue him and instead he

subdued you," the old dragon filled in so the priest could continue telling his story.

"Yes, and I was right this whole time!" Father Fernando nodded unhappily, "this Paulita, a blind beggar from the street I had crossed so many times, was a witch! She summoned the ugliest beast I have ever seen..."

"Really!" interrupted Bush, completely surprised. What *he* had seen had been beautiful beyond imagining. "What did it look like?"

"It had great big black feathered wings," shivered the man in recollection, "its body was a rotten skeleton and all over it, black smoke emanated slowly, threatening to choke me."

Bush nodded pensively, thinking about what this could all mean.

"What I saw was quite different. II Corinthians 11:14 says that Satan himself masquerades as an angel of light. You must have been looking through the eyes of the Holy Spirit because that devil did not fool you at all!"

Following this declaration, Bush stood up abruptly and smiled down at the priest.

"Okay, it's time we end this evil and overcome it with good, don't you think?"

"Yes, yes, I agree," Father Fernando nodded, resting his chin on his right hand, "I'll have to ask God and see what he wants me to do."

"He has already told you," Bush smiled broader, "heal the sick, forgive, and teach."

The religious man nodded slowly but his expression seemed lost.

"Here's what I know," the old dragon continued,

"that beggar girl is blind and she's looking for her father. Normally, I don't think you would ask for a demon's help to accomplish such a task so it's really something else that she wants. Clearly, going by what happened last night, what she wants is to see again, to be healed of her blindness."

"So you're proposing I pray over her for a healing?"

"Ah no," Bush shook his head, "I'll take care of that part."

Father Fernando raised an eyebrow and shrugged.

"What I need you to do is forgive her of the wrongs she did against you and take her in under your wings."

"Look," the priest answered, "I'm willing to do all that, but will she even cooperate?"

"I can teach her about my plants," Francesca piped in, "to keep her mind off witchcraft and focused more on helping people."

So the three made plans for Paulita's future and Bush found the little girl few miles down the road that same evening. The whole way back to Francesca's, she kicked and screamed and threatened the old magician; but of course, nothing could stop him. Once back at the healer's house, he made her eyes whole, flaky white scales falling out to reveal attentive brown eyes. In wonder, she touched her face in wonder, a smile never leaving her expression. As planned, she began her tutelage under the old lady and the priest the very next day.

Clever and quick on her feet, the young girl quickly learned Francesca's wares and was helping patients by the time she was thirteen. As for her learning with the priest, she listened attentively enough, but never showed interest in Jesus' redeeming love or in God's offer to adopt her as His daughter.

I would love to tell you that the three of them lived together happily ever after; but unfortunately, life did not turn out that way. By the time she was fifteen, Paulita's thirst for power overtook her and she could no longer resist the allure of witchcraft and demons. She ran away from her mentors, abandoned the good path, and continued to wreak havoc in the world. Things did not end well for her.

In the meantime, the two dragons had left a long time before all of these events and they were heading home.

Note 17

I missed Tundra so much, I had not seen her in months! Of course, for her, it would only be three weeks, but I felt certain she would be exhilarated to see me again! This adventure away from home taught me that I must take advantage and enjoy every day I have with my loved ones. You never know when will be the last time you see them.

Chapter 17 – Homecoming

To go home, Warthang had only to teleport directly to the continent of Atlantis and the right time and he would be there. However, since Bush traveled with him, he decided to take a few hours of flight before making the jump to discuss what had just happened. To his horror, the older dragon described the episode with the witch and the priest and all the information he had gathered about his mystery. Poor Warthang felt ashamed by his actions but constantly wondered if his companion had not left out some worse information to spare him the guilt trip. Unfortunately, he could never know.

"So what is this curse?" Bush asked at one point.

Warthang paused a moment, enjoying the gusts of wind in his scaly face as they glided over the clouds, then he looked at his companion.

"Let me start from the beginning," he said, "I want to tell you everything."

So he did. He told him about the prophecy that led to the creation of their species, the curse laid upon them by the wizards to force them into peace with their territorial nature, the annihilation of their creators and Warthang's role in that, his exile from the others, his acceptance by a blind human, his rage, and his vengeance for Benzady's murders of his only friends. He told him about Tundra who had brought light into his life and had given him a will to live after all of these horrible events, how she wanted so badly for the other dragons to be good and how she would sacrifice her life to help the humans. Finally, he explained about the result of the curse in the form of Gurb and his resolve to find a way to kill all dragons to end the madness.

"Wow," Bush murmured at the end of the tale, "so you left Atlantis to find a way to kill them—and yourself—only to learn in the end that God would take care of it? What do you suppose He'll do?"

"I'm not certain," shrugged Warthang, "but I'm pretty sure it's all connected with that prophecy that made the wizards create us in the first place. We're all going to die in the fire."

"But we're immune to fire," reasoned the old dragon.

For answer, Warthang raised his shoulders, smiled, and then indicated with his head for the other dragon to follow him. In a moment, he had disappeared in time and space and reappeared at the edge of his home island, Bush following close behind.

"Here it is!" Warthang yelled in the wind, a great big grin lighting his face.

Below them, the beautiful beach stretched inward toward the mountains. They flew close below the clouds, enjoying the peaks and the breathtaking sights of the home of the dragons. At one point, Warthang frowned and suddenly jumped over the clouds, dragging Bush behind him.

"What's the matter?" the old wizard asked him, rubbing the leg his companion had grabbed.

"Something's wrong," explained Warthang, worried. "Can you disguise yourself and come with me? I don't want anyone to know about you."

Bush nodded and suddenly he was a very normal looking sparrow—not counting the blue creepy eyes, of course. Nodding at him, the red dragon dove down through the clouds and continued plummeting to the valleys between the peaks. When he had neared the ground, he spread his wings and the wind caught his fall, helping him to land loudly on the rocky earth. Behind him, the little bird fluttered unto the branch of a scraggly conifer.

On all fours, Warthang walked a ways to the main cave where he had lived with Tundra, what seemed like ages ago. Close to the entrance of their lair, he paused and looked up. Thunderous laughter greeted him, echoing through the mountains like a trumpet.

"I told you, you would regret it if you left!" Gurb screeched at him from above.

Anxious, Warthang scurried into the cave to find it empty and filled with critters and cobwebs. No one had been home in a while. His heart heavy in his stomach, he cautiously walked back outside and sat in the sunlight, waiting for his green nemesis to fly down. Nearby, Bush peered between the pine needles of his tree, sad at seeing his friend and family so downhearted.

With a loud thud, Gurb landed in front of Warthang, a satisfied smirk on his scaly lips.

"What did you do?" asked the red dragon, very quietly.

"I have her *and* your young," sneered the evil creature.

"My young?"

At that moment, Warthang thought he was going to die. His heart had ceased in his chest and his breath had caught in his throat. In front of him, Gurb's sneer morphed into an elated leer.

"This is even better than I imagined!" he bellowed, crazed, "he didn't even know!"

From different directions, cackling emerged to join Gurb's giggles. Warthang began to pant uncontrollably and he collapsed to the ground, drained and defeated.

"Here's the deal," growled the young green reptile, "if you let me kill you, I will set them free."

Laying in the dirt, Warthang closed his eyes, trying to blot out the roar he heard in his ears.

"You don't have to decide now," continued Gurb, "but you have to stay in this cave. We'll be watching you, you see, and if you ever leave it, we'll send out the message and they will all die."

Hopping to a nearby ledge, Gurb turned away from the object of his hate but before he flew off, he added a last comment.

"When you're ready to die, just let us know. I'll be waiting."

Finally, the green reptile leaped to the sky and then perched himself on a high ledge, facing Warthang's cave, looking like a vulture who waits for its victim to die off so he can tear its flesh apart. For a while, Warthang did resemble a corpse for the lack of movement his body made; but in the end, he crawled his way into the cave, leaving the tip of his tail out into the sun to make sure that Gurb could see he would not vacate the premises.

"What am I going to do?" he moaned in the darkness of his dank home.

A small brown mouse with bright blue eyes scurried across the rocks toward the dragon and stopped at his scaly nose.

"You're not going to do anything," Bush squeaked in the language of mice, "you're going to stay there and I'll take care of everything."

A light sparkled in Warthang's yellow eyes, hope having returned. In receiving the news of Tundra and his eggs, the red dragon had completely forgotten about his friend listening out on the tree.

"I only need you to do one thing," the little voice squealed on, "look for Tundra with the wizard sight and I'll follow the magic wave with my own. That way, when you find her, I'll know where and who she is."

Dragons have very keen hearing and had this conversation not been in the tongue of furry little animals, the enemies outside would have heard everything. As it was, to the ignorance of his foes, Warthang did what Bush asked him to and he found Tundra weak and beaten, tied up in the gloomy marshes southeast of the continent. Some human had her in their barn, stabling with their chickens and ducks in dirty feces! Had it not been for the threat on the life of his young, the red dragon would have rushed to rescue her from her pathetic state, but now he had to rely on Bush. Although he had not known him for very long, he trusted in his friend's goodness and wisdom and felt certain that in the end, things would turn out for the best.

As planned, still in mouse form, Bush disappeared and appeared in the marshlands barn to visit Tundra, the mother of his ancestors. A cat having spotted him, he transformed himself to match one of the chickens and thus lost the predator's interest. Clucking noisily, he wobbled toward the weak blue dragon and pecked at her nose several times before she cracked an eye open. Right away, her dull stare noticed the strange bright sapphire eyes and she attempted to raise her head, but instead let it fall back into the wet muck.

"Is anyone listening?" the chicken eerily whispered in a voice that sounded like a clucking wind.

Now Tundra opened her second eye and she focused on the strange hen but she made no other movement and did not say anything. Understanding she was physically incapable of answering him, Bush told her,

"Blink once for yes and twice for no."

When her eyes closed and reopened twice, he had to restrain his feathered wing from patting himself on the back. No point in whispering now, or being a chicken for that matter. Without further ado, he turned himself into a mini version of his dragon self and laid down by Tundra's exhausted face.

"I'm here to rescue you, I'm a friend of Warthang's" he told her as he placed his clawed hand on her cheek, comfortingly.

Quickly, or as quickly as she could anyway, Tundra blinked twice, a horrified look entering her eyes.

"But I'm rescuing your eggs first," Bush explained, to try to alleviate her fear.

At her single blink, his little face was all smiles and he stood up, all the while trying to contain his great excitement.

"How many young do you have?" he asked quickly. Then, after a pause, he added, "blink for the number."

Tundra and Warthang had six beautiful eggs, six more to add to his family! However, after further questioning, the injured blue dragon had no other information to help him and he had to leave her there, alone and in bad shape. Not satisfied with this situation, Bush grew a plant from the ground, one that Francesca had taught him about, and he fed it to the poor broken down creature. Although the weed would not cure her in any matter, it would help numb her pain for a while and give her some respite.

When Bush finally emerged from the barn, he had taken on his human form, but the old man kept on tripping on everything and swaying from left to right as if dizzy. In a roundabout way, he reached the shack that stood by the barn, knocked loudly on its door and emitted a boisterous belch. Right away, a young man, probably in his mid-twenties, threw the door open and stared menacingly at the old wizard.

"What do you want?" he asked harshly.

"Losht," slurred Bush, "am tired. Can I resht shere and share shome drink?"

Slowly, the dragon opened a pouch he carried to reveal several bottles of golden spirit. At the sight of the alcohol, the young man snickered and invited the wizard inside his home. Before closing the door behind the two of them, he looked around to make sure no one had seen what had just happened.

"Sit there," the boy commanded, pointing at the kitchen table, "I'll get us some glasses."

"Naaaaah," Bush shook his head the way seals do so adamantly in our modern day animal shows. Then, as he sat down at the table, almost knocking his bench over and falling to the floor, he took out two full bottles and banged them down on the table. Taking a swig out of one bottle, he pointed the boy to the opposing chair and the drink waiting for him. With a smile, the young man took a seat and gulped down half the second bottle in one shot.

"What's wrong with your eyes?" he hiccupped,

already affected by the drink.

"Bad cayshe of ink eyesh" giggled Bush uncontrollably as he pointed to his very blue eyes.

As time ticked by and the two of them drank together, the young man's speech became more and more slurred as Bush's took back a firmer diction. The two of them talked, told jokes, laughed, sang and danced together. Then, when the moon had reached its zenith, Bush looked at the young man with a silly smile and poked him in the chest with his skinny finger.

"What's with the dragon in your barn?" he asked.

"Sssssshhhhhh," the boy repeatedly brought a finger to his lips and made his other hand to bat the air, "that'sh a shecret."

Bringing his hands down to the bottle, the young man took another long draft and then giggled at Bush.

"You noticed no dragon attacksh?"

For an answer, the old dragon explained he had not really been around to notice anything but that he would love to find out what was going on, since he seemed to be so far behind on the news. Amiably, the boy told him everything, all the while shushing him to secrecy. It took a long time to sort out everything the drunk told Bush; but in the end, he got the full story.

Apparently, two weeks back, the dragons had formed what they called the "Dragon Alliance," whose sole purpose was to get rid of Warthang and his meddling once and for all. Technically, Gurb was the only one with the right to kill him but because the wizard dragon had so much power, he was incapable of finishing the task and needed to find some other way of accomplishing it. Together, the dragons devised a plan that would basically force poor Warthang to throw himself at Gurb to be murdered, all to save his eggs and mate. It would be either his life or those of his loved ones, and the dragons knew that in the end, there was only one choice Warthang would make. So, they had beaten poor Tundra and put her away, stolen the eggs and placed them in the care of the different human towns, all but one, that is. In his cave, Gurb kept one of the eggs for his own pleasure.

As soon as he had all the information he could get out of the drunk boy, the conversation ended and the young man slowly drifted off to sleep between gulps of spirits. Leaving him in a hurry, Bush disappeared and reappeared in the mountains to the north where the dragons live in their dank caves. There, back as his dragon-self, he picked six different big stones and once he felt satisfied he had the right ones, he took flight back toward the south. After the high-peaked mountains, he crossed the farmlands and plains and finally found the river that led him to a large boulder that indicated the wizards' secret library. This was the same underground structure Warthang had entered at the age of four, the same place where he had stolen all the magic for himself.

Bush let his six large stones roll down the stairs to finally land in the dirt, and he made himself smaller so he could enter behind them. Sitting on the ground between the book shelves, he chiseled and polished the stones with his claws, shaping them into the likeness of dragon eggs. Having spent much time with his brother and sister eggs in his youth, creating fake replicas of them proved to be easy. The only bother was their gray color: dragon eggs were white. With that in mind and with some concentration, bird feces began to fly into his hiding place and splash themselves unto the stones. After a good hour, Bush had collected enough of the white nasty liquid to turn his stones white, and he felt ready to execute his rescue plan. Now, he only had to find where exactly in each town the humans had hidden Warthang's eggs.

Note 18

Losing a child is...I can't even describe what that feels like, but to try, it leaves a gaping hole inside you that threatens to swallow you whole and leave you empty, devoid of any will to live or love again. You teeter on the edge of that precipice, tempted to let yourself fall in and give up, to let the darkness, or the nothingness, overtake you so that the pain can stop. Can I ever forgive? I know I need to, but I cannot. Maybe with time. But for now, my hate is an ever black presence clouding my heart, permeating and saturating it.

Chapter 18 – Eggs

It did not take long for Bush to figure out where the marshland humans had hidden Warthang's first egg. The area, seeming like a nasty place to live, did not hold many inhabitants and so, after scrying their few homes, his attention fell on the only house with a guard at its entrance. Looking further in, he found one of the rooms, completely empty, with a small table in the middle of it that had a large locked box on top. To make it even more obvious, another guard sat in front of the precious chest and watched it intently, almost without blinking.

"Humans," Bush chuckled to himself, as he squatted in the secret wizard library.

He was still in his natural form but had adopted a smaller version of himself so he could fit inside the small cave. In the middle of the library, his six large fake eggs rested in a perfect row, waiting for him to deliver them to their new homes. Carefully, he caused the first white oval rock to float into the air and follow him outside the dark cavern. The tricky thing about teleportation is that you could not bring anything with you so because of that pesky rule, Bush had to fly to each location and back instead of taking his usual transportation shortcut. This rescue would take a while.

The egg flying behind him, the green dragon rose to the sky until he had hidden himself behind the clouds.

After forty minutes in the air, he finally dropped to the low hanging trees by the human village. Still above ground, he transformed into the old man and then soundlessly landed into the marsh water. His large rock came to rest in his hands and suddenly it fit perfectly into one of his closed fists. He deposited his treasure into a side pocket in his trousers and approached the back of the guarded house. Making sure no one could see him, he closed his eyes to look inside the room with his wizard sight. As before, a middle-aged man squinted at the locked chest, a large baton sitting in his lap. All of a sudden, he frowned and placed a hand over his stomach, but other than that, he remained at his post. A devious smile twitched on Bush's face and the man in the room jumped to his feet, clutching at his stomach, the baton falling to the floor noisily. Quickly, he ran out of the room just as Bush entered, passing straight through the wall. As he reached the chest, his hand passed through the box as if it were air and he took out the warm egg. In its place, he grabbed the rock from his pocket, passed it through the edges of the locked chest and grew the rock to its original size, not quite an exact replica of the real egg, but close enough. As soon as he had finished the switch, he ran through the wall back out of the house, just as a second later the outside guard came in to take over the other man's post. It had all taken close to five seconds and the marshland men had no idea of what had transpired. In their minds, inside that chest still lay a dragon egg and they had to guard it or destroy it if the signal were given.

Forty minutes later, Warthang's first egg rested safely in the cold fireplace of the wizard library. Once again, Bush squatted by the other five white stones, searching for egg number two in the desert lands to the west of the marshlands. A good twenty minutes flew by and he had searched everywhere without finding any clue as to its whereabouts. Frustrated, he laid his large green head on his clawed hands and thought. Apparently, the people living in the desert were cleverer than their neighbors and he would have to work harder to find their hidden prize.

Done pondering, Bush left the cave and flew southwest high above the clouds, a fake egg floating close behind. When he felt close enough to the sandy settlement, he landed in a dusty cloud, making sure no one would notice a dragon approaching the city. Once on the ground, he became again an old man and he placed the oval rock that had been following him into his pocket as he had done before. Then, he began his long trek toward the large city, this time dressed in the way of the marshland people, garbed in a green shirt and brown pants, and wearing simple shoes and a large hat that overshadowed his face, but mostly his blue opaque eyes. Once at the edge of town, he asked a passerby for directions, wanting to know where he could buy some clothes. They pointed him to the right place and he headed there amiably, greeting everyone he passed by.

Once at the bazaar, he stopped by a shopkeeper and asked her for the best clothes the area had to offer. When she showed him the long thin robes, he felt the fabric between his fingers and frowned.

"What kind of clothes are these?" he complained, "they're so thin they would tear at the first branch that clung to them!"

Patiently, the merchant lady took the garment off its perch and put it on Bush, then nodded approvingly.

"It's hot in the desert," she explained, "this will cover and protect you from the sun while keeping you cool at the same time. There are no trees in the desert so do not worry about ruining the clothes."

Bush grunted, sounding unimpressed, and he took the robes off to place them back on their perch.

"I like our clothes better back home," he commented, loud enough for her to hear.

Moving on to other items, he frowned again and pointed at some nice leather sandals the lady had for sale.

"What kind of shoes are those!" he mocked, "you stub your toes and you're in for real pain: there's no protection whatsoever."

As she tried to explain why one would wear sandals, Bush ignored her and went on to the next item, and the next, and the next, all the while commenting on how everything in the marshlands, in his home, was better made. After this long banter, the shopkeeper began tapping her foot impatiently and she crossed her arms, no longer saying anything to him. When she had gotten to that point, Bush swept some sweat off his brow and sighed.

"It's so hot here, is there some place I can get a drink?"

The merchant lady pointed to some tables a bit down the street and turned around, ready to get rid of this grumpy customer.

"Will you come have a drink with me?" Bush asked her.

When she ignored him, he took some gold out of his pocket and put it in front of her nose so she could see what he had in his hand.

"Please, I don't want to go by myself," he almost begged pathetically.

Seeing the precious metal, the shopkeeper grudgingly accepted and a few minutes later, she left her attendant at the shop while the two of them sat at a table further down the street, drinking some ale together. When Bush tasted the alcohol, he nodded slowly and said,

"That's not too bad, but still not as good as our ale."

Fed up with his comments, the woman set her cup down with a bang and pointed to the east as she said,

"If everything's so perfect in the marshlands, why don't you just go back home?"

Bush chuckled at her reaction and crooked a finger at her.

"So you're jealous of us, then," he laughed annoyingly.

Not believing this stranger's stupidity, the lady stared at him, her teeth clenched.

"You know what else we probably do better?" he continued his tirade, "I bet you we guard our dragon egg better than you guys do."

The shopkeeper harrumphed and crossed her arms.

"And what have you done with your egg, pray tell?" she asked, sarcastically.

"Ah!" Bush exclaimed excitedly, "Well, we've placed it in a locked chest, you see, and then put it in an empty room. There, we have a guard that watches it day and night. Then, to top it off, we also have a guard outside the house. There's no way in or out without us realizing it!"

"That is the stupidest thing I have ever heard!" the merchant woman spat the words at him. "You might as well put a flag on the house that says, 'here's the egg, come and get it!'"

Hurt, Bush pouted and looked away. After a few moments, he sighed and begrudgingly asked her, "How else would you do it, then?"

"Bury the egg some place that always has people," she explained, wisely, "the egg is out of sight and no outsider would suspect its whereabouts seeing as that would be a place that is normally frequented by people anyway."

"Wow, that *is* smart," consented the old man, "maybe I ought to go back home and tell them to do that."

"You do that," the merchant lady gave her permission, hoping he would leave the gold and leave town.

To her surprise, Bush did just that: he placed all the gold he had on the table, tipped his hat to her and began walking down the street, back where he had come from. Once he had walked out of the bazaar and out of her line of sight, he stopped the first passerby and asked about where he could go to watch people. You see, he was new in town and wanted to understand the local culture: he needed to find a place that had movement 24/7 so he could learn all about them. Raising his eyebrows, the man he had stopped in the street told him about a bar they had in town that never closed—that was the only place that fit the bill, in his opinion.

So, upon receiving directions to this ever opened bar, Bush searched for the place and finally found himself sitting at one of its tables an hour later. Although he seemed to be watching the other men and women milling about, in reality, he had his mind focused on the composition of the ground under his feet. For a long while, all he felt was dirt, sand and rocks. At one point, he found a very valuable necklace buried deep under one of the tables, probably some long lost token that had been trampled over the years, digging itself deeper and deeper with time. When he thought for sure he was in the wrong place, his searching led him to a large round object filled with liquid, limbs and a beating heart, buried right under where the bartenders stood to serve their customers.

Having found his ever illusive egg, Bush jumped up and uttered a small cry of triumph, drawing everyone's attention to his corner table.

"I know what I want to drink!" he burst, trying to explain his excitement. In his mind, he was berating himself for having reacted so explosively. Why did he always do that?

In self-importance, he walked up to the bar and banged on a stool with his fist.

"Some water!" he ordered.

The bartender scuffed and waved a rag toward the street.

"Get out!" he commanded, "this is a bar, we don't serve that here."

"Desert people," Bush mumbled under his breath, loud enough for the bartender to hear.

Then, he stumped out of the open air establishment and began walking around the area, looking for a quiet place, away from the crowds. Around five blocks later, a good distance away from where the egg rested deep in the earth, the dragon found just what he wanted: a narrow alley finishing in a dead-end. From there, he could easily spot if anyone were to walk by, and that way he could do his work in absolute confidence of not being discovered. At the end of the cul-de-sac, he suddenly became an overly large marmot with claws of steel and without further delay, he set out to dig himself a substantial tunnel. As he excavated the dirt, his fake egg, now back in normal size, floated behind him. By doing it this way, Bush knew that the tunnel's size would accommodate the real egg, when he would reach it.

Throughout the afternoon, Bush worked hard at his burrow, pausing a few times to take small breaks. As the sun began its descent, he changed his hard claws into soft paws and began shifting the earth packed hard above his body. Five minutes later, some dirt fell to the bottom of his tunnel to reveal the white shell of the dragon egg. Smiling radiantly, the brown marmot backed down into his hole and closed his eyes. Magically, the oval egg softly slid down after him and then rested at his feet. The big rock behind him then shrunk to the size of a pebble and flew past the animal and his treasure and arrived to where the egg had been just moments before. As it grew back to its original size, Bush caused the tunnel below it to collapse on itself and cushion the fake egg so that it would remain there until uncovered from above. After having finished that, he quickly padded the length of the tunnel, the precious egg following him like a happy puppy. Once outside into the alley with his cargo, all of his work caved-in and, except for the disturbed dirt, it seemed like he had never been there.

By then, night had fallen so it was easy for Bush to fly away with the egg without anyone noticing that a dragon had even been there. In a day's time, he had rescued two eggs, but he still had four more to go. Unfortunately, in his old age, he felt too tired to pull an all-nighter and when he arrived at the wizard cave, he rested the egg in the fireplace with the other one and collapsed in front of them to fall soundly asleep.

*   *   *

The farmlands did not have a village to speak of: what they had were houses spaced out among acres and acres of fields. By one of these homes, surrounded by fields of corn, the country people had placed the dragon egg in a dog house and had chained five massive black dogs to guard it. When Bush saw this, he clapped his hands excitedly. He would not have to deal with humans this time, but very sensible canines.

That morning, now in the form of an old, seasoned black guard dog, the dragon trotted between the stalks of corn, a ball-sized white rock between his teeth. When he reached the edge of the field, he dropped it to the ground and barked once. The five guard dogs by the farm house perked up their ears, stood up at seeing him and wagged their tails animatedly.

With his magic, Bush could freeze the animals and retrieve the egg without any problems, but he did not like the idea of distressing the poor beings who were just doing their jobs. Dogs were noble creatures, loyal and loving: they deserved some respect.

"Greetings!" Bush barked at them, also wagging his tail.

"Welcome," answered the smallest of the dogs, obviously the alpha male. "What brings you to these parts?"

"It smells interesting out here," answered the dragon as he sniffed the air.

All five dogs nodded and smiled with their long tongues hanging out of their mouths. Picking up his rock between his jaws, Bush trotted to the others, dropped his load at their feet and everyone began to smell everyone else, getting properly acquainted.

"Wow," the dog with a missing eye exclaimed, "you have come from so far. None of us have ever even left the farmlands, much less gone beyond the salt smell."

"You smell of wind and fire," alpha dog proclaimed, impressed.

The oldest of the five bent his head in respect and said, "You have lived beyond death."

"And you, my pups," Bush answered, "have guarded and loved your masters well. You do the race justice."

286

At his praise, the five animals bent their heads and slowed their wagging to a respectable speed. Looking toward the house, the old wizard dragon panted and sat down.

"When does the master check on you?" he asked them.

"Oh, only if we bark, don't worry," answered one-eye.

Satisfied, Bush stood back up and when he looked toward what they guarded, he sniffed the air and snorted twice.

"The ball you guard is not a ball."

Alpha dog looked at the egg and then back at Bush.

"Master likes the non-ball."

With a smile, the dragon pointed his long nose at what he had brought and his white rock began to grow. Excited, the five dogs jumped a few times around the fake egg and watched it grow and shrink until it finally stopped changing and remained the same size as their non-ball.

"Master would surely like *this* non-ball!" the long-haired dog replied.

"You can have my non-ball," Bush nodded, "but I would need yours in exchange."

"He would never know the difference," the oldest dog mused, "Master lives by eyes and not by nose."

"But Master wants us to guard *this* non-ball, not yours," Alpha dog loyally protested.

In shame, the other four dogs bent their long tails between their legs. They had been bad, only thinking of themselves instead of their Master.

"I will show you," Bush told them convincingly,

"that your Master wants you to guard my non-ball instead of this one."

With their permission, he moved the dragon egg out of the dog house and hid it a small distance away among the corn stalks. Then, he placed his oval white rock a few feet from the entrance of the small wooden structure and under his instructions, the five canines started to bark and growl loudly and all six of them began a ferocious looking fight filled with teeth and drool. From the house, an older man ran out with a large stick and started waving it at the foreign black dog. Seeming cowed, Bush ran off into the fields, chased by the farmer who yelled and screamed at him all sorts of curses. When the man felt he had scared the canine away, he returned to his guards and patted each of them on the head.

"Good dogs," he grunted.

Then, he picked up the egg-looking rock and placed it into the dog house.

"Now," he told the dogs, "guard this egg. This is very important, guard it with your lives."

In response, all five animals wagged their tails and barked several times. Content, the farmer smiled and headed back to his house. As he did so, Alpha dog looked at the opposite corn field from where Bush had escaped and nodded at the dragon, for he knew this was where he was. Understanding the signal, the old wizard grinned, lost his dog skin and took on his green wings to fly back to the cave with egg number three. As he flew to the air, the five dogs bade him goodbye and thanked him for their new non-ball.

Next, the old dragon focused his attention to the forest on the west side of the continent. The village in

Hall Forest had not even bothered to hide the dragon egg but had placed it in plain sight on a pedestal in the middle of town. Without wavering, all the townspeople in the vicinity constantly checked the skies and looked between the blue expanse and the white egg. On his way to the town with his floating white rock, Bush took his time making it to the forest, all the while gathering all the moisture in the air and making sure that the growing mass would follow behind him in a heavy gray cloud. When he had reached a point where he knew the humans still could not see him in the distance, he sent the thick fog forward, trailed by his home-made dragon egg. Quickly, the thick mist fell upon the whole village and the people looked astonished, barely able to see anything in front of their noses. A few of them began to head to the pedestal where they "guarded" the egg, feeling suspicious of this sudden fog. However, before they reached a place where they could see it, Bush, from his far off distance, caused the dragon egg to float up and deposited his replica in its place. Once that was done, he lifted the misty air back up with the precious cargo to head back where it had come from to his position. The humans, seeing their surroundings perfectly again, blinked and looked to the center of town to find that nothing had changed. It had just been some sort of weird fluke of nature.

Bush laughed to himself and soared back to the wizard library, egg number four following close behind. He only had two more to rescue and his task would be completed! Excited about the end nearing, Bush hurried to the cave and laid by the now four shelled babies resting in and around the fireplace. There, he continued in his search when all of a sudden, he gasped, the loud sound echoing throughout the large cavern. Valley City had broken their agreement with the dragons! He could not believe it and felt so appalled by what he saw that vomit threatened to bubble out of his throat uncontrollably. Breathing in deeply, he tried to control the nausea and the growing anger that welled up inside him. Then, remembering poor Warthang, sorrow replaced his ire and he offered a short prayer of consolation for his ancestor.

"There's nothing else I can do about it for now," he told himself out loud. "It's time I found the last egg, anyway."

Taking another deep breath, he closed his eyes and continued his search. A long time passed before he found the last eluding egg, but when he did, he furrowed his brow and frowned. Gurb himself had it! A dragon, not a human. Bush bit his lower lip and shook his head. Gurb would never be fooled by a fake egg of his own race and he would never, not even for one second, let his eyes wander from it. No trickery or magic could rescue this egg; Bush needed a more direct approach. His mind made up, the old dragon decided to sleep the night off since it was getting late and he needed all his energy, and in the morning, he would put his plan into action.

*   *   *

Unseen by the beady eyes watching Warthang's tail, for the dragon still lay in the cave with it sticking out, Bush scuttled into the dank structure in the form of a gray mouse. Inside, he found his ancestor motionless but red hot, like his blood was about to boil him alive. Cautiously, he scurried deeper in to find the ruby creature's face. The deeper into the cave he went, the more smoke permeated the air and the harder it was to breathe. Finally, when the mouse found the large dragon's head, he sat in front of the snout and created an air bubble that enveloped them both and purified the air around them.

"There," the Bush mouse nodded, "now we can talk without any unwanted ears hearing us."

Warthang cracked a yellow eye open but did not seem to see little Bush by his nose. Instead, smoke began to escape his nostrils profusely and he snorted and growled deeply. Uncertain, the mouse transformed into a small green dragon and jumped on the dragon's snout. For a second, Warthang tried to shake the diminutive reptile off his face but then he focused his eyes on Bush and seemed to take control of himself.

"I need your help," little Bush told him.

"How could they?" Warthang almost yelled, dislodging the tiny dragon from his face this time, causing the little being to plop to the ground. "How could they..." he repeated in a whimper.

After shaking the dust off his wings, Bush sat by Warthang's now contorted visage. Large tears slowly rolled down the red dragon's scaly cheeks.

"I protected them for so long...the first friend I ever made lived in that city."

Warthang scratched his face, trying to gouge the tears off his scales.

"They betrayed me!" he roared, lifting his head up and spitting a furnace of fire into the dark cave.

Then, he crumbled to the dirt, his eyes closed, his mouth open in a pant.

"She was so beautiful." The corner of Warthang's lip

curled upwards for a moment. "Purple: a perfect blend between Tundra and I."

Warthang's eyes popped open and instead of yellow, they seemed flaming red. At the sight, Bush backed a few steps, making sure he gave the dragon his space.

"I'll murder them all!" he yelled hysterically, "I'll do to them what they did to her!"

At this point, Warthang had stood up and he was clawing the walls, picturing and savoring the carnage in his mind. After a few crazy frenzied minutes, his eyes dimmed back to his normal yellow and he fell back down to the dirt, exhausted.

"Her frail helpless body," he sobbed uncontrollably, "they crushed her, broke her little limbs, her tiny wings, her weak neck, they gouged out her eyeballs. My little girl. They crucified her and let her dry out in the sun for everyone to see. What kind of sick creature does that? To my little girl!"

Sitting by the crumbled Warthang, Bush held his face within his clawed hands, remembering the helpless baby, and he cried silently along with his friend. Thus they stayed, silently mourning for that whole day and that whole night. There is nothing one can say in these situations. It'll be okay? I'm sure there's a reason why this happened? No. Just keep quiet and hold your friend. Your presence is what they need, not your meaningless words.

On the dawn of the next morning, Warthang languidly raised his gaze to Bush and sniffled.

"You needed help?" he quietly asked.

"Yes," Bush nodded as he sat up and made sure that the air bubble protecting what they said enveloped them properly, "Gurb has the last egg."

Two small flames burst from Warthang's nostrils but other than that, he did not seem to react.

"Since I can't be two places at once," Bush continued, "I'll need you to rescue Tundra while I save the last egg."

"Otherwise they would have the humans kill her when you would try to get the last egg," nodded Warthang, understanding. For a second, his face contorted and then became normal again. "What am I going to tell her..." he murmured.

Slowly, he stood up and picked up tiny Bush between his clawed hands and brought him up to his face.

"You have to do something for me," he intently looked into the little green dragon's eyes, "this can't happen again. You have to take them to a safe place."

Biting his lower lip to try and hold back the tears, Bush nodded, "I know just the place."

Warthang gave him a sad smile, "You know what this means, don't you?"

Sighing, the old green dragon grinned shortly.

"Go save her," he said, "I'll save the last egg and finally bring them all safely to my cave in the other continent. Then, I'm coming home, dad."

*   *   *

Intently and without blinking, Gurb stared at the tip of Warthang's tail that still lay in the sun, barely peeking out of the cave. These past few days, when he had been the one watching his enemy, that tail had never moved, had not even twitched once. Would Warthang surrender his life to save his family? Why was he taking so long to make a decision! Unhappily, the young green dragon tapped his claws on the egg he held in his left hand. His whole life, all he could think about was killing Warthang. It was an incessant, nagging urge that woke him up at night and brought a frown to his face whenever a tiny moment of happiness dared to engulf him, an urge he was ready to live without. What would life be without it? Would he be able to enjoy the company of others? To amass a vast treasure? To terrorize humans for the fun of it?

In the middle of his reverie, Gurb noticed a large shadow flying over him and his gaze twitched quickly from Warthang's tail basking in the sun to the shape in the sky. There, hovering directly above him, the biggest

green dragon he had ever seen, was looking down at him. The creature looked extremely old, his scales a bit dimmed, but even with his age, his shear mass bulged with muscle, causing Gurb's heart to skip a beat. Where did this one come from?

Mouth wide open, the young angry dragon completely forgot for a moment Warthang's tail and his claws stopped drumming the egg; in fact, his whole body froze. Seeing the desired reaction, Bush swooped down and landed like a boulder—or really, like the sound of a building landing, if one can think of such an analogy—and sat up, high enough that his eyes could not be seen.

"Hello," he greeted the guarding dragon.

Gurb blinked twice and the urge of vengeance returned, pulling his gaze away from the gigantean beast back to the cave he had been watching. At the site of the now empty clearing, he stood up abruptly and roared a series of loud bursts that echoed back to him from a distance in a different voice. Satisfied, he nodded and brought his attention back to his visitor.

"What was that?" Bush asked him.

"That," Gurb answered smugly, "is a signal to destroy my enemy's family."

"Hum," Bush grunted, "and what about this egg? You obviously can't destroy it or the curse will fall on you."

Looking up at the big dragon, Gurb squinted to see him better but the sun glared in his face.

"It's insurance," he explained, "now that Warthang knows that I won't stop at anything, he'll give himself over to save this last egg."

Unhappy with the sun blinding him, the smaller

reptile circled around Bush, careful not to crack the egg he held in his claws, to get a better look at his interlocutor.

"Where do you come from?" he asked, perplexed, "I know all of the dragons, plus you are so much older than any of us..."

Without a word, Bush pointed at the egg and then lowered his head to face the young dragon, his blue wizard eyes now in evidence. Afraid, Gurb backed away from him, clutching the white egg in both hands.

"How is this possible?" he stammered.

"You see these," Bush said, pointing to his opaque blue eyes, "they're wizard eyes. That means that I'm very powerful and can do all sorts of cool tricks."

At this proclamation, the old dragon displayed a quirky smile. Then, without preamble, a shadow crossed his visage and he became very serious.

"I need you to give me that egg. Now."

"No!" complained Gurb, holding the egg tighter, all the while distancing himself from the giant.

But every step he took, the egg grew larger between his claws until it became so big and heavy that he could no longer hang on to it and he dropped it to the ground.

"You can't do this!" Gurb begged, now hugging half the egg with his full arms.

"I am sorry, little one," Bush looked sadly at the distressed dragon, "I know this revenge is forced on you, and there will be an end to it someday, but that day is not today."

Without another word, Gurb crumbled to the ground, fast asleep. Sighing, Bush returned the egg to its normal size and he headed with it to the wizard's secret library to collect the rest of his family and begin his long journey to the other continent.

In the meantime, Warthang had been busy wreaking havoc in the marshlands, tearing apart the barn that had held poor Tundra prisoner for so long. They had a lot to talk about the two of them, especially before Bush's return from his journey; but first, he needed to heal her and reassure her that everything would be fine and that he would never leave her again.

Note 19

A lot of bad has happened in my life and much of it by my own fault. I understand that, and so I am so thankful for the good that has happened to me and I give the credit to God, because I certainly did not deserve any of it. But good or bad, each feeling seems to be accompanied with a face. When I think about the bad, I remember my parents who abandoned me, I remember Benzady who tormented me through every step, especially after I murdered him. Oh, and poor Gurb.

Nowadays, I try not to think about those things too much, I have a better outlook on life because of some other faces I remember. There's Maggie, my first friend, the first one to accept me for who I am, then, Tundra, my wonderful mate, and finally Bush, my son. They have made me a better soul and I know that without them, I never would have had even an ounce of happiness.

Thank you, God.

Chapter 19 – Farewells

"Did you see those wizards?" Bush asked Warthang as they walked quietly in the forest in human form. "Their skin was kind of transparent!"

Warthang looked back at his son and shrugged, a small smile plainly displayed on his face.

"Magic does that to human skin."

"Really? Well, if that's the case, then how come our skin isn't see-through when we're humans?"

Warthang raised an eyebrow as he focused on where he walked, making sure not to trip on stray branches.

"I don't know," he shook his head, "I guess we really aren't human at all even though we seem like it."

"We're such fakers," Bush chuckled, following his father carefully.

Abruptly, Warthang stopped walking, turned around and then shoved old Bush behind a ridiculously large conifer. Without a sound, he jumped behind the old man to also hide himself behind the tree.

"What is it?" Bush asked him as he rubbed his back.

"He's talking to my father," Warthang murmured.

"Grandpa Singe!" Bush whispered animatedly, "Remember that time when we made him think he had lost his tail?"

The red haired man sniggered in his hands.

"How could I forget? And then when his tail 'came back,' he lost all his teeth."

Like little children, the two dragon-men guffawed and patted each other's shoulders, all the while holding on to their mouths with one hand so that the minimum amount of sound could escape. Quickly, Warthang popped his head from behind the tree to see what was happening further into the forest and then squatted to the ground.

"I don't know what they're doing," he said, "but we may be here a while."

Looking down at his dad, Bush nodded.

"If that's the case, I think I'm going to go say goodbye to my brothers and sisters."

With that declaration, the old man disappeared into thin ear, leaving Warthang alone with his thoughts. After a moment of silence, the dragon sat down from his squatting position and began thinking about the past century. Truly, they had been the best years of his life. When he had met Tundra, she had taught him courage and love and had brought some light into his world. Now, with Bush in their lives, he had added laughter and a light-heartedness the red dragon had never known before. Having lived such a long time and alone among humans and creatures, his son had learned to live day by day and to make the most of everything. He had had so many wonderful adventures and had met countless amazing people; he always had a story to tell.

"That's funny," a voice startled him, "the first time I met you, *I* was the one hiding behind a tree."

Smiling, Warthang jumped up and grabbed Gala into his arms to engulf him into a warm hug. Embarrassed, the wizard raised one of his arms and patted the dragon on the back a couple of times. Warthang let go of the sorcerer and held on to his shoulders, looking straight into his eyes.

"Hello, my friend," he greeted.

"Wow," Gala exclaimed, "I think this is the first time you don't try to hide your eyes behind a hat...so, what's with the tree? You really don't like dragons, do you? Are you still trying to find a way to destroy them?"

Still wearing a smile on his face, Warthang shook his head and shrugged his shoulders.

"No. Really, I came to say goodbye."

Slowly, Gala's complexion lost its color and gradually became white.

"This is it, then?" he stammered, "we're about to die?"

"You're about to...?" Warthang asked and then when he understood he shook his head adamantly, "oh no, no. You guys have approximately another five years to go."

At hearing this, Gala sighed deeply and regained his natural color, the hand that he held up to his forehead shaking slightly.

"The last two times I saw you," he told the dragon, "I thought I would never see you again, so what's this visit about?"

"My death is approaching," Warthang explained, nonchalantly.

"You do look like you've aged just a little bit," Gala squinted at him, "but not enough to warrant your *dying*."

"You're right, it's got nothing to do with my health, but don't worry, I've lived a long enough life and I'm ready for it to end."

"You're kidding me, right? We seem to be around the same age and I only have five years left, apparently. I have no idea what to do with myself and I'm certainly not ready to die! How could you say such a thing about yourself?"

Out of nowhere, Bush appeared between the two men, startling Gala so much that he stumbled backwards and fell to the leafy floor. The old man brought a hand to his mouth to hide a giggle and then offered the other to help the wizard back up.

"Pardon the intrusion!" he apologized.

"Gala," Warthang said, "I want you to meet my son, Bush."

From the ground, Gala eyed Bush curiously and then accepted the hand. Once on his feet, he batted the leaves off his robes, all the while looking at the two men facing him.

"Two things," he said, thinking out loud, "your son is way older than you...so you both must be time travelers and somehow, you didn't meet until later in life. And secondly, wizards of your time are different than wizards of this time. How were you able to solve the problem of the transparent skin? I've been searching for years to figure it out!"

"Well now," Bush answered, shuffling his white hair around, "we can't divulge our secrets. We *are* from the future, after all."

"Warthang has already told me I have five years left to live, so I already know some of what will happen!"

"Some things are better left unknown, old friend," Warthang reasoned as he crossed his arms, "but the truth is, I'm more comfortable with you not knowing too much."

Frustrated, Gala looked down and drew circles in the leaves with his foot.

"So what's your story, guys? Will you tell me at least that?"

"From my point of view," the young dragon smiled, "I didn't even know I had a son. I was traveling ahead, looking for answers, when he found me. We traveled for a while and then it wasn't until later that we discovered our connection."

"If he's still with you," Gala surmised, "then you've never seen him as a baby. Why is that?"

"He was stolen from me," Warthang said with a hint of anger, "someone else rescued him and I let them bring him somewhere safe where my enemies could not harm him."

Gala raised his eyebrows, surprised. Warthang had enemies? He seemed like such a nice guy.

"As for me," Bush put in, "I was born without parents and I lived my whole life searching. I looked everywhere and it took years, but in the end, after all the hard work, I was able to achieve my goals."

Interested by the story, Gala looked into Bush's strange blue eyes and bit his lower lip.

"Did you know anything about your father?" he asked slowly.

"Absolutely nothing."

"Had he left clues behind for you to find?"

"Of a sort," Bush nodded, a quirky smile on his lips. "I only found a small message that had been left for me."

After a moment of silence, Gala tapped on his lips with his index finger and looked around the forest.

"It has to be possible then," he said.

303

"What's that?" asked Warthang.

Sighing, Gala let his arms drop to his sides and he looked back down to the ground.

"I don't know my father," he replied, then looked up at Bush. "I've been so busy with other things that I forgot all about him, I forgot about looking for him."

The old man nodded, looked at Warthang and then smiled.

"There's always hope," he acquiesced.

"I have five years left to live," Gala said, hope now filling his voice, "I will find my father, just like you did. And then, I will also be ready to die."

"I'm glad you have a purpose, something to look forward to," Warthang smiled at his friend, "as for us, we'll be heading back, now. I want to thank you for helping me all these years and I want to apologize for the harm that I've done. I am truly sorry."

"I'm not sure what you're talking about, but whatever it is, it's okay," Gala patted the yellow eyed man on the shoulder, "it's been fun. You definitely have made my life interesting. So I guess, I thank you too."

All three men shook hands in solemn silence and when that was done, Bush and Warthang walked away, trudging side by side in the forest. Once they had marched some distance away, they both stopped and faced each other.

"Are you ready?" Warthang asked his son.

For an answer, Bush nodded and the two men embraced. Still in that position, they time jumped to Warthang's present and they transformed back to their natural beautiful scaly forms. For a moment, they looked at each other and then at Tundra who joined them. All three of them formed a circle of red, blue and green, and

304

they watched the sky. The cloudless blue expanse was filled with a large fiery mass that grew bigger and bigger every moment, a large smoke cloud trailing behind it.

The dragons stretched their wings out and covered each other's bodies, waiting for the projectile to reach their precious continent. It did not take long.

Within seconds, the meteorite landed in the middle of the farm lands and decimated everything in its blast zone and everything miles beyond. Much of the ground blasted outward into the sea, killing and shredding every living thing in its path. What was not killed by the explosion, by the fire or by the debris, was then killed by the water that engulfed the whole continent of Atlantis, leaving a turmoil of waves in its place.

"Hear Atlantis, and learn:
By fire you will burn.
Flee, flee! For naught you hold
Can stop this tale foretold!"

With the end of the continent of Atlantis, came the end of the knowledge of true wizards, came the end of dragons. Now all that would be left, would be a few dragon-wizards, but no one would ever know what they truly were, where they came from or mostly that they even existed. But make no mistake, there is at least one out there in the world, roaming, looking for adventure, trying to find meaning in its life. If you ever see an animal or even a human being, and their eyes are a complete solid color, then know that you have had the rare occasion of seeing a dragon-wizard, a very rare, precious creature indeed.

Letter

Welcome to life, brother (or sister)!

I'm leaving you this letter because you need to know the truth. Our parents are dead. They died a very long time ago, some two thousand years, but they had all of us brought to this cave for our safety. They love us very much, you see, and want us to be able to have as full a life as possible.

Knowing that, I want you to look at the wall and see the inscription there. It says: *You are not the only dragon.* I wrote that for myself a very long time ago, and it was a message I needed, to give myself a purpose in life. But I tell you that this message is also for you. You are *not* the only dragon in the world, there are three more, and they are in those eggs, surrounding you right now. Take care of them, they are your brothers and sisters and they are very precious.

Here's another painful truth: they will never hatch while you are alive. Because of the nature of our magic, for we have many powers, only one of us is allowed to exist at one time. So here is what I really want to tell you: live your life to the fullest, discover the world, discover yourself and what you can do, discover God's purpose for you. Do good out there, but remember your brothers and sisters. If you ever feel lonely, remember them and know that you are not the only one.

About the Author

Although Sylvie Evdoxiadis enjoys the idea of wizards and magical creatures, the most important aspect in her life is God. Presently, she teaches French and Spanish at Harding University, a Christian Institution in Arkansas. On her time off during the summers, she travels with her husband, two children, and a team of students to New Zealand and Fiji for mission work: spreading God's good news and encouraging the churches there.

Made in the USA
Lexington, KY
12 April 2017